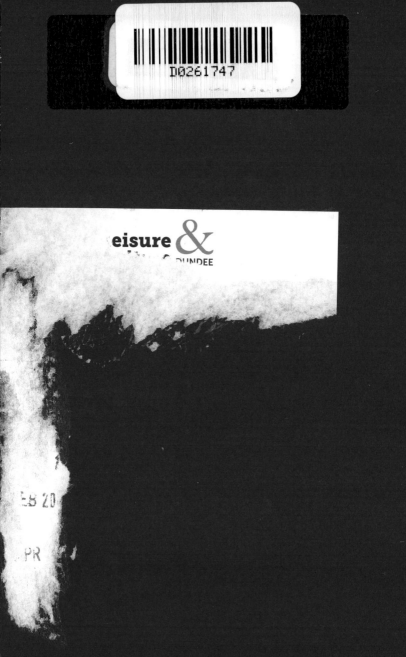

A Good
Woman

www.**rbooks**.co.uk

Also by Danielle Steel

* Published outside the UK under the title PASSION'S PROMISE

For more information on Danielle Steel and her books, see her website at
www.daniellesteel.com

DANIELLE STEEL

A Good Woman

BANTAM PRESS

LONDON · TORONTO · SYDNEY · AUCKLAND · JOHANNESBURG

TRANSWORLD PUBLISHERS
61–63 Uxbridge Road, London W5 5SA
A Random House Group Company
www.rbooks.co.uk

First published in Great Britain
in 2008 by Bantam Press
an imprint of Transworld Publishers

A CIP catalogue record for this book
is available from the British Library.

I3BNs 9780593056776 (cased)
9780593056783 (tpb)

Addresses for Random House Group Ltd companies outside the UK
can be found at: www.randomhouse.co.uk
The Random House Group Ltd Reg. No. 954009

The Random House Group Ltd supports The Forest Stewardship
Council (FSC), the leading international forest-certification organization. All our
titles that are printed on Greenpeace-approved FSC-certified paper carry the FSC logo.
Our paper procurement policy can be found at
www.rbooks.co.uk/environment

Typeset in Charter ITC
Printed and bound in Great Britain by
CPI Mackays, Chatham, ME5 8TD

2 4 6 8 10 9 7 5 3 1

Mixed Sources
Product group from well-managed
forests and other controlled sources
www.fsc.org   Cert no. TT-COC-2139
© 1996 Forest Stewardship Council
FSC

To the good women—the *great* women!
The *Best* women I know:
Beatrix, Sam, Victoria, Vanessa, and Zara.
Each one special and unique,
courageous, loving, wise, resourceful,
creative, persevering, honest, with integrity,
poise, and grace.
You are my heroes, my role models,
my treasures and my joy.
Thank you for the lessons you have taught
me, and the limitless love we share.

With all my love,
Mom/d.s.

A Good
Woman

Chapter 1

On the morning of April 14, 1912, Annabelle Worthington was reading quietly in the library of her parents' house, overlooking the large, walled-in garden. The first signs of spring had begun to appear, the gardeners had planted flowers, and everything looked beautiful for her parents' return in the next few days. The home she shared with them and her older brother Robert was a large, imposing mansion, at the northern reaches of Fifth Avenue in New York. The Worthingtons, and her mother's family, the Sinclairs, were directly related to the Vanderbilts and the Astors, and somewhat more indirectly to all the most important New York families. Her father, Arthur, owned and ran the city's most prestigious bank. His family had been in banking for generations, just as her mother's family had been in Boston. Her brother Robert, at twenty-four, had worked for her father for the past three years. And of course, when Arthur retired one day, Robert would run the bank. Their future, like their history, was predictable, assured, and safe. It was comforting for Annabelle to grow up in the protection of their world.

Her parents loved each other, and she and Robert had always been close and gotten along. Nothing had ever happened to upset or disturb them. The minor problems they encountered were always instantly buffered and solved. Annabelle had grown up in a sacred, golden world, a happy child, among kind, loving people. The past few months had been exciting for her, although tempered by a recent disappointment. In December, just before Christmas, she had been presented to society at a spectacular ball her parents had given for her. It was her debut, and everyone insisted it was the most elegant and extravagant debutante ball New York had seen in years. Her mother loved giving beautiful parties. The garden had been covered over and heated. The ballroom in their home was exquisite. The band had been the most coveted in the city. Four hundred people had attended, and the gown Annabelle had worn made her look like a fairy princess.

Annabelle was tiny, elfin, delicate, even smaller than her mother. She was a petite blonde, with long, silky golden hair, and huge blue eyes. She was beautiful, with small hands and feet, and perfect features. Throughout her childhood her father always said she looked like a porcelain doll. At eighteen, she had a lovely, well-proportioned slim figure, and a gentle grace. Everything about her suggested the aristocracy that was her heritage and that she and all her ancestors and relations had been born into.

The family had shared a lovely Christmas in the days following the ball, and after all the excitement, parties, and nights out with her brother and parents, in flimsy evening gowns in the winter weather, in the first week of January, Annabelle had fallen ill with a severe case of influenza. Her parents had been worried about her when it turned rapidly to bronchitis, and then nearly to pneumonia. Fortunately, her youth and general good health helped her to recover. But she had been sick and had run fevers in the evenings for nearly a month. Their doctor had decided finally that it would be unwise for her to travel in her weakened condition. Her parents and Robert had planned a trip for months, to visit friends in Europe, and Annabelle was still convalescing when they left on the *Mauretania* in mid-February. She had traveled on the same ship with them many times before, and her mother offered to stay home with her this time, but by the time they left, Annabelle was well enough for them to leave her alone. She had insisted that her mother not deprive herself of the trip she'd been looking forward to for so long. They were all sorry to leave her, and Annabelle was severely disappointed, but even she admitted that although she felt much better by the time they left, she still didn't feel quite up to a long journey abroad for two months. She assured her mother, Consuelo, that she would take care of the house while they were away. They trusted her completely.

Annabelle was not the sort of girl one had to worry about, or who would take advantage of their absence. They were just very sorry that she couldn't come with them, as Annabelle was herself. She was a good sport when she saw them off at the Cunard dock in February, but she returned home feeling a little dejected. She kept herself busy reading and taking on projects in the house that would please her mother. She did lovely needlework, and spent hours mending their finest bed and table linens. She didn't feel well enough to go out socially, but her closest friend Hortense visited her often. Hortense had also made her debut that year, and the two girls had been best friends since they were children. Hortie already had a beau, and Annabelle had made a bet with her that James would propose to her by Easter. She'd been right, as it turned out, and they had just announced their engagement the week before. Annabelle couldn't wait to tell her mother, who would be home soon. They were due back on the seventeenth of April, having set sail four days before from Southampton on a new ship.

It had been a long two months without them and Annabelle had missed them. But it had given her an opportunity to regain her health, and do a great deal of reading. After she finished her chores around the house, she spent every afternoon and evening in her father's library, poring over his books. Her favorites were the ones about important men, or science. She had never had much interest in the romantic books read by her mother, and even less so in the ones loaned to her by Hortense, which she thought were drivel. Annabelle was an intelligent young woman, who soaked up world events and information like a sponge. It gave her lots to talk about with her brother, and even he admitted privately that the depth of her knowledge often put him to shame. Although he had a good head for business, and was extremely responsible, he loved going to parties and seeing friends, whereas Annabelle appeared gregarious on the surface, but had a deep serious nature and a passion for learning, science, and books. Her favorite room in the house was their father's library, where she spent a great deal of her time.

On the night of the fourteenth, Annabelle read late into the night in her bed, and slept unusually late the next morning. She brushed her teeth and combed her hair when she got up, put on a dressing gown, and made her way slowly down to breakfast. She thought the house was strangely silent as she walked downstairs, and she saw none of the servants. Venturing into the pantry, she found several of them huddled over the newspaper, which they folded quickly. She saw in an instant that their faithful housekeeper Blanche had been crying. She had a soft heart, and any sad story about an animal or a child in distress easily reduced her to tears. Annabelle was expecting one of those stories as she smiled and said good morning, and with that, William the butler began crying and walked out of the room.

"Good lord, what happened?" Annabelle looked at Blanche and the two undermaids in amazement. She saw then that all of them were crying, and without knowing why, her heart skipped a beat. "What's going on here?" Annabelle asked, instinctively reaching for the newspaper. Blanche hesitated for a long instant and then handed it to her. Annabelle saw the banner headlines as she unfolded it. The *Titanic* had sunk during the night. It was the brand-new ship her parents and Robert had taken home from England. Her eyes flew open wide as she quickly read the details. There were very few, only that the *Titanic* had gone down, passengers had been put in the lifeboats, and the White Star Line's *Carpathia* had hastened to the scene. It said nothing of fatalities or survivors, but only that one could assume with a ship that size and that new that the passengers had been taken off in time, and the rescue would have been complete. The newspaper reported that the enormous ship had hit an iceberg, and although thought to be unsinkable, it had in fact gone down several hours later. The unimaginable had happened.

Annabelle flew into action immediately, and told Blanche to have the car and her father's driver brought around. She was halfway out the pantry door to run upstairs and get dressed, as she said that she had to go to the White Star office immediately, for news of Robert and her parents. It didn't even occur to her that hundreds of others would do the same.

Her hands were trembling as she dressed haphazardly in a simple gray wool dress, put on her stockings and shoes, grabbed her coat and handbag, and ran back down the stairs again, without even bothering to pin up her hair. She looked like a child with her hair flying, as she dashed out the front door and it slammed behind her. The house and everyone in it already seemed frozen in a state of anticipated mourning. As Thomas, her father's driver, took her to the White Star Line's offices at the foot of Broadway, Annabelle was battling a wave of silent terror. She saw a newsboy on a street corner, calling out the latest news. He was waving a more recent edition of the paper, and she made the driver stop and buy one.

The paper said that an unknown number of lives had been lost, and that reports were being radioed from the *Carpathia* about survivors. Annabelle could feel her eyes fill with tears as she read. How could this have happened? It was the largest, newest ship on the seas. This was her maiden voyage. How could a ship like the *Titanic* go down? And what had happened to her parents, her brother, and so many others?

When they reached the White Star offices, there were hundreds of people clamoring to get in, and Annabelle couldn't imagine how she could push her way through the throng. Her father's burly chauffeur helped her, but it still took her an hour to get inside. She explained that her brother and parents were first-class passengers on the ill-fated ship. A frantic young clerk took her name, as others went to post lists of survivors on the walls outside. The names were being radioed by the radio operator of the *Carpathia,* assisted by the surviving radio man from the *Titanic,* and they had boldly written at the top of the list that at present it was still incomplete, which gave many hope for the names they did not see.

Annabelle held one of the lists in her trembling hands, and could hardly read it through her tears, and then near the bottom she saw it, a single name. Consuelo Worthington, first-class passenger. Her father and brother were nowhere on the list, and to steady her nerves, she reminded herself it was incomplete. There were startlingly few names on the list.

"When will you know about the others?" Annabelle asked the clerk as she handed it back to him.

"In a few hours, we hope," he said as others shouted and called out behind her. People were sobbing, crying, arguing, as more outside fought to come in. The scene was one of panic and chaos, terror and despair.

"Are they still rescuing people from the lifeboats?" Annabelle asked, forcing herself to be hopeful. At least she knew her mother was alive, although who knew in what condition. But surely, the others had survived too.

"They picked the last ones up at eight-thirty this morning," the clerk said with somber eyes. He had already heard tales of bodies floating in the water, people screaming to be rescued before they died, but it wasn't up to him to tell the story, and he didn't have the courage to tell these people that lives had been lost by the hundreds, and maybe more. The list of survivors so far was just over six hundred, and the *Carpathia* had radioed that they had picked up over seven hundred, but they didn't have all the names yet. If that was all, it meant over a thousand passengers and crew members had been lost. The clerk didn't want to believe it either. "We should have the rest of the names in the next few hours," he said sympathetically, as a man with a red face threatened to hit him if he didn't hand over the list, which he did immediately. People were frantic, frightened, and spiraling out of control in their desperation for information and reassurance. The clerks were handing out and posting as many lists as they could. And finally, Annabelle and her father's driver, Thomas, went back to the car, to wait for more news. He offered to take her home, but she insisted she wanted to stay, and check the lists as they updated them over the next few hours. There was nowhere else she wanted to be.

She sat in the car in silence, some of the time with her eyes closed, thinking about her parents and her brother, willing them to have survived, while being grateful for her mother's name on the list so far. She didn't eat or drink all day, and every hour they went back to check. At five o'clock, they were told that the lists of survivors were complete, with the exception of a few young children who could not yet be identified by name. But everyone else that had been picked up by the *Carpathia* was on the list.

"Has anyone been picked up by other ships?" someone asked. The clerk silently shook his head. Although there were other ships recovering bodies from the freezing waters, the crew of the *Carpathia* were the only ones who had been able to rescue survivors, mostly in lifeboats, and a very few from the water. Almost all of those in the icy Atlantic had died before the *Carpathia* arrived, although the rescuers had been on the scene within two hours after the *Titanic* went down.

It was just too long for anyone to survive the frigid temperature of the ocean.

Annabelle checked the list one more time. There were 706 survivors. She saw her mother's name again, but there were no other Worthingtons on the list, neither Arthur nor Robert, and all she could do was pray that it was a mistake. Maybe an oversight, or they were unconscious and couldn't say their names to those who were checking. There was no way to get more news than they had. They were told that the *Carpathia* was due into New York in three days, on the eighteenth. She would just have to keep faith until then, and be grateful for her mother's survival. She refused to believe that her father and brother were dead. It just couldn't be.

She stayed awake all that night, after she got home, and still ate nothing. Hortense came to visit her, and spent the night. They said very little, just held hands and cried a lot. Hortie tried to reassure her, and her mother had come over briefly to comfort Annabelle as well. There were no words to soften what had happened. The whole world was shocked by the news. It was a tragedy of epic proportions.

"Thank God you were too sick to go," Hortie whispered as they lay in Annabelle's bed together after her mother left and went home. She had suggested that her daughter spend the night, and in fact stay there until Annabelle's mother returned. She didn't want Annabelle to be alone. Annabelle only nodded at the comment, feeling guilty for not having been with them, wondering if her presence could have helped in some way. Maybe she could have saved one of them at least, or someone.

For the next three days, she and Hortie roamed the house like ghosts. Hortie was the only friend she wanted to see or speak to in her shock and grief. Annabelle ate almost nothing, despite the housekeeper's exhortations. Everyone was constantly crying, and finally Annabelle and Hortie went for a walk to get some air. James came and escorted them, and he was very kind to Annabelle and told her how sorry he was about what had happened. The city, and the world, could think of nothing else.

There was still relatively little news from the *Carpathia,* except the confirmation that the *Titanic* had indeed sunk, and the list of survivors was complete and firm. Only the unidentified babies and children were not on the list, and would have to be identified by family members in port, if they were American. If not, they would have to be returned to Cherbourg and Southampton to their anguished families there. Half a dozen of them belonged to none of the survivors and were too young to say their names. Others were taking care of them in the absence of their parents, and there was no way of telling who they were. But everyone else, even the sick or injured, was on the list, they'd been assured. Annabelle still didn't believe it as Thomas drove her to the Cunard dock on the night of the eighteenth. Hortie didn't want to go with her, as she didn't want to intrude, so Annabelle went to Pier 54 alone.

The waiting crowd saw the *Carpathia* steam slowly into port, with tugboats, just after nine P.M. Annabelle could feel her heart pounding as she watched her, and the ship startled everyone by going to the White Star docks at Piers 59 and 60 instead. And there, in plain sight of all observers, she slowly lowered the remaining lifeboats of the *Titanic,* which was all that was left of her, to return them to the White Star Line, before the *Carpathia* docked herself. Photographers were crammed into a flotilla of small boats trying to get photographs of the lifeboats, and survivors of the disaster lined up at the rail. The atmosphere around them was half funeral, half circus, as the relatives of survivors waited in agonized silence to see who would come off, and reporters and photographers shouted to each other and jockeyed for the best positions and best shots.

After depositing the lifeboats, the *Carpathia* moved slowly to her own dock at Pier 54, and longshoremen and Cunard employees tied her up quickly. And then the gangway was finally let down. In silence, and with heartrending deference, the *Titanic* survivors were let off first. Passengers from the *Carpathia* hugged some of them and squeezed their hands. There were many tears, and little said, as one by one, the survivors came off, most of them with tears streaming down their faces, some still in shock from what they'd seen, and lived through on that awful night. No one would soon forget the hideous screams and moans from the water, the shouts and calls for help in vain as people died. Those in the lifeboats had been too afraid of picking people up, for fear they would capsize from the effort, and drown even more people than those who were already doomed in the water. The sights around them had been hideous, of dead floating bodies, as they waited for help to come and to be picked up.

As they came off the *Carpathia,* there were women with young children, a few women still in evening gowns from their last night aboard the doomed ship, with blankets over them. Some of them had been too shaken to change their clothes for the past three days, and had huddled in the space provided in the *Carpathia*'s dining rooms and main salons. The regular passengers and the crew had done all they could to help, but no one could change the death toll and the shocking loss of life, in circumstances no one could have foreseen.

Annabelle felt breathless until she spotted her mother the moment she reached the gangway. She watched Consuelo coming toward her in the distance, with borrowed clothes, a tragic face, and her head held high in grief-stricken dignity. Annabelle saw it all on her face. There was no other familiar figure with her. Her father and brother were nowhere to be seen. Annabelle glanced one last time behind her mother, but Consuelo was entirely alone amid a sea of other survivors, mostly women, and a few men who seemed to look slightly embarrassed as they got off with their wives. There was a constant explosion of flashbulbs, as reporters recorded as many reunions as they could. And then suddenly her mother was standing in front of her, and Annabelle took her in her arms so tightly that neither of them could breathe. Consuelo was sobbing, and so was she as they clung to each other, while passengers and families eddied around them. And then, with Annabelle's arm around her mother's shoulders, they slowly walked away. It was raining, and no one cared. Consuelo was wearing a rough wool dress that didn't fit her, and evening shoes, and still wore a diamond necklace and earrings from the night the ship sank. She had no coat, and Thomas quickly brought Annabelle the car blanket to put around her mother.

They were barely away from the gangway when Annabelle asked the question she had to ask. She could guess the answer, but she couldn't bear not knowing. She whispered it to her mother, "Robert and Daddy? . . ." Her mother only shook her head, and cried harder as Annabelle led her to the car. Her mother suddenly seemed so frail and so much older. She was a widow at forty-three, and she seemed like an old woman as Thomas gently helped her into the car, and covered her carefully with the fur blanket. Consuelo just looked at him and cried, and then quietly thanked him. She and Annabelle held each other tight in silence as they rode home. Her mother didn't speak again until they reached the house.

All of the servants were waiting in the front hall, to embrace her, hug her, hold her, and when they saw she was alone, to tell her how sorry they were. Within the hour, there was a somber black wreath on the door. There were many in New York that night, once it was clear who hadn't come home and never would.

Annabelle helped to bathe her mother and get her into a nightgown, and Blanche fussed over her like a child. She had taken care of Consuelo since she was a young girl, and had attended both Annabelle's and Robert's births. And now, it had come to this. As she plumped Consuelo's pillows up behind her, once they got her into bed, Blanche had to constantly wipe her eyes, and made little comforting cooing sounds. She brought up a tray with tea, porridge, bland toast, broth, and her favorite cookies, which Consuelo didn't eat. She just sat staring at both of them, unable to say a word.

Annabelle slept in her mother's bed that night, and finally in the darkest hours, when Consuelo shook from head to foot and couldn't sleep, she told her daughter what had happened. She had been in lifeboat number four, with her cousin Madeleine Astor, whose husband hadn't survived either. She said that the lifeboat had only been half full, but her husband and Robert had refused to get in, wanting to stay back to help others, and allow room for the women and children. But there had been plenty of room for them. "If only they'd gotten in," Consuelo said in desperation. The Wideners, Thayers, and

Lucille Carter, all known to her, had been in the lifeboat too. But Robert and Arthur had steadfastly stayed on board to help the others into lifeboats, and given up their lives. Consuelo spoke too of a man named Thomas Andrews, who had been one of the heroes of the night. And she made a point of telling Annabelle that her father and brother had been very brave, which was small consolation now.

They talked for hours, as Consuelo relived the last moments on the ship, and her daughter held her and cried as she listened. Finally as dawn streamed into the room, at last, with a sigh, Consuelo fell asleep.

Chapter 2

There were hundreds of funerals that week in New York, and elsewhere. Newspapers everywhere were filled with poignant stories, and shocking accounts. It was becoming clear to everyone that many of the lifeboats had left the ship half empty, carrying only first-class passengers, and the world was shocked. The much-acclaimed hero was the captain of the *Carpathia,* who had rushed to the scene and picked up the survivors. There was still little explanation as to why the ship had sunk. Once it struck the iceberg, they couldn't avoid her going down. But there was much comment and consternation about why the *Titanic* had pressed on through the icefield, after it had been warned. Fortunately, the *Carpathia* had listened to their desperate pleas for help on the radio, or perhaps none of them would have survived.

The doctor had come to check Consuelo, and found her in remarkably good health, although grief-stricken and shocked. All the life seemed to have gone out of her. And Annabelle was left to plan her father and brother's funerals in infinite detail. The joint service would be held at Trinity Church, which had been a favorite of her father's.

The service was somber and dignified, with hundreds of mourners there to pay their respects. Both caskets at the Worthington funeral service were empty, as neither body had been recovered, and sadly, never were. Of the 1,517 who died, only fifty-one bodies were ever found. The others disappeared quietly into a watery grave at sea.

Several hundred of the people who attended the service came back to the house afterward, where food and drink were served. Some wakes had a festive atmosphere to them, but this one didn't. Robert had been only twenty-four, and his father forty-six, both in the flower of life, and had died in such a tragic way. Both Annabelle and Consuelo were swathed in somber black. Annabelle with a handsome black hat, and her mother in a widow's veil. And that night, when everyone had left, Consuelo looked shattered beyond belief. So much so that Annabelle couldn't help wondering how much of her mother was left. Her spirit seemed to have died with her two men, and Annabelle was seriously worried about her.

It was a great relief to Annabelle when her mother announced at breakfast two weeks after the funeral that she wanted to go to the hospital where she did volunteer work. She said she thought it would do her good to think of someone else, and Annabelle agreed.

"Are you sure you're up to it, Mama?" Annabelle inquired quietly, with a look of concern. She didn't want her mother getting sick, although it was early May and the temperature was warm.

"I'm fine," her mother said sadly. As fine as she was going to be for a long time. And that afternoon, both women wore their black dresses, and white hospital aprons, and went to St. Vincent's Hospital, where Consuelo had worked as a volunteer for years. Annabelle had joined her mother there since she was fifteen. They worked mostly with the indigent, and dealt more with wounds and injuries than infectious diseases. Annabelle had always been fascinated by the work, and had a natural talent for it, and her mother had a gentle manner and a kind heart. But the medical aspect of it was what had always intrigued Annabelle, and whenever possible she read medical books to explain the procedures they saw. She had never been squeamish, unlike Hortie, who had fainted the only time Annabelle had convinced her to join them. The messier a situation got, the more Annabelle liked it. Her mother preferred to serve food on trays, while Annabelle assisted the nurses whenever they let her, changing dressings and cleaning wounds. Patients always said that she had an amazingly gentle touch.

They returned exhausted that night, after a long, tiring afternoon, and went back to the hospital again later that week. If nothing else, it was keeping both Annabelle and her mother distracted from their double loss. Suddenly, the spring that had been meant to be the most exciting time of Annabelle's life, after her debut, had turned into a time of solitude and mourning. They would accept no invitations for the next year, which worried Consuelo. While Annabelle would remain at home in somber black, all the other young women who had just come out would be getting engaged. She was afraid that the tragedy that had struck them would also now impact her daughter's future in a most unfortunate way, but there was nothing they could do. Annabelle didn't seem to think about what she was missing.

Appropriately, she was far more distressed about their losses than about her future, or the absence of a social life.

Hortie still came to visit them often, and in mid-May they quietly celebrated Annabelle's nineteenth birthday. Consuelo was very upset at lunch, and commented that she had married at eighteen, when she came out, and Robert had been born when she was the age that Annabelle was now. Thinking about it reduced her to tears again, and she had left the two girls in the garden, and went upstairs to lie down.

"Your poor mother," Hortie said sympathetically, and then looked at her friend, "and poor you. I'm so sorry, Belle. This is all so awful." She felt so badly for her that it took her another two hours to admit that she and James had set the date for their wedding, in November, and plans for an enormous reception were under way. Annabelle said she was thrilled for her, and meant it. "You really don't care that you can't go out right now?" Hortie asked her. She would have hated being stuck in the house for a year, but Annabelle accepted it with grace. She was only nineteen, and the next year wasn't going to be fun for her. But she had already grown up immeasurably in the brief month since her brother and father had died.

"I don't mind," Annabelle said quietly. "And as long as Mama is willing to work at the hospital, it gives me something to do when I go with her."

"Ergh, don't talk to me about that." Hortie rolled her eyes. "It makes me sick." But she knew that her friend loved it. "Will you still go to Newport this year?" The Worthingtons had a beautiful cottage there, in Rhode Island, next door to the Astors.

"Mama says we will. Maybe we can go up early, in June, instead of July, before the season starts. I think it would do her good." Caring for her mother was Annabelle's only concern now, unlike Hortie, who had a wedding to plan, a million parties to go to, and a fiancé she was madly in love with. Her life was what Annabelle's should have been, and no longer was. Her world, as she knew it, had been interrupted, changed forever.

"At least we'll be together in Newport," Hortie said happily. They both loved to go swimming, when their mothers would let them. They talked about the wedding plans for a while, and then Hortie left. For Annabelle, it had been a very quiet birthday.

In the weeks following the funerals, Consuelo and Annabelle had several visits, as was expected. Friends of Robert's came to call, several elderly dowagers came to offer their condolences to Consuelo, two men from Arthur's bank whom they knew well, and finally, a third one, whom Consuelo had met several times, and liked very much. His name was Josiah Millbank, he was thirty-eight years old, and was much respected at Arthur's bank. He was a quiet man, with gentle manners, and told Consuelo several stories about Arthur that she'd never heard before, and which made her laugh. She was surprised by how much she enjoyed Josiah's visit, and he had been there for an hour when Annabelle came in from a ride with Hortie. Annabelle remembered meeting him previously, but didn't know him well. He was more her father's generation than her own, and was even fourteen years older than her brother, so although they had seen each other at parties, they had nothing in common. But like her mother, she was impressed by his kindness and good manners, and he was sympathetic to Annabelle as well.

He mentioned that he was going to Newport in July, as he always did. He had a simple, comfortable house there. Josiah was originally from Boston, from a family as respectable as their own, and with even more money. He led a quiet life anyway, and was never showy about it. He promised to come and visit them again in Newport, and Consuelo said she'd like that. After he left, Annabelle noticed that he had brought a large bouquet of white lilacs that had already been put in a vase. Consuelo commented about him after he left.

"He's really a very nice man," Consuelo said quietly, admiring the lilac. "Your father liked him a lot, and I can see why. I wonder why he never married."

"Some people don't," Annabelle said, looking unconcerned. "Not everyone has to get married, Mama," she added with a smile. She was beginning to wonder if she was going to be one of those. She couldn't imagine leaving her mother now, to go off with a man. She wouldn't want to leave Consuelo alone. And it didn't seem like a tragedy to her if she didn't marry. It would have been to Hortie, but not to her. With her father and brother gone, and her mother shaken to her core, Annabelle felt she had more important responsibilities at home, and didn't resent it for a moment. Caring for her mother gave purpose to her life.

"If you're telling me you don't want to get married," her mother correctly read her mind, as she often did, "you can forget about that right now. We are going to do our year of mourning, as is proper, and then we're going to find you a husband. That's what your father would want."

Annabelle turned to face her seriously then. "Daddy wouldn't want me to leave you alone," she said as firmly as any parent.

Consuelo shook her head. "That's nonsense and you know it. I'm perfectly capable of taking care of myself." But as she said it, her eyes filled with tears again, and her daughter was not convinced.

"We'll see about that," Annabelle said firmly, and swept out of the room, to organize a tea tray to be taken up to Consuelo's room. When she returned, she put her arm around her mother, gently escorted her upstairs for a nap, and settled her on her bed, the bed she had shared with the husband she had loved and who was gone, which broke Consuelo's heart.

"You're much too good to me, my love," she said, looking embarrassed.

"No, I'm not," Annabelle said brightly. She was the only remaining ray of sunshine in the house. She brought her mother nothing but joy. And each was all the other had left. There were just the two of them now. She pulled a light shawl over Consuelo, and went back downstairs to read in the garden, hoping her mother would feel up to going back to the hospital the next day. It was the only distraction Annabelle had, and gave her something to do that was important to her.

She could hardly wait to go to Newport the following month.

Chapter 3

Annabelle and her mother left for Newport a month earlier than usual, in June. It was beautiful that time of year, and as they always did, the staff had gone ahead to open the house. Usually, the social season in Newport was dazzling, but this year they were planning a very quiet life. People could visit them at the house, but two months after her father and brother's deaths there was no way that Annabelle and her mother could go out. The now-familiar black ribbons were put on the front door in Newport, to indicate their state of mourning.

There were a number of families in the same situation in Newport that year, including the Astors. Madeleine Astor, who had lost her husband John Jacob on the *Titanic,* was expecting her baby in August. The tragedy had hit the New York social world hard, since it was the maiden voyage, and so many society types and aristocrats had been on the ship. And continuing news of the ineptitude of the crew getting people off the boat was increasingly disturbing. Almost all the lifeboats had left half empty. Some men had forced their way into them with the women and children. And almost no one from steerage had been saved. There were going to be official hearings about it in time.

Newport was extremely quiet in June, but started to liven up as people from Boston and New York began to arrive and fill their "cottages" in July. For the uninitiated, what people called cottages in Newport were actually mansions of mammoth proportions anywhere else. They were houses with ballrooms, enormous chandeliers, marble floors, priceless antique furniture, and spectacular gardens, bordering on the sea. It was a remarkable community made up of the scions of society from the entire East Coast, a watering hole for the very rich. The Worthingtons were right at home there. Their cottage was one of the largest and loveliest in town.

Annabelle started to have fun once Hortie arrived. They sneaked off to the sea together, went for walks, and Hortie's fiancé James often joined them for picnics on the lawn. Now and then he brought friends, which was fun for Annabelle, and her mother pretended she didn't notice. As long as they didn't go to parties, she had no objection to Annabelle seeing young people. She was such a good person and so devoted to her mother, she deserved it. Consuelo wondered if any of James's friends, or Robert's old pals, would spark Annabelle's interest. She was increasingly worried that the year of mourning would impact Annabelle's fate forever. Since the Christmas season, when all the girls had come out, six of the young women in Annabelle's age group had gotten engaged. And Annabelle wasn't going to meet anyone staying at home with her mother. After the past two months, she already seemed older and more mature than the others. Something like that could frighten young men away. And more than anything, her mother wanted her to get married. Annabelle continued to be unconcerned and was happy to see Hortie and the others, but none of the men was of even the slightest interest to her.

Josiah Millbank came to see them once he arrived in July too. He never failed to bring a gift with him when he visited, flowers in the city, and in Newport, either fruit or candy. He spent hours talking to Consuelo, as they sat together on the wide porch in rocking chairs, and after his third visit, Annabelle teased her about it.

"I think he likes you, Mama," she said, smiling.

"Don't be silly." Consuelo blushed at the suggestion. The last thing she wanted was a suitor. She intended to remain faithful to her husband's memory forever, and said so to anyone who would listen. She was not one of those widows who was looking for a husband, although she wanted one desperately for Annabelle. "He's just being kind to us," Consuelo added firmly, convinced of what she was saying. "He's younger than I am anyway, and if he's interested in anyone, it's you." Although she had to admit, there was no evidence of it. He seemed to be equally comfortable talking to mother or daughter, and he was never flirtatious, just friendly.

"He's not interested in me, Mama," Annabelle confirmed with a broad grin, "and he's only five years younger than you are. I think he's a very nice person. And he's old enough to be my father."

"Lots of girls your age marry men his age," her mother said quietly. "He's not that old, for heaven's sake. I think he's only thirty-eight, if I remember correctly."

"He's much better for you." Annabelle laughed and ran off with Hortie. It was a hot, sunny day and they wanted to go swimming, and James had promised to come over later. There was a big party planned at the Schuylers' that night, which James and Hortie and all their friends were going to, although Annabelle of course couldn't. She wouldn't have dreamed of asking her mother, and didn't want to upset her.

But that night, sitting on the porch, they could hear the party and the music in the distance. There were fireworks, and Consuelo knew it was to celebrate the engagement of one of the Schuyler daughters. It made her heart ache for Annabelle as they listened.

Much to their surprise, Josiah dropped by later in the evening to bring them each a piece of cake from the party. He was on the way back to his place, and both women were touched by the thoughtful gesture. He stayed for a glass of lemonade with them, and then said he had to leave, as he had a houseguest waiting for him at home. He promised to come back soon, when they thanked him. Even Annabelle was touched by the gesture of friendship She had no ro mantic interest in him, but in a funny way, she felt as though he were standing in for her brother. She liked talking to him, and he teased her in just the way Robert used to, and which she missed so much.

"I wonder why he didn't take his houseguest to the party," Consuelo mused, as she left their glasses and the pitcher of lemonade in the pantry.

"Maybe they're unsuitable," Annabelle teased, "a shocking, unsuit- able woman. Maybe he has a mistress," she said, chortling, as her mother guffawed. Given how well brought up Josiah was, and how po- lite, it seemed extremely unlikely. And he wouldn't have mentioned a guest at all if that were the case.

"You have a most unsuitable imagination," her mother scolded, and a moment later the two of them went upstairs, chatting amiably about Josiah and how nice he had been to bring them cake from the party. It was the first time Annabelle had actually been sorry she couldn't go out. All her friends had been there, and it had sounded like quite a celebration, with the fireworks and all. It was going to be a very quiet summer, except for Hortie and Josiah, both of whom were faithful about frequent visits, and a few other friends as well.

Josiah came back again the next day, and Consuelo invited him for a picnic lunch with Annabelle and Hortie. Josiah seemed perfectly at ease with both girls, even though Hortie giggled a lot and was often silly, and he said that he had a half-sister their age, from his father's second marriage after he was widowed. Annabelle still couldn't imagine Hortie as a married woman, which she would be in four months. She was still such a baby, but she was crazy about James, and often when she and Annabelle were alone, she made racy comments about their wedding night and honeymoon, which made Annabelle roll her eyes. Fortunately, Hortie said none of that in front of Josiah, and he commented that his sister had gotten married in April and was expecting a baby. He seemed to be perfectly familiar with the lives, pursuits, and interests of young girls, and they both enjoyed talking to him.

He mentioned his houseguest to them, and said he was a classmate of his from Harvard, and came up to visit every summer. He said he was a studious, quiet fellow, and usually avoided social events and parties.

Josiah stayed until the late afternoon, and walked Annabelle back up to the house when Hortie left. Her mother was sitting on the porch, chatting with a friend. It was fun for them there. Lots of people came to visit, and there was a sense of life swirling around them. It was particularly nice for Annabelle, who was dreading going back to the city. She had told Josiah about the hospital work she loved to do, and he had teased her about it.

"I suppose you want to be a nurse when you grow up," he said, knowing full well, as she did, that that would never happen. The closest she would ever get to it was volunteer work, but she still did a lot of reading about medical subjects. It was her secret passion.

"Actually," she said honestly, not afraid to be candid with him, "I'd rather be a doctor." She felt as though she could tell him anything, and he wouldn't laugh at her. He had become a good friend since her father died and he had begun his visits to them. But this time he looked startled. She had surprised him. She was a far more serious person than even he had guessed, and he could see from the look on her face that she meant what she had said.

"That's a pretty impressive ambition," he said, sobered for a minute. "Would you ever do that?"

"My mother would never let me. But I'd love to. If I could. I take medical books and books about anatomy out of the library sometimes. I don't understand everything they say, but I've learned some interesting things. I think medicine is fascinating. And there are a lot more women doctors now than there were." Women had been getting into medical schools for over sixty years now, but he still couldn't imagine Annabelle doing that, and he suspected she was right, her mother would have a fit. She wanted Annabelle to have a far more traditional life, to get married and have children, hence her debut.

"I never wanted to be a doctor," he confessed. "But I did want to join the circus when I was about ten or twelve." She laughed as he said it, it was such a funny thing to admit to. "I loved the animals, and I always wanted to be a magician, so I could make my homework disappear. I wasn't much of a student."

"I don't think I believe you, if you went to Harvard," she said, still laughing at him. "I think it would have been fun to join the circus. Why didn't you?"

"Your father offered me a job instead, although that was later. I don't know, maybe I just didn't have the gumption it took. But I never had ambitions like yours. Just thinking of all the years of school it would take would kill me. I'm much too lazy to be a doctor."

"I don't believe that," she said kindly. "But I know I'd love it." Her eyes shone brightly as she said it.

"Who knows, maybe someday you'll be able to use some of what you've learned in books, in your volunteer work. That's a noble pursuit." He admired her for doing it at least.

"They don't let you do much," she said, looking disappointed.

"What would you like to do?" he asked with interest.

"I do very nice needlework, everyone always says so. I'd like to try stitching someone up sometime. I'm sure I could." He looked shocked when she said it, and then smiled broadly.

"Remind me not to cut myself in front of you, or you'll be whipping a needle and an embroidery hoop out of your pocket!"

"I would enjoy that," she admitted, smiling impishly at him.

"Someone is going to have to keep you busy, Miss Worthington, or I get the feeling you'll be up to mischief."

"Medical mischief would suit me very well. Just think, if we weren't who we are, I could go to medical school and do anything I wanted. Isn't that annoying?" she asked, looking like a child and a woman all at once, and without thinking he hugged her, just as he would his little sister. She felt like that to him, just as she felt a bond to him almost like a brother. A nice relationship and friendship was developing between them.

"If you weren't who you are, you couldn't afford to go to medical school," he said practically, and she nodded in agreement.

"That's true. But if I were a man I could. Robert could have, if he'd wanted to, and my parents would have let him. Sometimes, it's very difficult being a woman. There is so much you can't do and that's not considered proper. It's really very boring," she said, kicking a pebble with the toe of her shoe, and he laughed at her.

"Don't tell me you're one of those women who want to fight for rights and freedom." She didn't seem the type to him, and it would have surprised him.

"No. I'm perfectly happy the way things are. I just wish I could be a doctor."

"Well, I wish I could be the King of England, but that's not going to happen either. Some things are just out of our reach, Annabelle, and we have to accept that. You have a good life as it is."

"Yes, I do," she agreed. "And I love my mother. I wouldn't do anything to upset her, and that would upset her a lot."

"Yes, it would."

"She's been through so much this year, and I just want to make her happy."

"You do," he said comfortably. "I can see it. You're a wonderful daughter to her, and a lovely person."

"No, she's not," Hortie said, as she appeared from nowhere and sidled up to them. She had come back to go swimming with Annabelle again. "She dissected a frog once. She read how to do it in a book. It was the most disgusting thing I've *ever* seen. She is definitely *not* a lovely person." All three of them laughed at what she said.

"I assume that's true," Josiah said, beginning to know Annabelle better. She was a most remarkable young woman, in many ways.

"Yes, it is," Annabelle said proudly. "I did it just like the book told me. It was very interesting. I wish I could dissect a real person. A corpse, you know, like in medical school."

"Oh my God," Hortie said, looking woozy, and Josiah looked shocked but amused.

"You two had better go swimming," he said, and shooed them off as he went up to the porch to say good-bye to Consuelo.

"What were the three of you talking about?" she asked him with interest.

"Oh the usual, parties, debuts, engagements, weddings," he said, covering for Annabelle, knowing that her mother would faint if she thought that Annabelle wished she could dissect a cadaver. He was still laughing to himself as he walked back to his own cottage. Annabelle Worthington was certainly an interesting young woman, and not the usual nineteen-year-old girl at all.

As he got back to his own place, his college roommate was just returning from lunch, and Josiah waved as he saw him. Henry Orson was one of his oldest friends, and he enjoyed the time they spent together every summer. They had been valued friends to each other since their college days, and Henry was a man of substance, whom everyone admired.

"How was lunch?" Josiah asked him. They were both good-looking men, and had always been able to have all the women they wanted, but were responsible about it. They never led women on nor took advantage of them. Henry had been engaged two years before and had been seriously disappointed when his fiancée fell in love with a younger man, a boy her own age. And he had had no serious involvements since, which made all the Newport mothers hopeful, as they were about Josiah.

"Boring," Henry said honestly. "How was yours?" Henry found many social gatherings tedious and preferred discussing business with other serious men to flirting with young girls.

"I had a picnic with a young lady who wants to dissect a human cadaver," Josiah said, grinning, and Henry laughed out loud.

"Jesus," Henry said, looking amused and impressed, and pretending to be frightened. "She sounds dangerous. Stay away from her!"

"Don't worry," Josiah said, laughing, as they walked into the house together, "I will."

The two men played cards for the rest of the afternoon, while discussing the state of the financial world, which was Henry's passion. It was a subject that made him tedious to women but interesting to men, since he was extremely knowledgeable and had an intelligent perspective, and Josiah was always happy to talk to him. He had gotten Henry a job at Annabelle's father's bank several years before, and he was extremely respected by his colleagues and superiors. Although less sociable than Josiah, he had done very well at the bank too. Henry had never met Annabelle or Consuelo, but Josiah promised to introduce him to them during his stay in Newport, as Henry shook his head, while frowning at his cards.

"Not if she's going to chop me up like a cadaver," Henry said ominously, and then smiled as he put down a winning hand.

"Damn," Josiah said, folding, and smiled at him. "Don't worry. She's just a child."

Chapter 4

Josiah visited the Worthingtons often during July and August, as did Hortie and James, and a number of other friends. Josiah introduced Henry to them, as promised, who extended his condolences to Consuelo, and taught Annabelle several new games of cards, which delighted her no end, particularly when she beat him several times. She was enjoying the company of the good friends they saw in Newport, and although they were removed from the social whirl that summer, she felt far less isolated than she did in the city. Life seemed almost normal again here, despite the absence of her father and brother, who had often stayed in the city to work anyway.

By the time they left Newport at the end of August, she looked healthy and brown and happy, and her mother looked better too. It had been an easy, peaceful summer for them, after their tragic spring.

Once back in the city, Annabelle joined her mother doing hospital work again. And she volunteered on her own one day a week at the New York Hospital for the Relief of the Ruptured and Crippled. They were doing extraordinary work that fascinated her. She told Josiah all about it when he came to the house in the city to have tea.

"You haven't gotten to work on any cadavers yet, have you?" he asked, pretending to be worried, and she laughed at him.

"No, I just bring food and jugs of water to the patients, but one of the nurses said I might be able to watch a surgery one day."

"You are a remarkable girl indeed," he said, with a broad easy grin.

And by the end of the month, Consuelo finally had the courage to go through her husband's and son's things. They put some of them away, and gave away most of their clothes, but left Arthur's study and Robert's bedroom intact. Neither of them had the heart to take the rooms apart, and there was no reason to. They didn't need those rooms.

They saw very little of Josiah in September, compared to his summer visits. He was busy at the bank, and they were still settling the estate. Although Arthur had no reason to think anything would happen to him, he had left his affairs in perfect order, and Annabelle and her mother were in excellent financial shape. Both of them could live easily for the rest of their lives on what he had left them, and there would still be a healthy estate to leave to Annabelle's children one day, although it was the last thing on her mind.

Annabelle saw very little of Hortie that month too. The wedding was only six weeks away, and Hortie had a lot to do. She had fittings for her wedding gown, a trousseau to be ordered, her father had given them a house, and she and James were buying furniture for it. They were going to Europe on their honeymoon, and would be gone until Christmas, and Annabelle knew she would miss her while she was away. Once she was married, it would never be quite the same.

Annabelle had seen it with other friends, and she missed Hortie already.

It was early October when Josiah finally came to visit again. Annabelle was at the Hospital for the Relief of the Ruptured and Crippled, and Consuelo was in the garden, enjoying a sunny afternoon with a cup of tea. She was surprised to see Josiah, but he was always welcome, and as she stood up to greet him, she looked genuinely pleased.

"We haven't seen you in ages, Josiah. How are you?"

"Fine." He smiled at her. "I've been in Boston for the past few weeks. My family had some things I needed to handle for them there. What have you and Annabelle been up to?"

"We're fine. Annabelle's been busy at the hospital again, but at least it keeps her occupied. There's nothing much else for her to do here." They had another six months in their formal mourning period, and Consuelo knew that although Annabelle never complained, it was hard on her. She hadn't been out with her friends in six months, and it was boring for a nineteen-year-old girl. She needed to be out in the world, but there was nothing Consuelo could do.

"I know this time must seem long to both of you," Josiah said quietly, as he sat down in the garden with her, and declined a cup of tea.

"I don't mind it for myself, but I do mind it for her," Consuelo admitted. "She'll be nearly twenty before she gets out in the world again. It really doesn't seem fair." But what had happened to Consuelo hadn't been fair either. Life just worked that way sometimes.

"She'll be fine," Josiah reassured her. "Annabelle's the sort of person who makes the best of every situation. She's never complained to me once about not being able to go out," he said honestly, and her mother nodded.

"I know. She's a dear. I'm sorry you missed her today, she'll be disappointed. She's always at the hospital on Monday afternoons." He nodded, hesitating for a moment, looking pensively into space, and then back at Consuelo with a surprisingly intent look.

"I actually didn't come to see Annabelle today. I came to see you, on a matter of business that I wanted to discuss with you privately." He looked proper and businesslike as he said it, as though he were on a mission from the bank.

"Something about Arthur's estate? Can't you handle that with the lawyers, Josiah? You know how bad I am at all that. Arthur handled everything. It's all a mystery to me."

"No, no, everything is fine. The bank is handling it with the attorneys, and everything's in order. This is a more private matter, and perhaps I'm premature, but I wanted to discuss it with you, and I'm hoping you'll be discreet." She couldn't begin to imagine what it was as she listened to him, nor why Annabelle shouldn't be around. For a fraction of an instant, she worried that Annabelle had been right months before, and that he was paying court to her. She hoped not. She liked him enormously, but if he had any romantic interest in her whatsoever, Consuelo was going to decline. She had no leanings in his direction, nor toward anyone else. As far as Consuelo was concerned, that chapter of her life was closed.

"I wanted to talk to you about Annabelle," he said clearly, so that neither of them would be confused. He realized that he was much closer to Consuelo's age than her daughter's, but he felt no romantic spark toward Consuelo, only respect, admiration, and warm friendship. The Worthingtons had been extremely hospitable to him since Arthur's death, and he had greatly enjoyed spending time with them.

"I know you're both in deep mourning for another six months, and that you're concerned about her. It is a shame that she has missed this whole year since her debut, and all the opportunities that would afford. At first I thought I should say nothing to you, whatever my feelings. She's extremely young, and I sincerely believed that she would be happiest with someone her own age. To be honest, I no longer think that's true.

"Annabelle is a very unusual young woman in many ways, intelligent, intellectual, thirsty for knowledge, and mature beyond her years. I have no idea how you would feel about it, but I would like your permission, when your period of mourning is over, to ask for her hand in marriage, and see how she feels. If you and I remain discreet about it, and keep this to ourselves, it will give her another six months to get accustomed to me. If you agree, I would plan to continue visiting you both often. But I wanted your permission first." Consuelo sat there staring at him. In her eyes, he was an answer to her prayers and a dream come true. She had been desperately worried about life passing Annabelle by during this year, and afraid she might wind up an old maid. And although he was nineteen years older, Consuelo thought Josiah was perfect for Annabelle.

Josiah was from an excellent family, well educated, exquisitely polite, charming, handsome, and had a very good job at Annabelle's father's bank. And from what she had seen, particularly over the summer, the two were becoming good friends, which Consuelo felt was a far more solid base for marriage than some starry-eyed girlish romance, which wouldn't last anyway. This was the way she and Arthur had started out. He had been a friend of her family's, had asked her father's permission to court her, and they had always been friends as much as husband and wife. She couldn't have thought of a better match for her daughter, and like Josiah, she thought Annabelle would do well with an older, more mature man. "I hope you're not shocked, or angry," he added cautiously, as Consuelo leaned over and gave him a motherly hug.

"No, how could I be? I'm delighted. I think you and Annabelle would be wonderful for each other." And in her eyes, their year of mourning had not been a waste after all. It was the perfect way for the two of them to come to know each other well. And there was no distracting competition at balls and parties from silly young men to turn Annabelle's head. Josiah was a solid, established man, and would have been a wonderful husband for anyone, particularly her daughter. And Annabelle didn't seem to mind him, in fact she liked him very much. "Do you think she suspects anything about your intentions?" Consuelo asked candidly. She had no idea if he had wooed her or not, kissed her, courted her, or hinted at what he had in mind. Annabelle had never said anything to her mother, which made her think that she had no idea what was in Josiah's head.

"I've never said anything," he told Consuelo honestly. "I wouldn't until I spoke to you, although I've been thinking about it all summer, but I thought it was too soon. And unfortunately, for the last few weeks I've been away. I don't think Annabelle suspects anything. I'd like to wait to talk to her about it, until your year of mourning is over in April. Perhaps I could speak to her about it in May." He knew she would be twenty then, and he would be thirty-nine, something of an old man to her. He was afraid she might have objections to that, but he wasn't sure. She wasn't flirtatious with him, but he had the feeling they had truly become good friends. And like her mother, he thought that was an excellent foundation for marriage. This was a first for him. He had never proposed to any woman before, but he hoped it wasn't too late. And recently, he had been thinking that he would love to have children with her. She seemed like the perfect lifetime companion to him. Consuelo was absolutely thrilled.

"I couldn't have found a better person for her, if I'd picked you myself," Consuelo said, looking pleased, and ringing for the butler. When William appeared, she asked for two glasses of champagne. Josiah was a little startled. He hadn't expected it to be this easy.

"I'm not sure we should celebrate yet. We still have to ask her, in May. She may not think it's as great an idea as we do. She's very young, and I'm twice her age."

"I think she's more sensible than that," Consuelo said as the butler returned and handed them each a glass of champagne. Arthur had had remarkable wine cellars, and the vintage was very good. "And she likes you, Josiah. I think the two of you get on very well."

"I think so too," he said, looking happy, and wishing he could ask Annabelle that afternoon, but it wouldn't be proper to propose to her so soon after Arthur and Robert's deaths. "I hope she agrees," Josiah said hopefully.

"That's up to you," Consuelo reminded him. "You have the next six months to win her heart and seal the deal."

"Without her knowing what I'm doing," he said cautiously.

"Maybe you could drop a little hint once in a while," his future mother-in-law suggested, and he laughed.

"She's too smart for that. If I start hinting, I might as well ask her. And I don't want to scare her off by doing it too soon."

"I don't think it's going to be as difficult as you think to convince her," Consuelo said, beaming at him, in the dappled sunlight of the warm October afternoon. Thanks to him, it had been a perfect day. She was only sorry she didn't have Arthur to share it with, and she suspected that he would have been pleased as well.

They were still chatting amiably with each other, about Josiah's plan, when Annabelle strode into the garden with her hospital apron on. There was blood on it, and her mother made a face.

"Take that thing off," Consuelo scolded her, "and go wash your hands. For heaven's sake, Annabelle, you're bringing germs into the house." She shooed her away, and Annabelle returned five minutes later, without the apron, in her severe black dress. She looked almost like a young nun. It was a sober look, but she was wreathed in smiles when she saw Josiah, and the only thing somber about her was her dress. She seemed to be in a great mood.

"I had a terrific day," she announced, then noticed the champagne they were drinking. She always observed everything, and never missed a detail. "Why are you two drinking champagne? What are you celebrating?"

"Josiah just came to tell me he got a promotion at the bank," her mother replied smoothly. "They've given him all sorts of new accounts to handle. And I thought we should congratulate him. Would you like a glass too?" Annabelle nodded. She loved champagne, and went to get a glass herself, and then duly congratulated Josiah on his promotion, although she never found banking very exciting. It had bored her when her father and Robert talked about it too. She was far more interested in science.

"What did you do at the hospital today?" he asked her gently. He suddenly felt as though she were already his wife, and he was feeling extremely tender emotions toward her, which he couldn't allow to show.

"Lots of interesting things," she said, smiling openly at him, and then taking a sip of the champagne. She had no idea she was toasting her own future engagement, and knowing that made both him and Consuelo smile too. They had become co-conspirators that afternoon. "They let me watch while they sewed up a nasty wound."

"If you tell me about it, I'll be sick," her mother warned, and Annabelle laughed, as they shifted the subject to something else. "You'll have to stop doing that someday," Consuelo said cryptically. "One day you'll be grown up and married, and you can't hang around hospitals, watching them sew up wounds."

"You do," Annabelle reminded her with a smile.

"I do not. I carry trays to patients in a far more civilized hospital, and I didn't have time to do that when you were small. You can go back to it when you're older."

"I don't see why I'd have to stop if I married," Annabelle complained. "Lots of women have children and still work at the hospital. Besides, I might never marry. Who knows?"

"I don't want to hear that!" her mother said, frowning, and then turned to Josiah. She could hardly wait for them to be married, and start having babies. It would be a whole new chapter in their lives, and she knew that Annabelle would be a wonderful mother. She was so patient and loving, and she thought she would make an excellent wife for Josiah.

They talked about Hortie's wedding then, which was only weeks away. She was so busy that Annabelle hardly saw her now. And Josiah said he was going to the wedding. Annabelle quietly said she couldn't, and then was surprised by her mother.

"I don't see why you can't go to the church service," Consuelo said benevolently. "There's nothing that says we can't go to church. In fact, we should probably go more often. You can come home after that, and avoid the reception. But at least you could see Hortie get married. After all, she is your oldest and dearest friend." And would probably be Annabelle's matron of honor, Consuelo knew, when she married Josiah.

"I'd be happy to take both of you," Josiah was quick to offer, as he turned to his future bride, who had no idea what he was thinking. It would be his first opportunity to escort her in public, and he was excited by the prospect.

"I don't think I should go," Consuelo said quietly. She wasn't ready to be out in public yet. "But it would be lovely if you escort Annabelle to the service."

"Would you like that?" he asked Annabelle directly. She smiled broadly as she nodded.

"I'd love it." All her friends would be there. Hortie had wanted her as maid of honor, and now she couldn't do it. This way, at least, she could be at the wedding. And it would be fun to go with Josiah, a little like going with Robert. Her brother had often escorted her to parties, although they had been small ones before her debut. And Hortie was having a gigantic wedding. Eight hundred people had been invited, and more than likely, most were coming.

"We'll have to find you something to wear," her mother said

thoughtfully. Annabelle would have to wear a suitable black gown, and she had nothing formal in dark colors.

"It's going to be so much fun!" Annabelle said, clapping her hands, looking like a child as her mother and Josiah smiled at her.

"It's all going to be fun from now on," her mother said to her with a loving look. She was so relieved by Josiah's intended proposal.

And with that, Annabelle put her arms around Josiah's neck and hugged him. He looked particularly delighted. "Thank you for taking me," she said happily.

"It's one of those sacrifices one has to make in life," he teased her. "I'll muddle through it." He could hardly wait for the next six months to pass, and then, with luck, they'd be going to their own wedding. Her mother had the same thought at the same moment, and she and Josiah exchanged a knowing look over Annabelle's head, and smiled. Annabelle didn't know it yet, but her future was secure now. It was all her mother had ever wanted for her since she was born.

Chapter 5

Annabelle was almost as excited as Hortie herself, as she dressed for her best friend's wedding. Her mother had called her dressmaker, and she had whipped up a beautiful black taffeta gown in record time. The bodice and hem were bordered in black velvet. And there was a matching black velvet jacket and hat trimmed in sable, which softened it as the fur lit up her face. Annabelle looked like a Russian princess. And bending the rules about no jewelry during a period of mourning, her mother had loaned her a pair of diamond earrings. She looked exquisite when Josiah came to get her. And so did he, in white tie and tails, and an elegant top hat he'd had made in Paris. They were a spectacular couple, and Consuelo had damp eyes as she watched them. She only wished that Arthur were there to see it. But if he were, perhaps it would never have happened. Josiah had only begun visiting them out of sympathy in their bereavement. So destiny took strange turns and pathways.

Consuelo had urged them to take her car, and Thomas the driver, and they drove to the wedding in the impeccable Hispano-Suiza that had been her father's prize possession, and was only used for important occasions. As far as Consuelo was concerned, this was an event of significant proportions. It was the first time her future son-in-law would be seen in public with her only daughter. How much more important could it get, except their wedding?

She watched them lovingly as they went out the door, and then went up to her bedroom, lost in her own thoughts. She was remembering the first time she had gone out with Arthur, after he had asked her father for her hand. It had been to a friend's coming-out ball. And she had been only a year younger than her daughter at the time.

The car drove them to St. Thomas Episcopal Church, on Fifth Avenue, and the chauffeur let Josiah out first. He turned and handed Annabelle out of the car. She was wearing her blond hair pulled back, under the velvet and sable hat, with a small face veil. She looked as stylish as any woman in Paris, and older than her years, because of the opulent black gown. Josiah had never been prouder.

"You know, for a girl who'd rather be scrubbing floors in a hospital and dissecting cadavers, you look very nice when you get dressed up," he said lightly, and she laughed, which only made her look prettier, as her mother's diamond earrings sparkled behind the thin veil. She looked elegant, sensual, and romantic, and Josiah was bowled over by the woman he hoped to marry. He hadn't fully realized how truly beautiful she was, because she made so little fuss about herself, and while in mourning she never wore fancy clothes or makeup. He had been at her coming-out ball the year before, but even then she hadn't looked this pretty. She had grown into her womanhood in the year since then.

An usher in white tie and tails escorted them to a pew near the front on the bride's side of the church. They had been expected, and Josiah noticed people looking at them with quiet admiration. They made a very dashing couple. Annabelle was oblivious to it, dazzled by the absolute forest of white orchids that Hortie's mother had ordered. Annabelle had seen the gown, and knew that Hortie was going to look gorgeous in it. She had a terrific figure. The gown was low-cut white satin, covered with white lace, with a train that would stretch out for miles behind her. There were sixteen bridesmaids in pale gray satin gowns, carrying tiny orchids. It was a very stylish wedding, and Hortie was going to carry a huge ball of lily of the valley.

They took their seats as Annabelle looked around. She knew everyone in the pews ahead of and behind them, and Josiah knew most of them as well. People smiled and made little gestures of greeting. They looked interested to see her with Josiah, and he noticed then that her mother had let her wear lipstick. In his opinion there was no more beautiful woman in the church than Annabelle as she sat beside him, including the bride as she came down the aisle, to Wagner's Bridal Chorus from *Lohengrin.*

All eyes were on Hortie, and her father had never looked prouder. It was then that Annabelle realized that on her own wedding day there would be no one to walk her down the aisle, neither her father, nor her brother. Thinking about it brought tears to her eyes, and seeing that, Josiah gently patted her arm. He had a feeling that was what she was thinking. He was developing good instincts about her, and getting to know her well. And although he hadn't been in her life for long, he was beginning to love her. He enjoyed sitting through the church service with her. Everything went smoothly, and when the bride and groom walked back down the aisle after the ceremony, to

Mendelssohn, everyone was beaming. All sixteen bridesmaids and an equal number of groomsmen walked out solemnly behind them, including a five-year-old ring bearer, and a three-year-old flower girl in a white organdy dress, who forgot to strew the rose petals and just clutched them in her hand.

Annabelle and Josiah greeted friends in the throng of people in the vestibule of the church. They passed through the receiving line to congratulate the bride and groom and both sets of parents, and finally, an hour after the ceremony, everyone left the church for the reception. Annabelle wished she could go with them, she knew it was going to be a fabulous party that would go on all night, but there was no question of it for her. Josiah rode home with her in the car, and walked her into the house, as Annabelle thanked him for going with her.

"I had a wonderful time," she said, looking ecstatic. It had been fun to catch a glimpse of all her friends, and even meet some of Josiah's who were, of course, much older than she was, but seemed very nice.

"So did I," he said honestly. He had been so proud to be with her. She was such a beautiful young woman.

"You should hurry, so you're not late to the reception," she said, as she took off her hat, kissed his cheek, and shooed him toward the door. She looked even prettier without the veil, and her mother's earrings were blinding.

"I'm in no rush," he said easily. "I declined the reception." He was smiling at her.

"You did?" She looked startled. "Why? It's going to be the wedding of the year." Hortie's parents had gone all out, and she didn't want Josiah to miss it. It didn't occur to her why he had declined.

"I've been to a lot of weddings of the year." He laughed, and added,

"For a lot of years. There are always others. Why would I go to the reception, when you can't? That doesn't seem right to me. The church service was fine. We saw lots of people. I can go to parties anytime. Why don't we go down to the kitchen and make something to eat? I make a terrific sandwich and a mean omelette." Neither of them had eaten dinner. The staff had disappeared for the night, and her mother was upstairs in her room, probably asleep.

"Are you serious? Don't you think you should go to the reception?" she pressed. She felt guilty for keeping him from going.

"It would be pretty strange if I showed up after I declined." He laughed again. "They'd think I was out of my mind, and I wouldn't have a seat. So let's check out what's in your icebox, and I'll dazzle you with my culinary skills."

"In that suit?" He was wearing white tie and tails, with handsome mother of pearl and diamond studs and cuff links.

"I might take off the jacket, if you won't be too shocked." He had on the traditional white piqué tie and vest, also with studs in the vest, all of which he'd had made in Paris with the top hat. He was a very handsome vision, and a perfect match for her.

"I won't be shocked. I'll take off my jacket too," she said, taking off the sable-trimmed velvet jacket that matched her dress, and exposing creamy white shoulders, and a well-shaped bosom that he glanced at discreetly.

"That's quite a dress," he said, smiling at her in admiration.

"I'm glad you like it," she said shyly. The evening suddenly felt very grown-up to her. Her debut ball was the only event of its kind she had ever attended. And she had very much enjoyed going to the wedding with Josiah at her side.

Annabelle led him down to the kitchen and turned on the lights. Everything was immaculate and had been left in perfect order. They checked the icebox and found eggs, butter, cooked vegetables, half a turkey, and some ham. She took most of it out and set it on the kitchen table. And then she found lettuce, and some fresh vegetables in the larder.

She set the table with the kitchen plates, in her evening gown, as Josiah took off his tailcoat and made dinner. He sliced the ham and turkey finely, made a salad, and cooked an excellent cheese omelette in a skillet. It was a delicious meal, as they sat at the kitchen table and chatted, and commented on who they'd seen. He told her little bits of gossip about some of the people she'd met, and she filled him in on some of her friends. It was a lively exchange, and they sat talking long after they finished the meal. She didn't have the key to the wine cellar, and he said he was delighted with a glass of milk. It was the nicest evening Annabelle had had in years.

They talked about the holidays, and he said he was going to Boston to be with his family for Thanksgiving, but said he would be in New York for Christmas. She reminded herself to ask her mother if they could invite him to Christmas dinner. It was going to be a tough one for them that year. It was hard to believe that a year after her ball their life had changed so dramatically, and she said as much to him.

"You never know in life," he said quietly. "You have to be grateful for what you have, for as long as you have it. Fate is unpredictable, and sometimes we don't know how blessed we are until things change."

She nodded and looked at him sadly. "I knew how blessed we were, and so did my mother. We all did. I always felt lucky to have the parents and brother that I did. I just can't believe they're gone," she said quietly, and as he looked at her, he gently put a hand over hers.

"Sometimes Fate ushers some people out, and when we least expect it, others enter. You just have to believe that things will continue to be good from now on. Your life is just beginning."

She nodded again. "But for my mother, it's over. I don't think she'll ever recover." Annabelle worried about her a great deal.

"You don't know that," he said gently. "Good things can happen to her too."

"I hope so," Annabelle said softly, and thanked him for the meal. It had been a lovely evening. He helped her put the dishes in the sink, and then she turned to him with a smile, their friendship blossoming between them. "You're a pretty good cook."

"Wait until you taste my soufflés. I also make the stuffing at Thanksgiving," he said proudly.

"How did you ever learn to cook?" She looked amused. None of the men in her family had ever cooked, she wasn't even sure they knew how to find the kitchen.

He laughed in answer. "If you stay single as long as I have, you either starve or learn to feed yourself. Or go out every night, which gets exhausting. A lot of the time, I'd rather stay home and cook."

"Me too, about the stay-at-home part. But I'm not much of a cook."

"You don't need to be," he reminded her, and she looked momentarily embarrassed. She had been waited on all her life. But so had he.

"I should still learn one of these days. Maybe I will." She had been impressed by how competent and organized he was in the kitchen.

"I can teach you a few tricks," he volunteered, and she liked the idea.

"That sounds like fun," she said, looking enthusiastic. She always had a good time with him.

"Just think of it as science, that will make it easier for you." She laughed as she turned off the lights and he followed her back up the stairs. They went through two doors, and came back out in the main hall, under the chandelier. He was carrying his tailcoat, and his top hat and gloves were on the hall table. He picked them up, slipped into his tailcoat, and put the hat back on his head. He looked as elegant as ever, and no one would have suspected that he had cooked dinner.

"You look very dashing, Mr. Millbank. I had a wonderful time with you tonight."

"Me too," he said, and kissed her chastely on the cheek. He didn't want to rush her, they had months still ahead of them as just friends, despite her mother's blessing. "I'll see you soon. Thank you for going to Hortie's wedding with me, Annabelle. Those things can be deadly boring, unless you have someone fun to go with."

"I think so too," she agreed. "And the best part was talking about it in the kitchen afterward." She giggled, and he smiled too.

"Goodnight, Annabelle," he said, opening the door, and turned to look at her before he closed it behind him. She picked her jacket up off the chair, stuck her hat back on her head at a crazy angle, and walked up the stairs to her bedroom with a smile and an enormous yawn. She had had an excellent time, and was so glad that she and Josiah were friends.

Chapter 6

Much to Consuelo's delight, at Annabelle's urging, they invited Josiah to dinner on Christmas Eve. It wasn't a romantic move on Annabelle's part, she just felt that he had been so nice to them that they should do something for him in return, since he was alone for Christmas. As they always did, they had Christmas Eve dinner in white tie. Annabelle and her mother wore evening gowns, and as directed, Josiah arrived in a well-cut tailcoat with an immaculately starched shirt and vest, with beautiful old pearl and diamond studs and cuff links that had been his grandfather's. And he touched them both by bringing presents.

Annabelle had bought a cashmere scarf for Josiah, and a cookbook partly as a joke, but he said he loved it. And Annabelle was embarrassed to discover that he had bought her a beautiful gold bracelet at Tiffany, and a handsome black silk scarf for her mother.

They shared a lovely, warm evening together, and sat in front of the fireplace after dinner. Josiah drank brandy, while the two ladies drank eggnog laced with rum, from a recipe Arthur had always made, and they admired the tree that Consuelo and Annabelle had decorated. It was a difficult Christmas for them that year, understandably, and Josiah avoided the topic of the current hearings that were in the news about the *Titanic*. He knew that whatever happened, they wouldn't want to hear it. It would change nothing for them now.

Annabelle announced to them that Hortie had gotten back from their honeymoon that afternoon, and had rushed over to tell her she was already pregnant. Hortie was certain of it and said that she and James were thrilled, although she found the prospect a little scary. She had just barely become a wife, and now was going to be a mother, sometime in late August, as closely as she could figure it. Hortie said the baby had been conceived in Paris, and then she had giggled mysteriously, like the little girl she still was despite her new status, and made all kinds of innuendoes about their sex life that Annabelle didn't want to hear. Hortie said that sex was fabulous, and James was incredible in bed, not that she had any frame of reference, but she had never had so much fun in all her life. Annabelle didn't mention any of that to her mother or Josiah, but just said that Hortie was having a baby and was very excited about it. Listening to the news, Consuelo hoped that the following Christmas Annabelle and Josiah would have the same kind of news to share, providing they were married by then, which she hoped fervently they would be. Consuelo couldn't see the point of a long engagement once they announced it.

Before he left that night Josiah said he was going skiing in Vermont over New Year's with his old classmate, Henry Orson. As they were the last single men left at their age, according to him, he said it was nice to still have someone to do things with. Their New Year ski trip to

Woodstock was a tradition they engaged in every year, and he was particularly looking forward to it this year, with a new ski jump recently added to the toboggan run. Josiah asked if Annabelle knew how to ski or snowshoe. She said she didn't, but would love to learn. A veiled look passed between him and Consuelo, and he promised to teach her sometime. He suggested that maybe he, Annabelle, and her mother could take a trip to Vermont together. Annabelle's eyes lit up, and she said it sounded like a lot of fun. He said they had wonderful sleigh rides in Woodstock too.

Josiah stayed till after midnight, and after he thanked them again for the presents and the delicious meal, Consuelo mysteriously disappeared while the two young people said goodnight. Annabelle thanked him profusely again for her bracelet, which she loved, and which was already on her arm.

"I'm glad you like it," he said warmly. "I know you're not supposed to wear jewelry right now, but if your mother objects, maybe you can wear it later." He hadn't wanted to offend Consuelo by giving Annabelle a bracelet while they were in mourning, but he had wanted to give her something that she'd enjoy for a long time. And he didn't want to give her anything too lavish, or she might suspect what he had in mind. He thought the simple gold bracelet was discreet, and Annabelle was thrilled with it.

"Have a good time skiing," she said as she walked him to the door. He was wearing an impeccably cut black coat and a white silk scarf over his tuxedo, with a homburg. As always, he looked extremely elegant. And Annabelle looked pretty and young in her simple black evening gown.

"I'll call you when I get back," he promised. "It will be after the first." He kissed her chastely on the cheek, and she did the same, as they said good-bye.

Annabelle found her mother in the library, thumbing through a book. It was one of her father's that Annabelle had read before.

"Why did you come in here?" Annabelle asked, looking surprised. Her mother wasn't much of a reader, and she turned to her daughter with a gentle smile.

"I thought you and Josiah might like to be alone to say goodnight." There was a deeper meaning in her eyes, and Annabelle looked momentarily annoyed.

"Josiah? Don't be silly, Mama. We're just friends. Don't start getting ideas about him. It would spoil everything, I love the friendship that we have."

"What if he wanted more?" Consuelo asked cryptically, and her daughter frowned.

"He doesn't. And neither do I. We like it just the way it is. Just because Hortie got married and is having a baby doesn't mean I have to. I can't even go out for another four months. So I'm not going to meet anyone for a while, and who knows if I'll ever meet someone I like and want to marry." She sighed and put her arms around her mother. "Are you trying to get rid of me, Mama?" she asked gently.

"Of course not, I just want you to be happy. And nothing makes a woman happier than a husband and a child. Ask Hortie. I'll bet she can't wait to have that baby in her arms."

"She sounds pretty happy," Annabelle admitted with a shy smile. "She was trying to tell me all about her honeymoon. It sounds like they had a lovely time." Mostly in bed, but she didn't say that to her mother, she didn't even want to know it herself.

"When is the baby due?"

"End of August, I think. She's not sure. She says it happened in Paris, and James is thrilled too. He wants a boy."

"All men do. But the ones they fall in love with are their girls. Your father did the minute he saw you." They both smiled at the memory. It had been a hard Christmas Eve for both of them, but having Josiah there had helped. Everything was easier and more pleasant when he was around.

Arm in arm, they walked up the stairs to their rooms, and they exchanged presents the next day. Her mother had bought her a magnificent fur coat, and Annabelle had gotten her mother a pair of sapphire earrings at Cartier. She had tried to get her the kind of gift her father would have given her, on a slightly more modest scale. He always bought wonderful gifts for all of them. And she wanted to somehow make it up to her mother this year, although she knew that she couldn't make up for all that they had lost. But her mother was deeply touched by the gesture, and the beauty of her daughter's gift, and put them on immediately.

They went downstairs together, and had a big breakfast cooked by Blanche. It had snowed during the night, and there was a blanket of white covering the garden. After breakfast, they dressed and went out for a walk in the park. It was going to be difficult for them to fill the day alone. They had lost half of their family, and on holidays like this, the absence of Arthur and Robert was sorely felt.

In the end, the day was less painful than they had feared. They had both dreaded it so much, and had tried to keep busy. Consuelo and Annabelle had lunch together, played cards that afternoon, and by dinnertime they were both tired, and ready for bed. They had gotten through it, that was the main thing, and as she undressed that night, Annabelle found herself thinking of Josiah in Vermont. She wondered if he and Henry had gotten there safely and were having fun. She would have loved to go skiing with them sometime, as he had suggested. It sounded like fun to her. And she hoped she got a chance to, maybe next year, if she could talk her mother into going.

The rest of the holiday was easier than Christmas. Annabelle spent some time with Hortie, and all her friend talked about now was the baby, just as she had talked about nothing but the wedding for six months before. She had little else on her mind or to keep her busy. Consuelo congratulated her when she saw her, and Hortie rattled on for half an hour about Paris, and all the clothes she'd bought, which very soon she would no longer be able to wear. She said they would still go to Newport that summer, and if she had the baby there, it was fine with her. She was going to have it at home anyway, in Newport or New York. Listening to her talk to Consuelo about it, Annabelle felt left out of the conversation. She had nothing to contribute. Hortie had turned into a married woman and mother overnight. But Annabelle still loved her friend, boring or not. Hortie had brought her a beautiful sweater from Paris, with pearl buttons. It was the palest pink, and Annabelle couldn't wait to wear it that summer.

"I didn't want to buy you a black one," Hortie said apologetically. "It's too grim, and you can wear it pretty soon. I hope that's all right."

"I love it!" Annabelle reassured her, and meant it. It had a beautiful lace collar, and it was the subtlest powder pink. It looked wonderful with Annabelle's skin and hair.

The two young women had lunch together several times that week, and felt very grown-up going to the Astor Court at the St. Regis Hotel. Hortie was taking her new status very seriously, dressed up, wearing the jewelry James had given her, and looked very grand. When they went to lunch, Annabelle wore the new fur coat her mother had given her for Christmas. And she felt a little like she was playing dress-up in her mother's closet. She was wearing Josiah's bracelet on her arm.

"Where did you get that?" Hortie asked when she noticed it. "I like it."

"So do I," Annabelle said simply. "Josiah Millbank gave it to me for Christmas. It was very nice of him. He gave Mama a scarf."

"You two looked great together at my wedding." And then suddenly Hortie's eyes lit up, as she had an idea. "What about him?"

"What about him?" Annabelle looked blank.

"For you, I mean. You know, as a husband." Annabelle laughed in response.

"Don't be stupid, Hort. He's twice my age. You sound like Mama. I swear, she'd marry me off to the milkman if she could."

"Is the milkman cute?" Hortie was laughing at the thought.

"No. He's about a hundred years old and has no teeth."

"Seriously, why not Josiah? He likes you. He's always hanging around."

"We're just friends. We like it that way. Getting mushy about it would mess everything up."

"That's a very nice bracelet to give to just a friend."

"It's only a present, not a proposal. He came to dinner on Christmas Eve. It was so sad this year," she said, changing the subject.

"I know," Hortie said sympathetically, forgetting about Josiah for the moment. "I'm sorry, Belle, it must be awful." Annabelle only nodded, and they moved on to other topics, mostly clothes. Hortie couldn't imagine what she'd wear when she got bigger. She was planning to go to her mother's dressmaker to figure it out in the next few weeks. She said her waistband was already getting tight, and her corset was killing her. And she swore her breasts had doubled in size.

"Maybe you're having twins," Annabelle suggested with a smile.

"Wouldn't that be funny?" Hortie said, laughing. She couldn't begin to envision what that entailed, and it was all one big thrill for her right now.

She was a little less thrilled two weeks later, when she started to get nauseous. And for the next two months, she hardly got out of bed. She felt awful. It was the middle of March before she felt decent again. Until then, Annabelle had to visit her, since Hortie wouldn't go out. Hortie hadn't been to a party since Christmas, and she wasn't nearly as delighted with her pregnancy as she'd been before. She felt fat and sick most of the time, and she said it was no fun at all. Annabelle felt sorry for her, and brought her books and flowers, and magazines to look at. It became her main mission in life to cheer Hortie up. And then finally, in April, Hortie got out of bed. She looked obviously pregnant by then, and she was already five months. All the women in her family said it was only one baby, but she was huge, and her mother said it was going to be a boy.

It was Hortie's only topic of conversation, and most of the time, she just lay there and complained. She said she felt like a whale. And she said that James hardly made love to her anymore, which was really disappointing. He went out with his friends most nights alone, and promised her that when the baby came, they'd make up for it and go out all the time. But her mother reminded her that she'd be nursing then and even if she wasn't, she'd still have a baby to take care of. So being grown-up didn't seem like so much fun after all. Annabelle was infinitely patient, listening to her whine and moan, and now Hortie cried all the time too.

Consuelo had planned a service for the anniversary of Arthur and Robert's deaths that month. It was held at Trinity Church again, with a luncheon afterward at the house. All her father's close friends were there, and several cousins including Madeleine Astor, whose late husband was Consuelo's cousin, and Josiah came, of course, as well as everyone from the bank, including Henry Orson.

Josiah had been at the house a lot in recent months, always helpful, always pleasant, always with a joke or a smile, or a little present. He had bought Annabelle a series of medical books, which she loved, and *Gray's Anatomy*. Other than Hortie, he had become her best friend in the world, and he was better company now since he wasn't pregnant, and feeling sorry for himself all the time. Annabelle always had a good time with him, and lately he had started taking her to nice restaurants for dinner. Once the anniversary date was behind them, she was looking forward to going to social events with him. She hadn't been anywhere, other than Hortie's wedding, for over a year. Before the sinking of the *Titanic,* her parents had been gone for two months, and she'd been sick for a month before that, so she hadn't gone out socially in fifteen months. At her age, that was a long time.

She was turning twenty in May. And two weeks after the church service for her father and brother, Josiah invited her to what promised to be a very fancy dinner at Delmonico's, where Annabelle had never dined, and she could hardly wait. She bought a new dress for the occasion, and her mother did her hair. Consuelo suspected what was coming, and for both their sakes, she hoped it would go well.

Josiah came to pick her up at seven. He had his own car this time, and the minute he saw Annabelle in the new dress, he whistled. It was a delicately pleated ivory silk that showed off her shoulders, and she was wearing a white silk shawl. It was in sharp contrast to the dismal black she'd been wearing for so long. Her mother was still dressed in mourning and had said that she didn't feel ready to give it up yet. Annabelle was afraid she never would. But she had been grateful to put her own black dresses away. It was time.

They got to the elegant restaurant at seven-thirty, and were shown to a quiet corner table. It felt so exciting to be out, and to have dinner with Josiah. Even more so than she had with Hortie, she felt terribly grown-up as she sat across the table from him and took off her shawl. She was still wearing the gold bracelet he had given her for Christmas. She never took it off.

The waiter asked her if she'd like a cocktail, and she nervously declined. Her mother had warned her not to have too much to drink, except some wine. It wouldn't make a good impression, she'd said to her daughter, if Annabelle got drunk at dinner. She had laughed at the prospect and told her mother not to worry. Josiah ordered a scotch and soda, which startled Annabelle. She had never seen him drink hard liquor before, and wondered if he was nervous too, though she couldn't imagine why, since they were such good friends.

"Would you like some champagne?" he offered when his drink came.

"No, I'm fine," and then she giggled. "My mother told me not to get drunk and embarrass you." He laughed too. There was nothing they couldn't say to each other. They discussed a thousand topics of interest, and they enjoyed each other's company. They both ordered the restaurant's famous Lobster Newburg, and Baked Alaska for dessert.

They had a lovely evening with each other, and with dessert, Josiah ordered champagne for both of them. The waiter brought the bottle to the table and opened it for them, and Annabelle smiled as she took a sip. She had only had one glass of wine with dinner, so her mother's warning had stood her in good stead.

"That's delicious," Annabelle commented. He had ordered a particularly fine bottle. Josiah had had more to drink than she had, but he was still sober too. He wanted to keep his wits about him for what he had to say. He had been saving it for a long time, and the day had finally come. He had butterflies in his stomach, as he smiled and toasted her.

"To you, Miss Worthington, and the wonderful friend you've become," he complimented her, and she smiled.

"So have you," she said gently, taking another sip of champagne. She didn't have the faintest inkling of what he had in mind. He could see it on her face. She was innocence itself.

"I have a wonderful time with you, Annabelle," he said simply, and it was true.

"Me too," she echoed. "We always have a lot of fun." She started to talk about the medical books he'd given her then, and he gently cut her off, as she looked surprised. He usually let her rattle off for hours about what she'd learned in those books.

"I have something to say to you." She looked at him blankly, wondering what it was. She hoped nothing was wrong. "I've waited a long time to say this. I didn't think it would be right to say it before April, because of the anniversary. And your birthday is coming up soon. So here we are."

"Are we celebrating something?" she asked naïvely, feeling a slight buzz from the champagne.

"I hope so," he said softly. "That depends on you. It's up to you to decide. What I've wanted to tell you since last summer is that I'm in love with you. I don't mean to upset the applecart of our friendship, or to startle you. But somewhere along the way, I fell in love with you, Annabelle. I think we're wonderful together, and I can't stay single forever. I've never met a woman who made me want to settle down But I can't think of a better foundation for doing that than being best friends, which we are. So I would like to ask you to do me the honor of marrying me, if you will." As he said the words, he saw Annabelle staring at him in complete amazement. Her mouth was slightly open and her eyes were wide.

"Are you serious?" she asked him when she finally caught her breath.

He nodded. "Yes, I am. I know this comes as a surprise to you, and you can think about it if you need to. Annabelle, I've been in love with you for a long time."

"Why didn't you tell me?" He couldn't tell if she was happy or angry. Most of all, she looked shocked.

"I thought I should wait until now." She nodded. It was proper and made sense. And Josiah always did the right thing. It was one of the things she loved about him. She was still staring at him in disbelief.

"Are you upset?" he asked, looking worried, and she shook her head. There were tears in her eyes when she looked at him.

"No, of course not. I'm very touched," she said, reaching out to take his hand.

"I know I'm a lot older than you are. I could be your father. But I don't want to be. I want to be your husband, and I promise I'll take good care of you forever."

She believed that as she listened to him, and then wondered, "Does my mother know?" It explained her occasional discreet suggestions about Josiah, all of which Annabelle had brushed off.

"I asked her permission in October, and she said yes. I think she believes it would be a good thing for both of us."

"So do I," Annabelle whispered with a shy smile. "I just never expected this to happen. I thought we were just friends."

"We still are," he replied, smiling too. "And if you accept, we always will be. I think a husband and wife should be best friends, along with everything else. I would like to share children with you, and the rest of my life. And I will always, always be your friend."

"So would I," she said, looking misty. And the thought of having children with him shocked her a little, but touched her heart. As she listened to him, she tried not to think about all the antics Hortie had described in Paris. What she shared with Josiah seemed so much more pure. She hated to spoil that. But Hortie had always been a little crazy, and now that she'd discovered sex, she'd gotten worse. The only thing that was slowing her down now was getting fatter day by day.

"Would you like some time to think about it? I know this came as a surprise. I've been biting my tongue for a long time." And then he laughed. "That's why I had a scotch, and half a bottle of wine tonight, and now champagne. I guess your mother should have warned me not to get drunk. It took a little courage to ask. I wasn't sure if you'd slug me or say yes."

"Are those my two choices?" she asked, reaching for his other hand. She was already holding one. "Slug you or say yes?"

"Essentially." He smiled at her, and squeezed both of her hands in his own.

"It's simple then. The answer is yes. If I slug you, it would make a terrible mess. They might throw us out of the restaurant. And you might not be my best friend anymore."

"Yes, I would." And then he asked her the same question she had inquired of him when he first proposed. "Are you serious?" He was referring to her timid "yes." It was gentle, but heartfelt.

"Yes, I am. I never thought of us that way before. And whenever my mother suggested it, I thought she was insane. But now that I think about it, there's no one else on earth I'd want to marry. Except Hortie maybe, but she can be such a pain in the neck. So if I'm going to marry my best friend, I'd rather marry you." They were both laughing while she explained.

"Have I told you that I love you?" he asked her.

"I think you did. But you can always say it again," she said primly, with an enchanting little smile.

"I love you, Annabelle."

"I love you too, Josiah. I love you very, very much. I guess this is the best way to protect our friendship forever." And then as she said it, he saw her eyes fill with tears, and her lip quiver, and he could see she was upset.

"What's wrong?" he whispered.

"I wish I could tell Robert and my father. This is the most important thing that's ever happened to me, and I have no one to tell. My mother already knows. And who will walk me down the aisle?" As she said it, tears rolled down her cheeks.

"We'll figure it out," he said gently, as he wiped her tears away with his hand. "Don't cry, sweetheart. Everything is going to be all right."

"I know," she said. She felt absolutely certain that with Josiah she would always be in good hands. Suddenly, it made perfect sense to her, although it never had before. But now it was his idea, and her own, not someone else's crazy suggestion that made no sense. Now it all did. "When do you want to do it?"

"I don't know. That's up to you. I'm at your disposal from today on. We can get married whenever you want."

"What about in Newport this summer?" she said, looking pensive. "In the garden. That would be less formal than a church." And there would be no aisle, which was so upsetting to her now. She had no uncles to walk her down the aisle, no one to stand in for her father or brother. There was no one at all. She'd have to walk down the aisle all by herself. "Maybe we could do the actual wedding very small, and have a big party later. With Daddy and Robert gone, it doesn't feel right to do a big wedding, and I think it would be too hard on my mother. What about Newport in August?"

"Sounds great to me." He beamed at her. Things were going even better than he'd planned, or dared to hope since last October. "Does that give you enough time to organize a wedding?"

"I think so. I don't want a wedding like Hortie's. And she's the only bridesmaid I want, and she'll be nine months pregnant."

"I'd say that sounds more like a matron of honor," he teased her.

They both knew that most people would be shocked to see her out socially in that condition.

"She says she might have the baby in Newport," Annabelle added.

"Maybe she could have it at the wedding." He chuckled. He had a feeling that with Annabelle, life was going to be interesting forever.

"Can I still do my volunteer work at the hospital?" Annabelle asked, looking worried.

"You can do anything you want," he said simply, smiling at her.

"My mother said I'd have to stop when I got married."

"You don't have to stop for me, except maybe when you're expecting. It might be a good idea to give it up for a while then." She could tell just listening to him that he was going to be reasonable, and always there to protect her. It seemed like the ideal marriage to her, and she couldn't imagine why she'd never thought of it herself before. She liked everything he said, and always had.

They chatted for a while longer about their plans. His mother had been dead for years, and his father was remarried to a woman Josiah didn't particularly like, but he thought they should invite them, and his half-sister with her husband. He had two uncles, and a brother. His brother lived in Chicago, and Josiah wasn't sure if he would come. He said his brother was a little eccentric. So he didn't think they'd be overrun by his family, and all she had now was her mother, and a wide assortment of distant cousins. She said she'd like to keep it below a hundred, maybe even fifty. And her mother could give them a big party in the city in the fall, which sounded great to him. He liked the idea of keeping their wedding personal and private, as a special moment just for them, and not a cast of thousands. He had never wanted a big wedding, and until now none at all.

"Where do you want to go on our honeymoon?" he asked happily. August was just around the corner.

"Anywhere we don't have to take a boat to get to. I don't think I could do that to my mother, and I'm not sure I'd want to either."

"We'll figure it out. Maybe California or somewhere in the Rockies. Or Canada, or maybe even Maine. New England is beautiful that time of year."

"I don't care where we go, Josiah," she said honestly, "just so I'm with you." It was exactly how he felt about her. He signaled for the waiter then and paid the check. Everything had gone perfectly and he had apologized to her for not having a ring yet. He had been nervous about choosing the right one.

He drove her home, and her mother was still up when they got there. Knowing what was happening, she had been too excited to go to sleep. She looked at them expectantly as they came through the door, and they were both beaming.

"Do I have a son-in-law?" she asked in barely more than a whisper.

"You will in August," Josiah said proudly, with an arm around his brand-new fiancée's shoulders.

"In Newport," Annabelle added, smiling ecstatically up at him.

"Oh my Lord, a wedding in Newport in August, with only three months to arrange it. You two don't fool around, do you?"

"We only want a small wedding, Mama," Annabelle said softly, and her mother understood why. Hearing that was a great relief to her too.

"You can have anything you want," she said generously.

"We really only want about fifty or sixty people, a hundred if we have to, in the garden."

"Your wish is my command," Consuelo said gamely, wishing she could call the florist and the caterer at that very moment. Instead she walked up to Josiah and hugged him, and kissed her daughter. "I'm so happy for you both. I think you're going to be very happy."

"So do we," they said in unison, and then all three of them laughed. Consuelo insisted on pouring each of them a glass of champagne, and then suddenly Annabelle remembered the day in October she had come home from the hospital to find her mother and Josiah drinking champagne in the garden.

"Did you really get a promotion that day?" Annabelle asked him, as her mother served their champagne.

"No, I got you, or your mother's permission. I told her I wanted to wait until May to ask you."

"You sneaky people," she laughed, as Consuelo toasted them.

"May you be as happy as Arthur and I were, may you live long and happy lives, and have a dozen children." Both Annabelle and Josiah raised their glasses and took a sip, and then Annabelle reached out to her mother and hugged her tightly. She knew that in some ways this was hard for her too. They all missed her father and brother so much. "I love you, Mama," Annabelle said softly, as Consuelo held her close.

"I love you too, sweetheart. And I'm so happy for you. And I know that wherever your father and Robert are, they are too."

Both women wiped their eyes, as Josiah cleared his throat and turned away, so they wouldn't see that he was crying too. It was truly the happiest night of his life.

Chapter 7

For the next several weeks, Consuelo was insanely busy. She had to organize the caterers and florist in Newport, speak to the minister, hire the musicians. She had already decided to open the house in June. Josiah's father had agreed to host the rehearsal dinner, and was planning to hold it at the Newport Country Club.

Consuelo also had to order invitations. Annabelle needed a wedding dress, and a trousseau. There were a million details to plan and organize, and it was the happiest Consuelo had been in a year. She was sorry that Annabelle wouldn't have her father there to see it, and Consuelo wanted to make it even more beautiful for Annabelle, to make up for it.

Their engagement was announced in the *New York Herald* the day before Annabelle's birthday and the following day Josiah presented her with her engagement ring. It was a ten-carat diamond that had been his mother's. And it looked spectacular on Annabelle's hand. He had decided that his mother's ring was more meaningful than a new one, and Annabelle loved it. She and her mother were already looking for wedding gowns by then. And by sheer luck, they found the perfect one at B. Altman's on the first of June. It was a slim gown of exquisite French lace, modeled after a Patou design, and just simple enough not to look out of place at a garden wedding in Newport. It had a long graceful train, and an enormous cloud of veil. Annabelle looked magnificent in it. And when she talked to Hortie about being her matron of honor, her old friend screamed.

"Are you insane? You can't get married until after I have the baby. If your mother is ordering a tent, she'd better order a second one for me. It's the only thing I can wear."

"I don't care how you look or what anyone says," Annabelle insisted. "I just want you to be there for me." It was still a sore subject for her and her mother, but she had decided to walk down the aisle alone.

"I'm not even supposed to go out in public once I'm that pregnant. All the old biddies in Newport will talk about me for years." Annabelle was well aware of that too, and Hortie was nearly in tears.

"Who cares? I love you, however you look. And we don't want to wait. August is perfect for us," Annabelle pleaded with her.

"I hate you. Maybe I can swim a lot and have the baby before. But I'll still be fat." When she realized that Annabelle couldn't be convinced to postpone her wedding for her, Hortie finally gave up, and promised that come hell or high water, she'd be there. It was the week before her due date, and she almost hit Annabelle when she suggested that maybe the baby would be late. She wanted it to come early. She was tired of feeling ugly and fat.

Annabelle and Hortie went shopping together, to look for items for her trousseau. And Annabelle and Josiah still had to figure out where to live. Josiah had a very respectable small summer house in Newport that he'd inherited from his mother, but his apartment in New York would be too small for them once they had children. They agreed to look for a bigger one after they got back from Wyoming, which they had chosen for their honeymoon. It was just too frantic trying to find a new place to live now. For the time being, his apartment was big enough for the two of them. And it was close to where her mother lived, which Annabelle liked. She hated to move out and leave her alone. She knew only too well how lonely she would be.

But for the moment, Consuelo was too busy to be lonely. She took two trips up to Newport to start planning the wedding and tell the gardener what she wanted planted. And they had managed to find a tent the perfect size, left over from a wedding the year before.

And much to Annabelle and Josiah's amazement, by the end of June, all the details were attended to and in place. Consuelo was a model of efficiency, and she wanted Annabelle to have the perfect wedding. Josiah was adorable throughout. He showed no sign of jitters or nerves, despite his long wait to get married at thirty-nine. Once he made up his mind, he was ready and completely calm about it. Even more so than his bride.

As soon as the announcement came out in the *Herald,* they were invited everywhere, and were out almost every night. They made a striking couple, and only two of Consuelo's friends made unpleasant comments that they thought Josiah was too old for Annabelle. Consuelo assured them that he was just right. Her own cousin, John Jacob Astor, in his forties, had married Madeleine at eighteen. Josiah was proving daily that he was the perfect husband for her. And Annabelle even managed to continue her volunteer work, with his blessing, until the end of June. She took a leave from it then until the fall.

The only thing Consuelo wanted from them, and she said it regularly, was grandchildren as soon as possible. Annabelle thought that if she heard her say it once more she would scream.

And Hortie couldn't stop talking about the surprises Annabelle had in store for her, and how great the sex would be. It unnerved her to hear all the unwanted advice her old friend gave her, as she got bigger every day. Hortie was huge, and Annabelle hoped that when she got pregnant, she wouldn't look like her. She said as much to Josiah one day, and he laughed.

"You'll be beautiful when that happens, Annabelle, and our babies will be too." He kissed her gently. They had so much to look forward to, and for the next two months so much to do.

It seemed as though everyone Josiah had ever known wanted to give them a celebration. At the age of thirty-nine, he was finally getting married. Henry Orson gave a bachelor party for him. The entire group had hangovers afterward for three days. Josiah admitted they'd had a hell of a lot of fun, although he didn't go into detail. None of the men who'd been present did.

Consuelo had already left for Newport in June, and Annabelle joined her there in mid-July. Josiah came up, to stay in his own house, at the end of the month. Henry Orson came with him, to lend moral support to the groom, who seemed to be doing fine. And he was going to stay in Josiah's house when they were on their honeymoon. Josiah had taken an additional three weeks of holiday this year, for their honeymoon. The bank was understanding about it, particularly since Annabelle was the bride.

Annabelle had come to love Josiah's friend Henry. He was smart, witty, kind, and a little shy. She was constantly trying to decide which of her young female friends to introduce him to. She had already introduced him to several and he admitted to liking two of them, though nothing serious had come of it yet, but Annabelle was hopeful. And when he and Josiah got together, they were funny and quick, and the sparks of their repartee flew. Henry had always been extremely nice to her. He was to Josiah what Hortie was to her, his oldest friend from school. And Annabelle admired him immensely.

Hortie had settled in Newport for the summer by then, in her parents' house, and James was there with her. They were almost sure they would have the baby there, and she came over to visit Annabelle every day. And Annabelle helped her mother whenever she could. But Consuelo insisted she had everything in control. Annabelle had brought her wedding dress up with her. There were more parties for them in Newport. And the Astors gave an enormous dance for them. Consuelo complained that she had never had so many late nights in her life, but she enjoyed them all.

The number of guests for the wedding had already slipped over the hundred mark, and was hovering at one twenty. Every time someone gave a party for them, they had to be added to the list. But the young couple was visibly having a ball. Josiah commented to her dryly at lunch one day, when he had come over with Henry for a picnic, that if he'd known getting married was so much fun, he'd have done it years before.

"It's a good thing you didn't," Annabelle reminded him, "because then you wouldn't be marrying me."

"You have a point," he chuckled, as Hortie arrived. She was waddling now, and every time Annabelle saw her, she couldn't help laughing at her. It was hard to believe that in the next month she'd get any bigger than she was. She looked like she was about to explode. It took both Josiah and Henry to help her sit on the lawn, and even more effort and nearly a crane to get her back up.

"This isn't funny," she said, as all three of them laughed at her. "I haven't seen my feet in months." She looked and insisted that she felt like an elephant.

"What are you wearing to the wedding?" Annabelle asked her with a look of concern. She couldn't imagine a dress big enough for her by then.

"My bedspread, I think. Or the tent."

"Seriously, do you have anything you can fit in? You're not getting off the hook."

"Don't worry, I'll be there," she reassured her. "I wouldn't miss it for the world." She had actually had her mother's dressmaker make something for her. It was a giant, pale blue tent, and she'd had shoes made to match. It wasn't exactly a matron of honor's dress, but it was all she'd be able to wear. She hated it, but it was all she had.

Consuelo had had a dress made in emerald green with a matching hat, and she was planning to wear the emeralds Arthur had given her. It was a beautiful color on her, and Annabelle knew she would look lovely as the mother of the bride.

Finally the big day arrived. Josiah's father and stepmother had driven down from Boston, with Josiah's half-sister and her husband

and their baby. Annabelle liked them all. And the rehearsal dinner was fine. Consuelo got along with Josiah's family, and she had them to lunch the day before the wedding. Both families were thrilled with the match. It was the union of two highly respected families, and two people whom everyone loved. And as Josiah had predicted, his odd-ball brother, George, who lived in Chicago had decided not to come. He was playing in a golf tournament instead. It was just the way he was, and Josiah's feelings weren't hurt. He would have been too much trouble if he had come, so his absence was a relief. His family had never been as normal, well balanced, and cohesive as Annabelle's had been. And his stepmother got on his nerves. She had a high squeaky voice, and complained every chance she got.

Consuelo had brunch with Josiah's relatives the morning of the wedding, without either the bride or groom. Out of superstition, Annabelle didn't want to see Josiah before the wedding, and he and Henry were relaxing at his house, and trying to keep cool. It was a blistering hot day, and Consuelo was worried that the flowers would wilt and the wedding cake would melt before the ceremony even began. The service in the garden was planned for seven o'clock that night, and they were sitting down to dinner at nine. There was no doubt in everyone's mind that the party would go late.

There were a hundred and forty people coming finally, almost equally divided between the bride and groom. And Henry Orson, of course, was going to be the best man.

Hortie was the matron of honor, and if she didn't have the baby before the wedding, she looked as though she could. She'd admitted to Annabelle, just to warn her, that she'd been having contractions for two days, and she was praying that her water wouldn't break at the altar. It was bad enough, she said, just looking the way she did. She knew that everyone would be horrified to see her at the wedding, and would probably find it shocking. But she couldn't let her best friend down. Annabelle had told her that it was sad enough not having her father or brother there, so Hortie couldn't be absent too.

Blanche had come to Newport with them to be at the wedding. She was bustling around Annabelle's bedroom in the afternoon, and fussing over her like a baby. And when the time came, she and Consuelo helped her into her wedding dress and did up the tiny buttons. The cinched-in waist and narrow gown were exquisite on her. And with a sharp intake of breath, Consuelo set the headpiece on Annabelle's blond hair and settled the cloud of veil around her. Both women stood back to look at her, as tears rolled down their cheeks. Without question, Annabelle was the most beautiful bride they'd ever seen.

"Oh my God," Consuelo whispered, as Annabelle beamed at them. "You look incredible." Annabelle was the happiest woman alive, and she could hardly wait for Josiah to see her. And they all wished that her father had been there. Consuelo knew that he would have had a lump in his throat the size of a fist, walking her down the aisle. Annabelle had always been his pride and joy.

The two women helped her down the stairs, carrying her long train. Then one of the maids handed her the enormous bouquet of lily of the valley, and with that, Annabelle, her mother, and Blanche slipped out a side door. Blanche went to warn the ushers that she was coming. The guests were in their places, Josiah and Henry were at the altar, Hortie was beside them, looking like a gigantic pale blue balloon. There had been several gasps when the dowagers of Newport saw her. But everyone also knew that it was an unusual wedding. The groom was nearly twenty years older than the bride, had never been married, and the family had been struck by tragedy barely more than a year before. Some allowances had to be made.

Consuelo stood for a last moment in the side garden, looking lovingly down at her daughter, and then took her in her arms and held her.

"Be happy, my darling...Daddy and I love you so much," and then, with tears streaming down her face, she rushed to take her place in the front row of chairs that had been set up in the main garden for the wedding service.

All hundred and forty people were there, and as soon as Consuelo took her place, the musicians began playing the Bridal Chorus from *Lohengrin,* as they had at Hortie's wedding. The big moment was here. The bride was coming. Consuelo glanced up at Josiah, and he smiled at her. A warm glow passed between them. And more than ever, Consuelo knew that he was the right man. And she was sure that Arthur would have thought so too.

All the wedding guests stood up at a signal from the minister, and all heads turned. The tension was enormous, as slowly and solemnly, the exquisite bride crossed the length of the garden in measured steps, alone. There was no one at her side, no one to lead her there, protect her, or hand her over to the man she was to marry. She was coming to him proudly, and quietly, with total certainty and dignity, on her own. Since there was no one to give her to Josiah, she was giving herself to him, with her mother's blessing.

There was a sharp intake of breath as they saw her, and the force of the tragedy that had impacted them hit the guests as well as they saw the tiny, lovely bride gliding toward them, with the huge bouquet of lily of the valley in her hands, and her face covered by the veil.

She stood before Josiah and the minister, as Henry and Hortie stepped aside. The bride and groom stood looking at each other through her veil, and he gently took her hand. She had been very brave.

The minister addressed the assembled company, and began the service. When he asked who gave this woman in marriage, her mother responded clearly from the front row, "I do," and the marriage ceremony went on. At the appointed moment, Josiah lifted her veil ever so gently and looked into her eyes. They said their vows to each other, he slipped the narrow diamond band on her finger, and she a simple gold band on his. They were proclaimed man and wife, kissed, and then, beaming, walked back down the aisle. Tears were streaming unchecked down Consuelo's face as she watched them, and as her daughter had, she walked back down the aisle alone behind Henry and Hortie, who waddled along happily on Henry's arm. He had never before seen a woman so extremely pregnant in public, nor had anyone else. But she had decided to enjoy the wedding and was delighted she was there. She quickly found James in the crowd, and Consuelo, Annabelle, and Josiah formed a reception line to greet their guests.

Half an hour later everyone was mingling, talking, and enjoying the champagne. It had been a beautiful, tender, and poignant wedding. Annabelle was looking up at Josiah adoringly as Henry came to kiss her and offer his best wishes, and congratulate the groom.

"Well, you did it," he chuckled, "you've civilized him. They said it couldn't be done," he said to Annabelle.

"You're next," she teased as she kissed him. "Now we have to find someone for you." He looked nervous as she said it and pretended to shake in fear.

"I'm not sure I'm ready for that," he confessed. "I think I'd rather hang out with you, and enjoy the thrills of marriage vicariously. You don't mind if I tag along, do you?" He was only half-kidding, and Annabelle told him he was welcome anytime. She knew how close he and Josiah were, just as she was with Hortie. There was room in their new life for their old friends.

Annabelle and Josiah greeted all the guests, and then just after nine o'clock it was time to sit down. Annabelle and Consuelo had been meticulous about the seating, making sure that all the most important people in Newport had been deferred to properly. Consuelo was seated with Josiah's family, and at the bride and groom's table, they had placed Henry, one of Annabelle's female friends, James and Hortie, and three other young couples they were fond of. Most of the guests were people they truly wanted there. There were very few guests invited out of obligation, with the exception of a few men from Arthur's bank, with whom Josiah worked. It seemed only proper to include them.

Josiah shared the first dance with Annabelle, a slow waltz they executed to perfection. It was a song they both loved and had danced to often. Both were proficient dancers, and they looked dazzling on the dance floor. Everyone sighed as they watched them. And then Josiah's father danced with the bride, and Josiah with Consuelo, and after that the rest of the guests joined them on the floor. It was nearly ten before people started eating the sumptuous repast Consuelo had ordered. They danced between courses, talked, laughed, enjoyed each other, and commented on how good the food was, which was rare at weddings. The newlyweds cut the wedding cake at midnight, danced some more, and the guests didn't start leaving until two in the morning. The wedding had been a huge success, and as they got into Arthur's Hispano-Suiza to go to the New Cliff Hotel for the night, Josiah bent to kiss her.

"Thank you for the most beautiful night of my life," Josiah said, as rice and rose petals began to pelt them, and he gently pushed his bride into the car. They had already thanked her mother profusely for the perfect wedding, and had promised to stop by in the morning, before they drove back to the city to take the train to Wyoming. They had all their luggage packed and ready at the hotel. Annabelle would be wearing a pale blue linen suit when they left the next morning, with a huge straw hat with pale blue flowers on it, and matching blue kid gloves.

They waved at their well-wishers as the car pulled away to take them to the hotel, and for an instant Annabelle wondered what was in store for her. The last thing she saw as they drove away was Hortie's enormous form as she waved at them. Annabelle laughed, as she waved back and hoped that if she got pregnant, she wouldn't look like Hortie nine months from now. Henry had been the last one to kiss her and shake Josiah's hand. The two men had looked each other in the eyes and smiled, as Henry wished them well. He was a good man, Annabelle knew, and more of a brother to Josiah than his own.

They sat in the living room of their suite for a while, she still in her wedding gown and he in his white tie and tails, talking about the wedding, their friends, how beautiful it was, and what an extraordinary job Consuelo had done. The absence of her father and brother had been painful for Annabelle, but even that had been tolerable. She had Josiah now, to lean on, love, and protect her. And he had Annabelle to count on and adore him, for the rest of their lives. They couldn't ask for more.

It was three A.M. when both went to separate bathrooms and finally emerged. He was in white silk pajamas someone had given him as a gift for the occasion, and she in a delicate white chiffon nightgown, the top encrusted in tiny pearls, with a matching dressing gown. She giggled like the young girl she was as she got into bed beside him. Josiah was waiting for her and took her in his arms. He suspected how nervous she was, and they were both tired after the long night.

"Don't worry, darling," he said quietly, "we have lots of time." And then, much to her delight and amazement, he held her gently, until she fell asleep, dreaming of how beautiful it had all been. In her dream, they were at the altar, exchanging their vows, and this time her father and brother were standing near and looking on. She had sensed them there anyway, and she drifted off to sleep as Josiah held her gently, like the priceless jewel she was to him.

Chapter 8

As promised, Annabelle and Josiah stopped off to say good-bye to her mother on the way out of town. The Hispano-Suiza, driven by Thomas, was taking them into the city, to meet their train that afternoon. They were going to Chicago for the first leg of the trip and from there would change trains to continue their journey west to Wyoming, to a ranch Josiah had been to once and loved. They would ride horses, and go fishing and hiking amid the incredible scenery of the Grand Tetons. Josiah had told her it was more beautiful than the Alps in Switzerland—and they didn't have to take a ship to get there. They would be staying for almost three weeks. Then they would come home to New York to start looking for a new home big enough for them and the children they hoped to have. Consuelo was hoping that, like Hortie, Annabelle would come home pregnant from their honeymoon.

Consuelo searched her daughter's face the next morning, looking for changes, and the tenderness of a woman loved that hadn't been there before, but what she saw was the beaming child she had loved all her life. Nothing had changed. Consuelo was pleased to see that she had adjusted well. There was no recalcitrance, or look of frightened amazement that one saw sometimes on brides' faces after the wedding night. Annabelle was as happy as ever, and still treated Josiah more like an old friend than a new love. Before saying goodbye to her mother they had stopped at Josiah's house to say good-bye to Henry too.

Consuelo was having lunch with Josiah's father and stepmother when the new couple stopped by. Everyone was in good spirits and talking of the delights and beauty of the night before. Her mother hugged her tightly again, she and Josiah thanked his father for the rehearsal dinner, and they left in the Hispano-Suiza moments later.

She would have liked to stop and say good-bye to Hortie too, but her mother said that James had sent a message that she was in labor. She had made it through the wedding, and gone into labor during the night. Her mother and the doctor were with her, and James was having lunch with friends. Annabelle hoped it would go well for her. She knew Hortie was nervous about the size of the baby, and how difficult it might be. One of their friends, who had made her debut at the same time they did, had died in childbirth only months before. It had been sobering for all of them. It happened, and sometimes couldn't be avoided, and often there were infections afterward, which almost always killed the mother. So Annabelle said a quiet prayer for Hortie as they left, wondering if her own mother was right, and it would be a boy. It was an exciting thought, which made her wonder too if she would return from their honeymoon pregnant, with a baby conceived in the wilds of Wyoming.

She was grateful that Josiah had been kind and respectful of her the night before. Adding the newness of sex to such an overwhelming day would have been too much, although she would have been willing if he'd insisted. But she had to admit, she was glad he hadn't. He was the perfect, kind, understanding husband, and as he had promised in the beginning, still her very best friend. She looked at him adoringly as they drove into the city, and they chatted some more about their wedding, and he described Wyoming to her again. He had promised to teach her how to fish. To Annabelle, it seemed like the perfect honeymoon. And Josiah agreed when she said it to him.

They got to New York at five o'clock, in perfect time for their train at six, and settled into the largest first-class compartment on the train. Annabelle clapped her hands in delight when she saw it.

"This is so much fun! I love it!" she giggled as he laughed happily at her.

"You are such a silly girl, and I love you." He put his arms around her and kissed her as he drew her close to him.

They were spending the next day in Chicago, before getting on another train and heading west that night. He had promised to show her the city during their brief stopover, and had taken a suite at the Palmer House Hotel, so they could rest comfortably between trains. He had thought of everything. He wanted Annabelle to be happy. She deserved it after all she had lost, and all they'd suffered, and he vowed to himself as the train left Grand Central Station that he would never let her down. He meant every word of it. It was a solemn promise to him.

By six o'clock that afternoon, as Josiah and Annabelle's train left the station, Hortie's baby had not yet been born. It had been an arduous and agonizing labor. The baby was large, and she was small. She had been screaming and writhing for hours. James had come home after lunch, and found her screams so piercing and disconcerting that he had poured himself a stiff drink and gone out again to dine with friends. He hated to think of Hortie going through that, but there was nothing he could do. It was what women did. He was sure that the doctor, her mother, and two nurses were doing all they could.

He was drunk when he came home at two o'clock that morning, and stunned to hear the baby still hadn't come. He was too inebriated to discern the look of terror on his mother-in-law's face. Hortie was so weak by then that her screams had diminished, much to his relief, and a piteous, animal moaning sound drifted throughout the house. He put a pillow over his head, and went to sleep. A sharp rapping on the guest-room door, where he was sleeping, as far away as possible from the bedroom where his wife was delivering, finally woke him up at five A.M. It was his mother-in-law telling him that his son had been born, and weighed just under ten pounds. The baby had made mincemeat of her daughter, but she didn't mention that to James. If he'd been more sober, he might have figured it out for himself. He thanked her for the news, and went back to sleep, promising to see Hortie and the baby in the morning when he woke. He couldn't have seen her then anyway, the doctor was sewing her up, after the tears the birth had caused.

Hortie had been in hard labor for twenty-six hours, with a ten-pound boy. She was still sobbing miserably as the doctor made careful stitches, and they finally gave her chloroform. It had been a difficult birth, and she could easily have died. They still had to worry about infection, so she wasn't out of the woods yet. But the baby was fine. Hortie was a lot less so. Her initiation into motherhood had been a trial by fire of the worst kind. Her mother would whisper about it to her friends for months to come. But all that would ever be said publicly was that the baby had arrived, and mother and child were fine. The rest could only be said among women, behind closed doors, keeping the agony of childbirth, and its appalling risks, carefully hidden from the ears of men.

When Consuelo heard about it from Hortie's mother the next day, she was sorry that Hortie had had such a rough time. Robert had been easy for Consuelo, but Annabelle had been more challenging, as she was born breech, feet first, and miraculously they'd both survived. She just hoped that Annabelle herself would have an easier delivery than Hortie's. They were doing everything possible so infection wouldn't set in now. After such a difficult birth, it was often hard to avoid, although no one knew why.

Consuelo said she would come to visit her in a few days, but her mother admitted that Hortie wasn't up to it yet, and might not be for a while. They were planning to keep her in bed for a month. She said that James had seen Hortie and the baby for a few minutes, and they had pinked up her cheeks and combed her hair, but she just cried. He was over the moon about his son. It made Consuelo think of Arthur, who had always been so kind to her after their children's births. For a young man, he had been unusually compassionate and understanding. And she had a feeling Josiah would be too. But James was barely more than a boy himself, and had no idea what delivering a baby entailed. He had said at the wedding that he hoped they had another one soon, and Hortie had laughed and rolled her eyes. Consuelo felt sorry for her, knowing what she had just been through. She sent over a basket of fruit and a huge bouquet of flowers for her that afternoon, and prayed that she'd recover soon. It was all that one could do. She was in good hands. And Consuelo knew only too well that after this birth, Hortie would no longer be the carefree girl she had once been. She had paid her dues.

As it turned out, Hortie made it out of bed in three weeks instead of a month. The baby was thriving, they had a wet nurse for him, and they had bound Hortie's breasts to stop her milk. She was still a little wobbly on her feet, but looking well. She was young and healthy, and she had been lucky to escape infection, and was no longer at risk. Consuelo had been to visit her several times. James was bursting with pride over his enormous son, whom they had named Charles. The baby got fatter every day. And three weeks after his birth, they drove Hortie back to New York in an ambulance, to continue her recovery in town. She was happy to go home. Consuelo left Newport on the same day.

It was lonely for her once she got back to New York. The house was deadly quiet without Annabelle, who was always so full of light and life and fun, always checking on her mother, and offering to do things with her. The full weight of her solitude and the loneliness of her future hit Consuelo like a bomb when she got home. It was hard being there alone. And she was grateful that the newlyweds were due back from their honeymoon in two days. She had run into Henry Orson on the street and he seemed lonely too. Josiah and Annabelle brought so much light and joy to those around them, that without them, everyone felt deprived. Consuelo, Hortie, and Henry could hardly wait for them to come back.

And then in a burst of cheer, they returned. Annabelle insisted on stopping in to see her mother on the way home from the station, and Consuelo was delighted to see her, looking healthy, happy, and brown. Josiah looked well too. They still bantered with each other like children in a schoolyard, teasing, laughing, making jokes about everything. Annabelle said that Josiah had taught her fly fishing and she had caught an enormous trout on her own. Josiah looked proud of her. They had ridden horses, gone hiking in the mountains, and thoroughly enjoyed life on the ranch. She looked like a child who had been away for the summer. It was hard to believe she was grown-up and married. And Consuelo could see none of the subtleties and innuendoes of womanhood on her face. She had no idea if a baby had been conceived, and she didn't want to ask. But Annabelle looked like the same gentle, loving, happy young girl she'd been when she left. She asked how Hortie was, and Consuelo said she was doing well. She didn't want to frighten Annabelle with stories about the birth, and it wouldn't have been suitable for Josiah's ears anyway, so she simply said that all was fine, and told her the baby had been named Charles. She left it to Hortie to tell Annabelle the rest, or not. And she hoped not. Most of it was too frightening for a young woman to hear. Particularly one who might be going through the same thing soon. There was no point terrifying her.

They stayed for an hour and then said their good-byes. Annabelle promised to visit her mother the next day, and they both would dine with her that night. And then after hugging Consuelo, the young couple went home. It had cheered Consuelo immeasurably to see them both, but the house seemed emptier than ever when they left. She was hardly eating these days, as it was too lonely sitting in the dining room alone.

True to her word, Annabelle came to have lunch with her mother the following day. She was wearing one of the outfits from her trousseau, a very grown-up-looking navy-blue wool suit, but she still looked like a child to her mother. Even with the trappings of womanhood, and a wedding ring on her finger, she acted like a young girl. She seemed very happy as they chatted over lunch, and Annabelle asked her what she'd been doing. Her mother said she hadn't been in town for long, and had stayed in Newport later than usual, enjoying the September weather, and now she was planning to start her volunteer work at the hospital again. She expected Annabelle to say she'd join her, or mention that she was going back to the Hospital for the Ruptured and Crippled again, but she surprised her mother and said that she wanted to begin volunteering at Ellis Island instead. The work there would be more interesting and challenging for her, and they were so shorthanded that she would have more opportunity to help with medical work, and not just observe or carry trays. Hearing about it, her mother was upset.

"Those people are so often sick, they bring in diseases from other countries. The conditions there are terrible. I think that's a very foolish thing for you to do. You'll wind up catching influenza again or worse. I don't want you to do that." But she was a married woman now, and it was up to Josiah what she did. She asked her daughter if he knew what she had in mind. Annabelle nodded and smiled. Josiah was very sensible about things like that, and he had always been understanding and enthusiastic about her medical interests and the volunteer work she did. She had told him about her new plans.

"He thinks it's fine."

"Well, I don't." Consuelo frowned, gravely upset.

"Mama, don't forget that the worst case of influenza I ever had, I caught in a bunch of ballrooms, going to parties when I came out. Not working with the poor."

"That's all the more reason for you not to do it," Consuelo said firmly. "If you can get that sick at parties among healthy, well-kept people, imagine how sick you will get working with people who live in terrible unsanitary conditions and are riddled with diseases. Besides, if you get pregnant, which I hope you will or are, that would be a terrible idea and would put you and the baby at risk. Has Josiah thought of that?" Something crossed her daughter's eyes that Consuelo didn't understand, but it vanished in a flash.

"I'm in no hurry to start a family, Mama. Josiah and I want to have some fun first." It was the first time Consuelo had heard her say that, and she was surprised. She wondered if she was using one of the new, or even ancient, methods to keep from having a child. But she didn't dare to ask.

"When did you decide that?" Her daughter's comment had answered Consuelo's question about whether Annabelle had gotten pregnant on the trip. Apparently not.

"I just feel too young. And we're having so much fun without a baby to worry about. We want to take some more trips. Maybe to California next year. Josiah says that San Francisco is beautiful, and he wants to show me the Grand Canyon. I can't do that if I'm expecting."

"The Grand Canyon can wait," her mother said, looking disappointed. "I'm sorry to hear it. I'm looking forward to grandchildren," she said sadly. She had nothing in her life now, except visits with Annabelle, rather than living with her, which she loved. Grandchildren would have filled a void for her.

"You'll have them," Annabelle reassured her. "Just not yet. Don't be in such a hurry. As Josiah says, we have lots of time." He had said it more than once on the trip, and she had no choice but to agree. He was her husband after all, and she had to follow his lead.

"Well, I still don't want you working on Ellis Island. I thought you liked the volunteer work you were doing." The Hospital for the Ruptured and Crippled was bad enough, in Consuelo's opinion. Ellis Island was unthinkable.

"I think Ellis Island would be more interesting, and give me more of a chance to improve my skills," Annabelle repeated, and her mother looked startled by what she said.

"What skills? What do you have up your sleeve?" Annabelle was always full of new ideas, particularly about medicine and science. They were clearly her passion, even if she didn't get to exercise them in any official way.

"Nothing, Mama," Annabelle said seriously, looking a little sad. "I just wish I could help people more, and I think I'm capable of doing more than what they let me do at the hospitals here." Her mother didn't know that she wished she could be a doctor. It was one of those dreams that Annabelle knew would never come to fruition, so why talk about it and upset her? But at least she could come as close as possible, as a volunteer. Ellis Island, and their acute need there, understaffed and overpopulated, would give her a chance to do that. It was Henry Orson who had suggested it to her. He knew a doctor there and had promised to introduce her. And because it was Henry, Josiah had approved the plan.

Annabelle went to visit Hortie after lunch with her mother. She was still in bed some of the time, but getting up more and more often.

Annabelle was shocked by how thin she looked, and how tired. The baby was big and beautiful, but Hortie looked like she'd been through the wars, and said she had.

"It was awful," she said honestly, with eyes that still told the tale. "No one ever said it would be like that. I thought I was dying, and my mother said I nearly did. And James says he wants another one soon. I think he's trying to start a dynasty, or a baseball team or something. I still can't sit down, and I was lucky I didn't get an infection. That probably would have killed me like Aimee Jackson last year." Hortie looked seriously impressed and badly shaken by what she'd been through. And Annabelle couldn't help wondering if the baby was worth it. He was adorable, but it wouldn't have been adorable if his arrival had killed Hortie, and it sounded like it nearly had. It seemed terrifying when Hortie told her what it had been like. "I think I screamed for all twenty-six hours. I'm not even sure I want to do that again. And imagine if it were twins, I think I'd kill myself rather than go through it. Imagine having two in one night!" She looked horrified, whereas six months before she had thought having twins would be funny. Having babies had turned out to be far more serious business than she'd previously thought. And the story she told was scaring her old friend. Enough so that Annabelle was grateful that she wasn't pregnant. "What about you?" Hortie asked, looking mischievous suddenly and more like her old self. "How was the honeymoon? Isn't sex fabulous? It's a shame it has to end up in childbirth, although I guess it can be avoided, if you're lucky. Do you think you're pregnant yet?"

"No," Annabelle said quickly. "I'm not. And we're in no rush. And what you're telling me makes me never want to do it."

"My mother says I shouldn't talk about it to women who haven't had babies." Hortie looked guilty then. "I'm sorry if I scared you."

"That's all right," Annabelle said sunnily. She had offered no comment about their sex life and didn't intend to. "You just make me glad I'm not pregnant." Hortie lay back in bed then with a tired sigh, as the wet nurse brought the baby in to show them how fat and handsome he was. He was a lovely baby, and sleeping soundly in the nurse's arms.

"I suppose he was worth it," his mother said, sounding uncertain, as the nurse left again. Hortie didn't like to hold him often. Motherhood still scared her, and she hadn't forgiven the baby yet for the agony he'd caused her. She knew she'd remember that for a long, long time. "My mother says I'll forget eventually. I'm not so sure. It was really awful," she said again. "Poor James has no idea, and I'm not allowed to tell him. Men aren't supposed to know." It seemed a strange principle to Annabelle, since they would have told him if she died. But failing that, it was supposed to remain a mystery, and one was supposed to pretend that everything had been easy and fine.

"I don't see why he can't know. I would tell Josiah. There's nothing I can't say to him. And I think he'd worry about me, if I didn't."

"Some men are like that. James isn't. He's a baby. And Josiah is a lot older, he's more like your father. So did you have fun?"

"We had a wonderful time." Annabelle smiled. "I learned to fly-fish, and we rode every day." She had loved galloping over the foothills with Josiah amid seas of wildflowers.

"What else did you learn?" Hortie asked with an evil look, and Annabelle ignored her. "I learned some pretty interesting stuff from James on our honeymoon in Paris." Everyone in town knew that before his marriage at least, James had gone to prostitutes constantly. There were whispers about it. And he had probably learned things from them that Annabelle didn't want to know, although Hortie didn't seem to mind. Annabelle much preferred being married to Josiah, even if they didn't start a family for a while. And they needed to find a house first anyway, since his apartment was too small.

Hortie got nowhere with her questions and racy innuendoes, and eventually she got tired and had to nap, so Annabelle left her and went home. It had been good to see her, and the baby was beautiful, but the story of his birth had shaken Annabelle. She wanted a baby, but had no desire to go through all that. And she wondered how long it would be before she had a baby of her own. She would have liked to hold Charles for a moment, but Hortie had never offered, and seemed to have no desire to hold the baby herself. But given what had happened to her, Annabelle told herself that it was understandable, and she wondered if it took time to develop maternal instincts, just as it took time to get used to the idea of being a husband or wife. Neither she nor Josiah had fully gotten used to all of that yet.

Chapter 9

By the time the social season in New York got fully under way in November, Hortie was back on her feet, and Josiah and Annabelle were invited everywhere. They frequently ran into Hortie and James at parties, and Hortie was in good spirits again. The baby was nearly three months old, and Annabelle and Josiah had been married for as long.

Overnight, Annabelle and Josiah had become the most desirable, popular couple in New York. They looked fabulous together, and still had the same easy, lighthearted relationship. They teased each other constantly and were playful, and had long serious discussions on political and intellectual issues, often with Henry when he came to dinner. They talked about books, the ideas they shared, and conversations with Henry were always lively. Sometimes the three of them played cards and laughed a lot.

Josiah and Annabelle dined with her mother at least twice a week and sometimes more often. Annabelle tried to spend as much time as possible with her in the daytime, since she knew how lonely her mother was now, although Consuelo never complained about it. She was dignified and loving. Consuelo didn't press Annabelle about starting a family, but wished she would. And she couldn't help noticing that Annabelle spoke to her husband as she had her brother Robert. There was a part of Annabelle that simply hadn't grown up yet, in spite of all that had happened, but Josiah seemed enchanted by it, and treated her like a child.

As promised, Henry had introduced her to his doctor friend on Ellis Island, and Annabelle had begun working there as a volunteer. She worked long, grueling hours, often with sick children. And her mother was right, although Annabelle never admitted it to her, that many of them were seriously ill when they arrived, and contagion was rampant. But the work was fascinating and she loved it. Annabelle thanked Henry for it every time she saw him. Josiah was very proud of how hard his wife worked, although she rarely shared the details of it with him. But he knew how dedicated she was to the hospital, the immigrants, and the work.

She went to Ellis Island three times a week, was there for exhausting but rewarding days, and often came home late. Annabelle worked in the hospital complex on the south side of the U-shaped island. Sometimes they sent her to the Great Room in the Great Hall. A fire had destroyed it sixteen years before, and the area where she worked had been rebuilt three years after the fire. In the Great Room, immigrants were held in large caged areas, where they were interviewed to make sure that their papers and questionnaires were in order. Most of the immigrants were sturdy laborers, many with wives and young children, or alone. Some had brides waiting for them whom they'd never met or scarcely knew. Annabelle often helped with the interview process, and about two percent of them were sent back, in tears and despair, to the countries where they came from. And in terror of deportation, many people lied in answer to the interviewers' questions. Feeling desperately sorry for them, Annabelle had jotted down vague, or incorrect, answers more than once. She didn't have the heart to make them eligible for deportation.

Fifty thousand people arrived at Ellis Island every month, and if Consuelo had seen them, she would have been even more terrified for Annabelle than she was. Many of the people who arrived there had suffered terrible hardships, some were ill, and had to be sent to the hospital complex. The lucky ones left Ellis Island in a matter of hours, but those whose papers were not in order, or were sick, could be quarantined or detained for months or even years. They had to have twenty-five dollars in their possession, and anyone whose entry was in question was sent to the dormitories, if not released. The sick ones went to the 275-bed hospital where Annabelle was normally assigned, doing the work she loved so much.

The doctors and nurses were understaffed and mostly overworked, which meant that they assigned tasks to volunteers that Annabelle would never have gotten to undertake otherwise. She helped deliver babies, cared for the children who were sick, assisted in eye exams for trachoma, which many of the immigrants were afflicted with. Some of them tried to hide their symptoms for fear of being deported. And there were quarantine wards for measles, scarlet fever, and diphtheria, which Annabelle could not enter. But she handled almost everything else, and the doctors she worked with were frequently impressed by her instinctive sense for diagnosis. For an untrained person, she had an impressive amount of knowledge from the reading she'd done, and an innate ability for anything medical, and she had a gentle way with her patients. The patients loved and trusted Annabelle completely, and she sometimes saw hundreds of patients in a single day, on her own for minor complaints or assisting the doctors and nurses on more serious cases. There were three full buildings set up for contagious diseases, and many of the patients there would not be leaving Ellis Island ever.

The tuberculosis ward was one of the saddest in the hospital, and Consuelo would have been frantic to know that Annabelle volunteered there often. She never told her mother, or Josiah either, but the sickest patients were those who interested her most, and where she felt she learned the most about the management and treatment of desperately ill people.

She had been working in the TB ward all day and into the evening one night when she came home late and found Henry and Josiah talking in the kitchen. Josiah commented on how late she was, and she apologized, feeling guilty. She'd had a hard time tearing herself away from her patients in the children's TB ward. It was ten o'clock when she got home and Henry and Josiah were cooking dinner and talking animatedly about the bank. Josiah gave her a big hug. She was bone tired, and still cold from the boat ride back. He told her to sit down at the kitchen table, handed her a mug of soup, and cooked dinner for her as well.

The conversation between them at the table was lively, as it always was between the three of them, and it revived her to think of something other than her sick patients. They loved batting new and old ideas around, argued about politics, questioned the social rules that had been accepted in their world for centuries, and generally had a good time. They were three bright people with lively minds, and were the best of friends. She had come to love Henry almost as much as Josiah did, and he was yet another brother to her, since she still missed her own so much.

She was too tired to join the conversation much that night, and Josiah and Henry were still in a heated debate about some political issue when Annabelle said goodnight and finally went to bed. She had a hot bath, put on a warm nightgown, and slipped gratefully between the sheets, thinking of the work she'd done on Ellis Island that day. And she was sound asleep long before Henry left and Josiah came to bed. She woke when he came in, and looked at him sleepily as he slipped between the sheets beside her, and she cuddled up to him. And within minutes, she was fully awake, having already had several hours' rest.

"Sorry I was so tired," she said sleepily, enjoying his warmth beside her in their bed. She loved sleeping with him, and cuddling. She loved everything about him, and always hoped he loved her as much. Sometimes she wasn't sure. Relationships with men, and their foibles, were unfamiliar to her. A husband was very different from a father or a brother. The dynamics with a husband were far more subtle and confusing at times.

"Don't be silly," he whispered easily, "we talk too much. You had a long day. I understand." She was selfless, and never hesitated to work hard for the good of others. She was an incredible human being with a good heart, and he truly loved her. There was no doubt in his mind about that.

There was an odd silence between them for a moment then, as Annabelle hesitated, and wanted to ask him something. She was always shy about bringing it up. "Do you suppose . . . could we maybe . . . start a family soon . . . ," she said in a whisper, and for a long moment he said nothing, but she felt him stiffen beside her. She had said it to him once before, and he hadn't liked it then either. There were times, and subjects, about which Josiah did not like to be pushed. And this was one.

"We have lots of time, Annabelle. We've only been married for three months. People need to get used to each other. I've told you that before. Give it time, and don't push."

"I'm not. I'm just asking." She wasn't anxious to go through what Hortie had, but she wanted to have his child, and was willing to brave it for him, no matter how bad it was or might be.

"Don't ask, and it will happen. We need to settle in." He sounded very firm, and she didn't want to argue with him, or make him mad. He was always very kind to her, but when she annoyed him, he backed away and got very cold with her, sometimes for several days. And she had no desire to cause a rift between them now.

"I'm sorry. I won't mention it again," she whispered, feeling chastised.

"Please don't," he said, turning away from her, his voice sounding suddenly cold. He was warm and loving on all subjects, but not this one. It was a sensitive point for him. And a few minutes later, without a word, he got up again. She lay waiting in bed for him for a long time, and then finally fell asleep before he came back. And in the morning, when she woke up, he was already up and dressed. It happened that way most of the time. It reinforced what he had said about not annoying him by pushing, and reminded her not to bring the subject up again.

The following week she went to visit Hortie, and found her in tears when she arrived. She was beside herself, and had figured out that she was pregnant again. The baby would be born eleven months after Charles, in July. James was delighted about it, and hoped it would be another boy. But with the memory of her first baby's birth still so fresh in her mind, Hortie was terrified of going through it again, and she just lay on her bed and cried. Annabelle tried to console her, but didn't know what to say. All she could think of to comfort her was that it probably wouldn't be as bad the second time. Hortie wasn't convinced.

"And I don't want to look like a cow again!" she wailed. "James never came near me the whole time. My life is ruined, and maybe this time I'll *die!*" she said miserably. "I almost did last time."

"You won't die," Annabelle said, hoping it was true. "You have a good doctor, your mother will be there. They won't let anything happen to you." But they both knew that other women died in childbirth and just after, even with excellent care. "It can't be worse than last time," Annabelle reassured her, but Hortie was inconsolable. "I don't even *like* babies," she confessed. "I thought he'd be so cute, like a giant doll, and all he does is eat and poop and scream. Thank God I'm not nursing him. And why should I risk my life for that?"

"Because you're married, and that's what women do!" her mother said sternly, as she walked into the room, and gave her daughter a disapproving look. "You should be very grateful that you're able to bear children and make your husband happy." They all knew of women who were unable to conceive, and were left by their husbands for women who could. But listening to them, Annabelle was suddenly grateful that it was not an issue between her and Josiah, although she found Hortie's baby a lot more appealing than his mother did. But in spite of that, Hortie was going to have two children by next July, within less than two years of her marriage. "You're a very spoiled, selfish girl," her mother scolded her and left the room again, with no sympathy whatsoever, although she'd been present at the agonizing experience Hortie had gone through. She said only that she'd been through worse herself, with equally big babies, several miscarriages, and two stillbirths, so Hortie had no reason whatsoever to complain.

"Is that all we're good for? Just breeding?" Hortie said to her friend angrily, after her mother left the room. "And why is it so damn easy for men? All they do is play with you, and then you get all the misery and the work, you get fat and ugly and throw up for months, then you risk your life having a baby, and some women die. And what do men do about it? Nothing, they just do it to you again, and run out with their friends and have fun." Annabelle knew, as Hortie did, that there were stories around town that James was playing a little too much, and seeing other women on the side. It reminded Annabelle that no one's life or marriage was perfect. Josiah wanted to wait before starting a family, but she was sure he wasn't cheating on her, he wasn't that kind of man. In fact, the only perfect marriage she knew of was her parents', and her father had died, and now her mother was a lonely widow at forty-four. Maybe life really wasn't fair.

She listened to Hortie rail and whine for several hours, and then went home to Josiah, relieved that their life was simpler, although he was still cool to her that night. He hadn't liked her comments of the night before. He went out to dinner with Henry that night at the Metropolitan Club, and said he had some business matters to discuss with him. Annabelle stayed home and pored over her medical books. The next day she was going to Ellis Island again. She was reading everything she could on infectious diseases, particularly tuberculosis.

Even though exhausting and challenging, she loved everything about what she did there. And as often happened, she was sound asleep when Josiah came home that night. But when she woke up briefly in the night, he was holding her. She smiled as she went back to sleep. All was well in their world.

Chapter 10

Since Josiah wasn't close to his family, he and Annabelle spent both Thanksgiving and Christmas with her mother. And since he was alone, to be kind to him, they invited Henry on both occasions. He was bright, charming, and attentive to Consuelo, so he was a happy addition in their midst.

Hortie eventually calmed down, and got used to the idea of another baby. She wasn't thrilled, but she had no other choice. She wanted more children anyway, she just hadn't been ready for it quite so soon after her ordeal in August, but she was hoping this time would be easier, and she wasn't as sick.

And Annabelle was dedicated to her work on Ellis Island, despite her mother's continuing objections. She hadn't asked Annabelle about grandchildren again, and had gotten the message loud and clear that it wasn't going to be happening imminently, and although she was anxious for them, she didn't want to intrude unduly. And she treated Josiah like a son.

It shocked all of them in April to realize that it had been two years since the sinking of the *Titanic*. In some ways, it felt like yesterday, in others a lot longer. So much had happened. Annabelle and her mother went to church that day, and had a special mass said for her father and brother. Her mother was lonely, but had adjusted to the losses in her life, and she was grateful that Josiah and Annabelle spent so much time with her. They were very generous about it.

In May, Annabelle turned twenty-one. Consuelo gave her a small dinner, and invited a few of their friends. James and Hortie came, several other young couples from their set, and Henry Orson, with a very pretty girl he had just met. Annabelle hoped that something might come of it for him.

They had a wonderful evening, and Consuelo had even hired a few musicians, so after dinner they all danced. It had been a lovely party. And that night, when Josiah and Annabelle went to bed, she asked Josiah the fateful question again. She hadn't mentioned it in months. He had given her a beautiful diamond bracelet for her birthday, which everyone had admired, and was the envy of all her friends, but there was something else she wanted from him, which was far more important to her. It had been gnawing at her for months.

"When are we going to start a family?" she whispered to him, as they lay in bed side by side. She said it, staring up at the ceiling, as though if she were not looking at him, he would be better able to come up with an honest answer. There was much between them now that was unsaid. She didn't want to make him uncomfortable, but after nine months of marriage, some things were hard to explain, and he couldn't keep telling her they "had time" and didn't "need to rush." How much time?

"I don't know," he said honestly, looking unhappy. She could see it in his eyes when she turned to look at him. "I don't know what to say to you," he said, sounding near tears, and suddenly she was frightened. "I need some time." She nodded, and gently turned to touch his cheek with her hand.

"It's okay. I love you," she whispered. There was so much she didn't understand and no one she could ask. "Is it something about me that I can change?" He shook his head and looked at her.

"It's not you. It's me. I'll work on it, I promise," he said, as tears filled his eyes and he took her in his arms. It was the closest they'd ever been, and she felt as though he was finally letting walls down and letting her in.

She smiled then as she held him, and gave his own words back to him. "We have time." As she said it, a tear rolled down his cheek.

In June, Consuelo left for Newport. With less to do in the city now, she liked being there before the season began. Annabelle had promised to come up in July, and Josiah at the end of the month.

Consuelo had already left the city, when the news from Europe riveted everyone's attention. On June 28, 1914, Archduke Franz Ferdinand, heir to the Austro-Hungarian Empire, and his wife, Sophie, were visiting Sarajevo in Bosnia on a state visit, and were shot and killed by a young Serbian terrorist, Gavrilo Princip. Princip was a member of the Black Hand, a much-feared terrorist Serbian organization determined to end Austro-Hungarian rule in the Balkans. The Grand Duke and his wife were each killed by a single bullet shot at close range to their heads. The shocking news reverberated around the world, and the consequences in Europe were rapid and earthshattering and mesmerized everyone in the States.

Austria held the Serbian government responsible and turned to Germany for support. Within weeks of diplomatic floundering, on July 28, Austria-Hungary declared war on Serbia, and opened fire on the city of Belgrade. Two days later, Russia mobilized its troops and prepared for war. France was then obliged, under the conditions of the treaty they had with them, to support Russia in its plans for war. Within days, the house of cards that had held the peace together in Europe began to fall. The two shots that had killed the Austrian Archduke and his wife were drawing every major country in Europe into war. On August 3, despite its protests as a neutral country, German troops marched through Belgium to attack France.

Within days, Russia, England, and France allied and declared war on Germany and the Austro-Hungarian Empire. Americans and their government stood aghast at what had happened. By August 6 all the major powers in Europe were at war, and Americans could talk of nothing else.

Annabelle had delayed going to Newport as events in Europe unfolded. She wanted to stay home and be close to Josiah. It wasn't their battle, although their European allies were going to war. But the United States showed no sign of getting involved. And Josiah reassured her that even if the United States did get pulled in at some point, which seemed unlikely, Annabelle had nothing to fear since, he reminded her, she was married to "an old man." At forty-one, there was no risk whatsoever that he would be sent to war. President Wilson was assuring the American public that he had every intention of staying out of the war in Europe. But it was deeply disturbing anyway.

Annabelle went to Newport with Josiah at the end of July, two weeks later than she'd planned. She'd been busy working at Ellis

Island as usual. Many of the immigrants were panicked over the safety of their relatives. It was obvious that the war, having been declared in many of the countries they came from, would affect their families, and stop some who had planned to join them in the United States. Many of their sons, brothers, and cousins had already been mobilized at home.

In New York, before they left, Annabelle, Josiah, and Henry talked about the war in Europe constantly during late-night dinners in the Millbanks' garden. And even sheltered Newport was agog at what had happened. For once, the social life there, and everyone's involvement in it, was taking a back seat to news of world events.

At Josiah and Annabelle's first anniversary dinner, Consuelo noticed that the pair were closer than ever, although she found both of them serious, which was entirely understandable, given what was happening in the world. Henry had come up from New York to spend their anniversary with them.

Hortie had had her baby by then, which arrived two weeks late on the first of August, a girl this time. The delivery was long and arduous again, but not quite as bad as it had been with Charles. And Louise, as they called her, only weighed eight and a half pounds. Hortie couldn't come to Annabelle and Josiah's anniversary dinner at Consuelo's house, as she was still in bed, being fussed over by her mother and a nurse. But James came to dinner of course. As he always did, he went to every party in Newport that summer, which he also did in New York, with or without Hortie.

August in Newport was quieter than usual, with news of the war in Europe. It seemed to be a cloud that hung over all of them, as they talked about their allies on the other side of the Atlantic and worried about their friends. Annabelle and Josiah discussed it constantly and enjoyed some quiet days together after Henry left. There seemed to be a peaceful understanding between Josiah and Annabelle, but Consuelo found them more serious than in the early days of their marriage. She was sad to see that they still hadn't started a family, and Annabelle never mentioned it to her. Once, when she saw a sad look in her daughter's eyes, she wondered if something was wrong, but Annabelle shared none of that with her, and seemed more devoted than ever to her husband. Consuelo still believed them to be a perfect match, and enjoyed being with them and their friends. She just hoped that a grandchild would appear one day, hopefully soon.

The young couple went back to New York in early September, Josiah to his duties at the bank, and Annabelle to hers on Ellis Island. She was getting more and more involved there, and had a deep affection and respect for the people she ministered to and assisted, most of whom seemed to be Polish, German, and Irish. And her mother still worried about her health, being in such close contact with them. They had so many illnesses, the children were often sick, and Consuelo knew that tuberculosis was rampant. What she didn't know was that Annabelle was fearless and unconcerned in their midst. She worked there more than ever that fall, despite her mother's warnings and complaints.

Josiah was busy at the bank, handling some very sensitive matters. As a neutral power, the U.S. government, although sympathetic to their plight, had refused to officially finance or supply the Allies' war efforts in Europe. As a result, private enterprise and some very wealthy individuals had stepped in to offer their assistance. They were sending money, as well as shipping goods, not only to the Allies, but sometimes to their enemies as well. It was creating a huge stir, and managing those transfers required the ultimate discretion, and Josiah found himself handling many of them. As he did with most things, he had confided in Annabelle about it, and shared his concerns with her. It bothered him considerably that certain important clients of her late father's bank were sending matériel and funds to Germany, due to ties those clients had there. It didn't sit well with him to play both sides of the fence, but he had to fulfill their clients' requests.

It was an open secret that transactions of that nature were happening, and in order to stop the influx of supplies to Germany, Britain had begun mining the North Sea. In retaliation, the Germans were threatening to sink any ship belonging to Britain or her allies. And German U-boats were patrolling the Atlantic from beneath the seas. It was surely not a good time to be crossing the Atlantic, but in spite of that, a steady stream of immigrants continued to appear on Ellis Island, determined to find a new life in the States.

The people Annabelle was seeing there were sicker and in worse shape than she had seen in years. In many cases, they had left dire conditions in their home countries and kissed the ground when they disembarked in the States. They were grateful for every kindness offered and everything she did. She had tried to explain that to her mother, to no avail, about how desperately she and others were needed, to assist the immigrants when they arrived. Her mother remained staunchly convinced that she was risking her life every time she went, and she wasn't completely wrong, although Annabelle didn't admit it to her. Only Josiah seemed to understand and be supportive of her work. She had bought a number of new medical books, and studied them now every night before she went to bed. It kept her occupied when Josiah was busy, had to work late, or went out with his men friends to events at clubs that didn't welcome women. She never minded when he went out without her. She said it gave her more time to read and study late into the night.

By then, she had seen several operations performed, and had read conscientiously everything she could lay her hands on about the contagious diseases that plagued the people she ministered to. Many of the immigrants died, particularly the older ones, after rigorous trips, or from the illnesses they were carrying when they arrived. In many ways, Annabelle was considered, among the medical staff there, as a kind of untrained, unofficial nurse, who often proved to be as competent as they, or more so. She had great insight, and an even greater talent for diagnosing her patients, sometimes in time to make a difference and save their lives. Josiah often said she was a saint, which Annabelle brushed off as generous but undeserved praise. She continued to work harder than ever, and often her mother thought that she was trying to fill the void in her life that a baby would have filled. She mourned the continued absence of children for her, even more than Annabelle seemed to herself. She never mentioned having children to her mother.

Henry joined them at her mother's for Christmas again that year. The four of them shared a quiet dinner on Christmas Eve. It was their third Christmas without Arthur and Robert, and on the holidays their absence was sorely felt. Annabelle hated to admit it, but she could see that so much of the life and spirit of her mother had gone out of her after her husband and son died. Consuelo was always grateful for the time they spent with her, and interested in what was happening in the world, but it was as though after the terrible tragedy on the *Titanic* more than two years before, she no longer cared what happened to her. Henry seemed to be the only one who could still make her laugh. For Consuelo, the double loss had just been too hard. She only wanted to live long enough now to see Annabelle with children of her own. She was growing more and more worried that something was wrong and that her daughter was unable to get pregnant. But the bond between her and Josiah continued to seem strong.

And as always, even on Christmas Eve, their conversation turned to the war by the end of the meal. None of the news was good. It was hard not to believe that, at some point, out of sympathy if nothing else, America would get into the war and that many young American lives would be lost. President Wilson was staunchly insisting that they would not get involved, although Josiah had begun to doubt it.

Two days after Christmas, Annabelle stopped in to see her mother for a visit, and was surprised when the butler told her that she was upstairs in bed. Annabelle found her shivering under the covers, looking pale, with two bright red spots on her cheeks. Blanche had just brought her a cup of tea, which she had refused. She looked very ill, and when Annabelle touched her forehead with a practiced hand, she could tell that she had a raging fever.

"What happened?" Annabelle asked, looking concerned. It was obviously influenza, and hopefully nothing worse. It was precisely what her mother always feared for her. But Annabelle was young and her resistance to illness was good. Particularly in the last two years, Consuelo had become more frail. Her ongoing sadness over her losses had diminished both her youth and her strength. "How long have you been sick?" Annabelle had seen her only two days before and had no idea she was unwell. Consuelo had warned Blanche not to worry her daughter, and said that she'd be fine in a few days.

"Just since yesterday," her mother said, smiling at her. "It's nothing. I think I caught a chill in the garden on Christmas Day." This looked like a lot more than a chill to Annabelle, and Blanche was worried too.

"Have you seen the doctor?" Annabelle asked, frowning as her mother shook her head. "I think you should." As she said it, her mother began coughing, and Annabelle saw that her eyes were glazed.

"I didn't want to bother him right after Christmas. He has more important things to do."

"Don't be silly, Mama," Annabelle chided her gently. She left the room quietly, and went to call him. She was back at her mother's bedside a few minutes later, with a bright smile that was more assured than she felt. "He said he'd come over in a little while." Her mother didn't argue with her about seeing the doctor, which was unusual too. Annabelle realized that she had to be feeling very ill. And unlike with the people she nursed so capably on Ellis Island, she felt helpless at her mother's bedside, and somewhat panicked. She couldn't ever remember seeing her mother so sick. And she had heard nothing about an influenza epidemic. The doctor confirmed that to her when he arrived.

"I have no idea how she got this," he said in consternation. "I've seen a few patients with it over the holidays, but mostly older people, who are more frail. Your mother is still young and in good health," he reassured Annabelle. He felt sure that Consuelo would feel better in a few days. And he left some laudanum drops to help her sleep better, and aspirin for her fever.

But by six o'clock her mother was so much worse that Annabelle decided to spend the night. She called Josiah to let him know, and he was very sympathetic and asked if there was anything he could do to help her. She assured him there wasn't and went back to her mother, who had been listening to the call.

"Are you happy with him?" Consuelo asked her daughter faintly, which Annabelle thought was an odd question.

"Of course I am, Mama." Annabelle smiled at her, and sat down on a chair next to the bed and reached for her mother's hand. She sat there holding it, just as she had when she was a child. "I love him very much," Annabelle confirmed. "He's a wonderful man."

"I'm so sorry you haven't had a baby. Has nothing happened yet?" Annabelle shook her head with a serious expression and gave her their official line.

"We have time." Her mother only hoped that she wasn't one of those women who was never able to have a child. She thought it would be a tragedy if they never had children, and so did Annabelle, although she wouldn't admit it to her mother. "Let's just get you well," she said, to distract her. Consuelo nodded, and a little while later she drifted off to sleep, looking like a child herself, as Annabelle sat next to her and watched her. Her mother's fever rose over the next hours, and by midnight Annabelle was bathing her forehead with cool cloths, as Blanche prepared them. They had far more comforts at their disposal than she did when she worked on Ellis Island, but nothing helped. She spent the night awake at her mother's bedside, hoping the fever would break by morning, but it didn't.

The doctor came to see her morning and afternoon for the next three days, as Consuelo continued to get steadily worse. It was the worst case of influenza the doctor had seen in a long time, and far worse than the one Annabelle had had three years before, when she missed the fateful trip on the *Titanic*.

Josiah came to sit with his mother-in-law one afternoon, so that Annabelle could get a few hours' sleep in her old bedroom. He had left the bank to do so, and was surprised when Consuelo woke and looked at him with clear bright eyes. She seemed far more alert than she had the day before, and he hoped she was getting better. He knew how desperately worried his wife was about her mother, with good reason. She was very, very sick, and people had died of influenza before, although there was no reason why she should with such good care. Annabelle hadn't left her side for a moment, except to sleep for half an hour here and there, when Blanche or Josiah sat with her mother. Consuelo hadn't been left alone for an instant. And the doctor came twice a day.

"Annabelle loves you very much," Consuelo said softly from where she lay, smiling at him. She was very weak and deathly pale.

"I love her very much too," Josiah assured her. "She's a remarkable woman, and a wonderful wife." Consuelo nodded, and looked pleased to hear it from him. More often than not, she thought he treated her like a younger sister or a child, and not a wife or a grown woman. Perhaps it was just his way, since she was so much younger than he was. "You have to rest and get better," he encouraged his mother-in-law, and she looked away, as though she knew it wouldn't make any difference, and then she looked directly at him again with an intense gaze.

"If anything happens to me, Josiah, I want you to take good care of her. You're all she has. And I hope that you'll have children one day."

"So do I," he said softly. "She'd be a perfect mother. But you mustn't speak that way, you'll be fine." Consuelo didn't look as sure, and it was obvious to him that she thought she was dying, or perhaps she was just afraid.

"Take good care of her," she said again, and then her eyes closed and she went back to sleep. She didn't stir until Annabelle came back into the room an hour later, and checked her fever. Much to her dismay, it was higher, and she signaled that to Josiah as her mother opened her eyes.

"Feeling better?" Annabelle asked with a bright smile, as Consuelo shook her head, and her daughter had the frightening feeling that she was giving up the fight. And so far, nothing they had done for her had helped.

Josiah went back to the apartment then, and told Annabelle to call for him in the night, if there was anything she wanted him to do. Annabelle promised she would, and as he left the Worthington house, he was haunted by what Consuelo had said. He had every intention of taking care of Annabelle. And the fact that he was all she had in the world, other than her mother, was not lost on him. In some ways, particularly if her mother died, it was a heavy burden for him.

On New Year's Eve the doctor told them that Consuelo had pneumonia. It was what he had feared would happen from the first. She was a healthy woman, and not of a great age, but pneumonia was a dangerous illness, and he had the feeling that Consuelo was far too willing to let go of life, and they all knew why. She seemed to be slipping away before their eyes, and they couldn't win this fight alone. They needed her help, and even with it, a happy outcome was not sure. Annabelle was looking terrified as she sat at her bedside. The only time she seemed to perk up was when her mother was awake, and she was trying to coax her to eat and drink, and assuring her that she would be fine soon. Consuelo didn't comment, was barely eating enough to sustain herself, and was being devoured by the fever. She wasted away day by day, while the fever refused to abate. Blanche looked as devastated as Annabelle as she ran trays up to the sickroom, and the cook tried to concoct meals that Consuelo would eat. The situation was frightening for them all.

And on the sixth of January, Consuelo quietly gave up the fight. She went to sleep in the early evening, after a long, difficult day. She was holding Annabelle's hand, and they had talked for a little while that afternoon. Consuelo had smiled at her before she went to sleep and told Annabelle she loved her. Annabelle had been dozing in the chair next to her at eight o'clock that night, when she suddenly sensed something different and woke up with a start. She looked at the smooth expression on her mother's face and instantly saw that she wasn't breathing, as Annabelle gasped. For the first time in two weeks, her mother's face was cool, unnaturally so. The fever had left her, and taken Consuelo's life. Annabelle tried to shake her awake, and saw that it was useless. She knelt at her mother's bedside, holding her lifeless form in her arms, and sobbed. It was the final goodbye she had never been able to say to her father or brother, and she was inconsolable as she cried.

Blanche found her there a little while later, and started to cry herself. She gently stroked Consuelo's hair, and then led Annabelle away, and sent Thomas to get Josiah. He was at the house moments later, and did all he could to comfort his wife. He knew all too well how great the loss would be to her, and how much she had loved her mother.

The doctor came that night to sign the death certificate, and in the morning the mortician came to prepare her. They laid Consuelo in state in the ballroom with flowers everywhere, as Annabelle stood by, looking devastated, with Josiah holding her hand.

Friends came to visit all the next day, after seeing the shocking announcement in the paper that Consuelo Worthington had died. Their home was plunged into deep mourning yet again, so soon after their double loss nearly three years before. Annabelle realized that she was an orphan now, and as her mother had said to him, Josiah was all she had in the world. She clung to him through the next days like a drowning person, and at her mother's funeral at St. Thomas Episcopal Church. His arm was ever around her shoulders, and he was true to his word. Josiah never left her side, and even slept with her in her narrow bed in her childhood room in her parents' house. She didn't want to go back to their apartment, and insisted on staying at her house with him. She talked about their moving into the house, which was stately to be sure, but he felt it would be grim, and too hard for her. But for now he let her do as she wished. It was a nearly intolerable loss for Annabelle. Henry was often with them, and was a great comfort to her too. He came to visit frequently and he and Josiah talked quietly in the library late at night or played cards, while Annabelle lay upstairs on her bed, in a state of shock and grief.

It was a full month before she left the house. She had touched nothing in her mother's bedroom. All Consuelo's clothes were still there. Josiah was handling the estate at the bank. Her parents' entire fortune was hers now, including the portion that would have gone to Robert. She was a very rich woman, but it was of no consolation to her. She didn't care. And although it pained him to do so, in March, Josiah had to relay to her an offer to buy the house, from a family that knew hers. Annabelle was horrified and didn't want to hear it, but Josiah told her gently that he didn't think she'd ever be happy there. She had lost all the people she had loved in that house, and the house was filled with ghosts for her. And the offer was a good one, probably better than any they'd get if she decided later to sell it. He knew it would be painful for her to do, but he thought she should.

"But where will we live?" she asked with a look of anguish. "Your apartment will be too small for us once we have a family, and I don't want another house." She was strongly inclined to decline the offer, but she also knew the truth of what he said. She and Josiah still needed a house, but had done nothing about it since Josiah wasn't ready to have children, and all she would ever see in that house were the visions of her parents and brother, all gone now. Even if they filled it with children, it would never fully balance the sadness she felt there, and the memories of those she'd lost.

She talked about it with Hortie, who was pregnant with her third child and sick again. She complained that James had turned her into a baby factory, but her own problems seemed minimal now compared to Annabelle's, and she tried to advise her as sensibly as she could. She thought Josiah was right, and that he and Annabelle should sell the Worthington mansion, and buy a new house for themselves, that had no bad memories for her, or sad ones.

It broke Annabelle's heart to do it, but within two weeks she agreed. She couldn't even imagine giving up the house where she had been so happy as a child, but now it was filled with loss and grief. Josiah promised to handle everything for her, and assured her that they would find a new one, or even build one, which would be a happy project for them. And whatever issues they had between them had gone unaddressed during her period of mourning. She was no longer worried about the family they hadn't started yet. She was in no mood to think of anything but her grief.

She spent all of April packing up the house, and sending everything to storage. And whatever was of no interest or value to her went to auction to be sold. The servants, Josiah, and Henry were tireless in their efforts to help her, and she spent hours crying every day. She hadn't been to Ellis Island since her mother's death. She missed it terribly but was too busy now closing her parents' house. The last of it went to storage in May, the anniversary of the day she and Josiah had gotten engaged two years before. She was relinquishing the house in June, and going to stay at the cottage in Newport, which she insisted she would keep. She and Josiah were going to spend the summer there.

Six days after she closed the house in New York, the Germans sank the *Lusitania,* killing 1,198 people, in a terrible tragedy at sea, which revived all her memories of the *Titanic,* and once again rocked the world and yet another of her mother's cousins died, Alfred Gwynne Vanderbilt, who stayed back to help others into lifeboats as her father and brother had on the *Titanic.* And like them, Alfred lost his life, when the ship exploded and sank in less than twenty minutes. Two weeks later, Italy entered the war and joined the Allies. And there were terrible stories in the news of nerve gas being used at the front and untold damage to the men it affected. All of Europe was in a state of turmoil, which seemed to mirror the despair and anguish that Annabelle felt.

She spent the rest of May in Josiah's apartment before she left for Newport in June. She took Blanche and those of her mother's servants who still remained to Newport with her. At the end of the summer, most of them would be moving on to other jobs, and life as she had known it would be forever changed. Blanche and William the butler would be staying in Newport with a few of the others.

Josiah had promised to come to Newport in mid-June, he was planning to take a longer vacation than usual that year, as he knew that Annabelle needed him with her. She looked heartbroken when she left town. The city home she had loved so much was already in other hands.

Once in Newport, Annabelle spent some time with Hortie, who had come up early with her children, their nanny, and her mother. Although only six months pregnant, she was huge again, and Annabelle was too restless to spend much time with her. She had felt sad and anxious since her mother's death, and it was hard being in Newport without her. In some ways, it felt to her like a replay of the summer after the *Titanic*, and she was relieved when Josiah arrived.

They would be staying at her mother's house and not Josiah's, and living in Annabelle's girlhood room. They went on long quiet walks near the sea. He was almost as pensive and silent as she was, but she didn't press him about it. He got that way sometimes, moody and even despondent. Neither of them was in great spirits. She asked him when Henry was coming up to see them, hoping it would cheer him, and he was vague about it and said he wasn't sure.

Josiah had been there for nearly a week when he finally turned to her one night as they sat by the fire and said he had to talk to her. She smiled, wondering what he was about to say. Most of the time now they talked about the war. But this time he sighed deeply, and she saw that there were tears in his eyes when he turned toward her.

"Are you all right?" she asked, looking suddenly worried, and all he did was shake his head slowly, and her heart sank like a stone at his words.

"No, I'm not."

Chapter 11

Nothing in Annabelle's life prepared her for what Josiah had to say. The impact of his words on her was as powerful as the morning she had seen the headlines about the *Titanic.* Everything he said to her hit her like a bomb. At first, he didn't know where to start. She reached out to him, and took his hand in her own.

"What's wrong?" she asked him kindly. She couldn't imagine a problem that would reduce him to the despair she was seeing. He looked devastated. He took a breath then, and began.

"I don't know how to say this to you, Annabelle," he said, squeezing her hand. He knew how innocent she still was, and how hard this would be for her to understand. He had wanted to say it to her six months before but thought it would be best to wait until after the holidays, and then her mother had gotten so sick. And he couldn't tell her after Consuelo died. Annabelle had been too devastated by her mother's death to sustain yet another blow, and worse yet at his hands. It had been almost six months since Consuelo's death, and selling the house had been a shock as well. But he just couldn't wait any longer. She had to know. He couldn't live a charade anymore, it was driving him insane.

"I don't understand what's wrong," she said, tears filling her eyes now too, before she even knew. "Have I done something to upset you?" He shook his head vehemently.

"Of course not. You've been nothing but wonderful to me. You're a perfect, devoted wife. It's not you who's done something wrong, Annabelle, it's me . . . right from the beginning. I truly thought I could be a good husband to you, that I could give you a good life. I wanted to—" He started to say more, but she instantly cut him off, hoping to stem the tide. But it was a tidal wave now, which even he couldn't stop. It had to be faced.

"But you are a good husband, and you do give me a good life." There was the sound of pleading in her voice, which broke his heart to hear.

"No, I don't. You deserve so much more. So much more than I can give you. I thought I could, I was certain of it at first, or I would never have done this to you. But I can't. You deserve a man who can give you everything you want, all your heart's desires, and who can give you children."

"We're in no hurry, Josiah. You always say that we have time."

"No, we don't," he said, looking resolute, his mouth hardening into a firm line. This was much harder to do than he had feared. The worst part of it was that he loved her, but knew he had no right to that now, he never did. And he felt guilty too for breaking his promise to her mother to take care of her, but the situation was far more complicated than Consuelo could have imagined. "We've been married for almost two years. I've never made love to you. I've given you a thousand excuses and fobbed you off." She had wondered once or twice before if he had a physical problem he'd been too embarrassed to tell her about. But she had always had the feeling that it was emotional and a matter of adjustment, which she hoped he would resolve over time, and never had. They both knew that after nearly two years of marriage, she was still a virgin. She had never admitted it to anyone, not even Hortie or her mother. She had been too ashamed, and feared it was because of something she was doing wrong, or that Josiah didn't find her attractive. She had tried everything imaginable, from new hairdos to different clothes, and ever more seductive nightgowns, until she'd finally given up on those as well, and decided that he was anxious and it would happen when it was meant to, and he was ready. But she had worried about it a great deal, although she tried to make light of it now to him. "I truly thought when I married you, that I was capable of being a man to you. I'm not. Every time I thought about it, I knew it was wrong, and I could not trade your virtue for a lie."

"It's not a lie," she said valiantly, fighting for her life, and that of their marriage. But she had lost before she began. She never had a chance. "We love each other. I don't care if you never make love to me. There are more important things in life than that." He smiled at how innocent she still was. There were many of both sexes who wouldn't have agreed with her, and he didn't himself. She just didn't know any better, and if she stayed with him, she never would.

"You deserve better than I can give you. Annabelle, you must listen to me. It may be hard for you to understand, but I want to be honest with you." He knew he should have been from the beginning, but he had to be now. He was about to take all her innocence from her in a single night, and perhaps destroy her faith in men forever. But he had no other choice. He had thought about this for a long time, and waited longer than he should have, for both their sakes. He couldn't do this anymore. He loved her. But everything about their marriage was wrong.

Her eyes were wide as she watched him, and her fingers shook in his hand as she tightened her grip, bracing herself for what he was about to say. Her whole body was shaking, although she wasn't aware of it. He could see her shoulders tremble as she waited. "It's not women that I want to make love with," he said in a hoarse voice of confession. "It's men. I thought I could be a decent husband to you, that I could go counter to my own nature, but I can't. That's not who I am. It's why I never married before. I love you deeply, I love everything about you, but not in that way." And then he added what seemed like the final blow. "Henry and I have been in love with each other since we were boys." Her eyes were so wide as she stared at him that for a moment he thought she would faint. But she was braver than that, and she refused to give in to the dizziness and nausea that engulfed her.

"Henry?" Her voice was barely more than a squeak. Henry, who had been their constant companion, and who she thought was their dearest friend? He had betrayed her totally, and had the part of her husband that she would never have. And Josiah had betrayed her as well.

"Yes. He understood that I wanted to marry you, and have children with you. I genuinely loved you, and I felt so sorry for you when your father died. I wanted to be everything to you. Father, brother, friend. The one thing I found I couldn't do, and wanted to, was be your husband. I couldn't bring myself to take the lie any further. And I couldn't lie to my own nature. Everything in me refused." She was nodding quietly, trying to absorb what he had said. It was a lot to take in all at once. Everything about their marriage to each other, their vows, their honeymoon, the promises they had made each other, the two years since, had been a fraud. "I thought that I could force myself to lead a double life, but I can't. And I can't keep doing this to you, while you gently try to ask me why nothing has ever happened between us, and now it can't. I discovered something six months ago that changed everything, and now I'm grateful that I was never able to overcome my reservations. I discovered in December that I have syphilis. Under no circumstances would I lay a hand on you now, or try to give you the babies I know you want so much. I wouldn't risk your life. I love you too much for that." Two lone tears streamed down his cheeks as he spoke, and she threw her arms around him and buried her face in his neck, sobbing hysterically. It was the worst news she'd had from him so far, even worse than the other.

"Josiah ... it can't be ..." She raised her tearstained face then to look at him. He looked the same to her, but she didn't know the signs. And for now, there were none. But in time, there would be. Eventually, he would go blind, and even die. His fate was sealed, and Henry's as well. They had discovered it together, and at least had the comfort of knowing that neither would have to survive the other. Theirs had been a powerful love for twenty years, for all of their adult lives, and it would follow them now to the grave. "Are you sure?"

"Entirely. And as soon as I found out, I knew I had to be honest with you, but then your mother got sick ... I just didn't have the heart to add to that. But we have to do something about it now. I can't let this go on forever."

"I don't want to do anything," she said staunchly, letting go of his hands and wiping away her tears with both of hers. "I want to stay married to you till the end."

"I won't let you do that. That's not fair to you. Henry and I want to go away with each other, and enjoy whatever time we have." She was shocked to realize that he didn't want to spend his last days with her, he wanted to be with the man he loved. It was the cruelest rejection she would ever know. Josiah took another breath then, to tell her the rest. "I have spoken to my attorney in confidence. He has already arranged for us to be divorced. We'll do it as quietly as possible. If anyone asks, you can say I was a dreadful husband, and you're well rid of me."

"But I don't want to be rid of you," she sobbed, clinging to him again. And they both knew that adultery was the only grounds for divorce and if he divorced her, people would imagine she'd been unfaithful and she didn't want to divorce him, and wouldn't. He knew that too. If he wanted to free her, for her own sake, he would have to divorce her, so she couldn't refuse. "Can't we just stay married?" she asked, sounding panicked, as he shook his head. He was determined, and nothing would sway him from his decision. She knew how he was when he got like that. He was an easy man to live with much of the time, except for the occasional melancholy mood, and his stubbornness, which he said he got from his father.

"We can't stay married, Annabelle," he said gently. "We could try to have our marriage annulled, but not without saying why, which would be embarrassing for both of us. And after two years, I'm not even sure we could. It's far simpler and quicker if we get divorced. I want you to be free to move on with your life as soon as possible. At least I owe you that. You need to find another man, get married, and have the married life you deserve. You need a real husband and a real marriage. Not this fraud."

"But I don't want to move on, and be married to someone else," she said, sobbing.

"You want children, and I could be sick and linger for years. I don't want you tied to me, wasting your life for all those years." He was forcing her to give him up, so he could go away, which was everything she didn't want. All she wanted was him. She loved him just as she had from the beginning. She wasn't angry at him, she was heartbroken by what he had said. And the last thing she wanted was a divorce.

"You must listen to me," Josiah insisted. "I know what's right. I made a terrible mistake, and we must correct it now. We could get divorced in Kentucky, which seems stupid and sneaky. It makes more sense to do it in New York, since we live there. No one will know the details. We'll get a private hearing, and be discreet about it." He took a sharp breath then. "I'm going back to the city tomorrow, to see my attorney again. And then Henry and I will go away. We're going to Mexico for a while." They would have preferred to go to Europe, but it was no longer reasonable or practical to do so, so they had chosen Mexico instead. There, they wouldn't see anyone they knew and could quietly disappear, which was all they wanted now, for the time they had left.

"When will you come back?" Annabelle asked weakly. After losing everyone else, now she was losing him.

"Not for a long time," he said, sounding harsher than he meant to, and not wanting to say "Never." But he wanted her to accept that it was over for them. It should never have started in the first place, but now he wanted the end to be quick. It seemed kinder to him. But the look on Annabelle's face said he was wrong. She looked completely undone by everything he had said, particularly that he was leaving her the next day.

She couldn't imagine how she would survive without him. She would be completely alone in the world when he left. He had Henry, and always had as it turned out, and she had no one. Neither parents, nor brother, and now not him.

"Why can't we stay married?" she asked plaintively, sounding almost like a child. "It's no different than it was before."

"Yes, it is. You know the truth now, and so do I. I need to free you, Annabelle. I owe you at least that. I've wasted two years of your life." Worse than that, he had destroyed it. She had nothing now, except her inheritance. She no longer even had a house in town. She'd have to stay in a hotel. She couldn't even stay at his apartment if they were divorcing. But he had thought of it as well. "You can stay at the apartment until you get your bearings, until you decide what you want to do. I'll be gone in a few days." He and Henry had already made their plans.

"I wish I hadn't sold the house," she said weakly, but they both knew it had been the right thing to do. It was too much house for her, and she couldn't stay there all alone, particularly not as an unmarried woman. She needed a more manageable establishment of her own. And he felt certain that she would remarry in a short time. She was a beautiful girl and only twenty-two years old. And she had all the innocence and freshness of youth. At least he hadn't spoiled that, although she felt as though she had aged a dozen years in the past hour. He stood up then and put his arms around her. He hugged her, but did not kiss her. The fraud he had perpetrated on her was over. He no longer belonged to her, and never had. He had been Henry's all along, and they were about to pay a high price for his trying to be something he wasn't. He loved her but not in the ways he needed to in order to be her husband. It had been a sad discovery for him too. And even worse now for her. He held out no hope. He was relieved now that he had never made love to her. He would never have forgiven himself if he had infected her as well. What he had done was bad enough. He felt terrible about lying to her for all this time. Worse than that, he had lied to himself. He loved her, but his wedding vows had been empty and meant nothing.

He walked her up to her room, but refused to stay with her that night. He said it was no longer proper. He slept in the guest room downstairs, and she lay in her bed and sobbed all night. Eventually, she crept downstairs and tried to get into bed with him, just so they could hold each other, but he wouldn't let her. He sent her back upstairs to her own room, feeling like a monster, and after she was gone, he lay in his own bed and cried. He truly loved her and it broke his heart to leave her, but he felt he had no other choice. He knew how troubled she had been by what had never happened between them, and he didn't want her with him now as he deteriorated slowly or rapidly, and ultimately died. He had no right to do that to her, and he planned to stay away until the end. The disease was already advancing at a rapid rate, and Henry was starting to show signs of it as well. They had both taken arsenic treatments, and it hadn't helped at all. They wanted to be away from New York now, and all those they knew, for what came next. It was time to leave Annabelle and let her begin a new life. He knew that in time, when she adjusted to it, she would understand that it was right.

She stood sobbing on the front steps when he left the next day. She was wearing black for her mother, and looked tragic as he drove away. Leaving her was the hardest thing he had ever done, and he felt ill and cried intermittently all the way back to New York. If he had killed her with his bare hands, it would have been no harder than this, and he wouldn't have felt worse.

Chapter 12

Annabelle saw no one after Josiah left. Blanche knew something terrible had happened, but she didn't dare ask what. Annabelle stayed in her room, and took meals on a tray, which she hardly touched. Once a day, she went out for a walk along the sea, but she saw no one and spoke to nobody. Hortie came by one afternoon, and Annabelle refused to see her. She had Blanche tell her that she was ill. Annabelle was too heartbroken to see even her best friend, and too ashamed to tell her she was getting divorced, even if through no fault of her own, and she couldn't tell her why. The truth was unthinkable and she wanted to protect Josiah. She panicked every time she thought of never seeing him again.

She knew that once people heard of the divorce, no one would believe her, and that everyone in New York and Newport would be shocked. She wondered how long it would take for news of it to get around. In mourning for her mother, she wasn't expected to go out, but people would find it strange that they never saw Josiah. Blanche already suspected what had happened, although she thought it was a lovers' quarrel, and had no idea it would end in divorce. She and the butler whispered that he must be having an affair, but no one could possibly have suspected it was with Henry, or that his and Annabelle's marriage was over. Blanche tried to tell her that everything would be all right, and all Annabelle could do was cry and shake her head. Nothing would ever be all right again.

Josiah's attorney came up to see her in July. Josiah had resigned his position at the bank and left for Mexico by then. Two weeks before, Henry had claimed illness in his family and resigned as well. It had never occurred to anyone to link the two events, but the departures of both men were a loss to the bank.

Josiah had sent her a letter before he left, apologizing to her again for his terrible perfidy and betrayal. He said he would bear the guilt of it all his life, and assured her that his love for her had been sincere. The divorce had already been filed in New York, and the attorney brought her a copy of the papers. The only grounds that he had been able to file them under was infidelity, which rocked her to the core when she read it. She had known it, but seeing it was worse. She had told Josiah she wouldn't file a divorce, so Josiah had no choice but to do it himself.

"Everyone will think I cheated on him," she said with an anguished look at the attorney, and he shook his head. She had hoped Josiah wouldn't file it, but he had, on the only grounds that existed.

"No one will ever see these papers," the attorney assured her. "There was no other choice, since you wouldn't agree to file a divorce." She would have died first. She loved him.

As it turned out, Josiah and his attorney's confidence in the system was gravely misplaced. A clerk at the court sold a copy of the divorce papers to the newspapers, and in August it was published that Josiah had filed for divorce for adultery. In a single stroke, Annabelle's life and reputation were ruined. Overnight, she became a pariah.

She was still in Newport when she heard of it from her father's bank, and news of it spread like wildfire. Everyone in Newport was talking about Josiah and Annabelle's divorce. It took her a full two weeks to have the courage to visit Hortie to talk to her about it, and when she did, she was in for another shock. Instead of allowing her to run straight upstairs to Hortie's room, where she was languishing on her bed as usual, the butler ushered her into the drawing room, as Hortie's mother swept out of the room and brushed past her with a disapproving scowl. She said not a word to Annabelle, and it was another ten minutes before Hortie appeared, looking considerably larger than the last time Annabelle had seen her. She looked extremely nervous and didn't sit down. Instead, she stood looking at Annabelle uncomfortably as tears rushed to Annabelle's eyes, and Hortie turned away and pretended not to see it.

"I suppose you've heard the news. Everybody has," Annabelle said miserably, and blew her nose discreetly on a lace handkerchief that had been her mother's. She was carrying her parasol too, as she had walked over from the house on an unusually hot day.

"I had no idea that there was someone else," Hortie said in a choked voice, and she made no move toward her friend, nor said anything to comfort her. She stood like a statue across the room from Annabelle, her arms firmly at her sides.

"There isn't, and never was," Annabelle said clearly. "Adultery was the only grounds they allowed. Josiah wanted the divorce, I didn't. He thought it was best . . . he couldn't . . . he didn't want . . ." Her words trailed into a choked sob. She had no idea how to explain it, because none of what had really happened made sense, and she couldn't say it, even to her best friend. She didn't want to betray him, no matter how great his betrayal of her had been. She couldn't do that to him. He would be ruined forever if she said he had left her for a man, and she didn't have the courage to tell Hortie she was still a virgin, so she just sat in the chair and cried. And there was no way she could tell her of his shocking illness. "I don't know what to do," Annabelle said miserably. "I want to die." Hortie mistook her agony for guilt. Her mother had said that she deserved everything Josiah did to her now, that a man of Josiah's moral stature would never divorce a woman for no reason, and that Hortie could rest assured that whatever Annabelle had done had been unforgivable. Otherwise he'd have stayed married to her. And if he had divorced her as an adulteress, then she was. She said she felt extremely sorry for Josiah, and not at all for Annabelle, who got just what she deserved. And James had told Hortie in no uncertain terms that she was strictly forbidden to ever see Annabelle again. He didn't want her evil influence on his wife.

"I'm very sorry this happened," Hortie said uncomfortably. "You must have made a terrible mistake." She tried to be charitable with her, but she actually thought her mother was right. Josiah was too kind a man to do this lightly. For him to divorce Annabelle, quit his job, and leave town, she must have behaved abominably. She had never thought Annabelle capable of it before, but it only proved that you never knew even your best friends. She was severely disappointed in her, and from the flood of tears Annabelle was shedding, she could see just how guilty she felt. Her mother and James were right.

"I didn't make a mistake," Annabelle hiccuped as she sobbed. She looked and felt like an abandoned child, and she was shocked that Hortie wasn't being nicer, after all they'd been through together since they were children. Hortie was looking very distant and sounding very cold.

"I don't think I want to know what happened," Hortie said, reaching for the door. "I'm sorry, but you'll have to go. James said I can't see you again. Good-bye, Annabelle, I have to go upstairs and lie down, I'm not feeling well." And with that, she walked out of the room and closed the door behind her, without another word. Annabelle sat staring after her, unable to believe what had just happened. She was shaking violently when she stood up, ran out of the house, and all the way home. She thought of throwing herself into the sea and killing herself, but she didn't have the courage to do it. She would have liked to, because then she would see her parents and Robert again, she was sure of it. She couldn't believe that Hortie had abandoned her too, and said she would never see her again. And then she realized that everyone she knew would do the same. Every door in Newport and New York would be closed in her face, once she could go out again.

Annabelle slammed the door behind her as she ran into her own house and up the stairs to her room. She threw herself on the bed, too shocked to even cry. She was still lying there when Blanche let herself into the room and spoke softly to the woman she had known as a child.

"I know you didn't do what they say, Miss Annabelle. I've seen you almost every day, all your life. I know you were a good wife to him. I don't know what happened between you two, but I know it has nothing to do with you." And with that, she moved forward and put her arms around Annabelle and they cried together. Annabelle couldn't tell her what had really caused the divorce, but at least Blanche knew she wasn't capable of what she was accused of. And as they cried and hugged, Annabelle missed her mother more than ever. She couldn't even imagine what her life would be like now. She had refused to divorce him, and thinking he was saving her from a worse fate, he had branded her as an adulteress forever.

She got a taste of what it meant in the last weeks of August, as the summer season drew to a close. She went to the store a few times, and the post office, and each time she did, the people she saw on the way turned away and refused to speak to her. Men glared at her in disapproval, and women looked right through her. She had in fact become the pariah she had warned Josiah she would be. He had thought this would be best for her, and had freed her out of love and remorse, and in so doing he had condemned her to a life sentence of disapproval and contempt. She had been banished by her own from her own world. She knew then that her life was over in Newport and New York, and she would never again be admitted into proper homes, or into polite circles. She would forever be the adulteress whom Josiah Millbank had divorced. He might as well have taken her out and hanged her. The decent woman she had always been was as good as dead.

Chapter 13

Annabelle went back to New York in the first week of September, and left Blanche, William, and several other servants at the Newport house. It was no longer her parents' house, but her own. She took Thomas back to New York with her, and she was planning to sell all but one of her father's cars.

She stayed at Josiah's apartment, and knew she had to find a house, but she had no idea where to start or how to do it, and she knew Josiah wasn't coming back soon, if at all. He had said that he and Henry would be gone for many months, or longer, and she had heard nothing from him since he left for Mexico. He had completely abandoned her, and so had everyone else. And Josiah thought he had done it for her own good.

She went back to work on Ellis Island while she tried to figure out what to do. People were still coming in from Europe, even though the British had mined the Atlantic, and the Germans were still sinking boats. And it was while talking to a French woman one day about her experiences that Annabelle knew what she had to do. It was the only thing she could think of, and it made more sense than staying in New York, and being shunned by everyone she knew. She didn't care now if she died crossing the Atlantic, or once she was in Europe. In fact, she would have welcomed the release from the fate Josiah had unwittingly condemned her to with the divorce.

She spoke to several people at Ellis Island about what to do. The doctor she had worked for gave her a letter, as witness to her skills, which she planned to use at a hospital in France. He told her about a hospital that had been set up in an abbey in Asnières-sur-Oise near Paris, staffed only by women. It had been established the year before by a Scotswoman, Dr. Elsie Inglis, who had proposed to do the same in England and had been refused. The French government had welcomed her with open arms, and she had taken over and personally set up the hospital at the abbey, using women's medical units to staff it, both doctors and nurses, with only a few male physicians, and Annabelle's doctor friend at Ellis Island had encouraged her to go there, once she told him her plan.

Elsie Inglis was a forward-thinking woman and suffragette, who had studied medicine at the Edinburgh School of Medicine for Women. She had established her own medical college, and taught at the New Hospital for Women. The physician who had referred Annabelle to her was certain that any medical establishment Inglis set up would be medically sound and impeccably run. She had had the Abbaye de Royaumont up and running by December 1914, after the outbreak of war. And from all the referring doctor had heard, they were doing a great job caring for the wounded soldiers who were being brought to them from field hospitals at the front. Everything Annabelle heard about it told her that it was where she wanted to be, and that more than likely she would be most welcome. She didn't care if she drove an ambulance or worked in the hospital. Whatever they needed from her, she was more than willing to do.

She had no reason to stay in the States now. She had no home, no relatives, no husband, and even her best friend had said she couldn't see her anymore. Her parents' friends and Josiah's would be even more shocked. And since he had left the city, everyone assumed that she had broken his heart. She had been disgraced in every possible way, and no one would ever know the truth of what had happened. She had absolutely no reason to stay and every possible reason to leave.

Annabelle spent the next several days packing up everything she wanted to send to storage, and getting a new passport, since she hadn't traveled in six years, since she was sixteen. She booked passage on the *Saxonia* going to France, and bought some sturdy clothes to wear once she got there. She had no need for frills or elegance anymore, and left all her jewelry and her mother's in a vault at her father's bank, and made the financial arrangements she'd need in Europe. She told no one what she was doing, and at the end of September she went back to Newport to say good-bye to Blanche, and the rest of the staff. There were five of them in the house for the winter, to take care of it and tend the grounds. It was enough, given the size of the cottage, but not too many. She told Blanche what she was doing and that she might not be back for a long time.

The old woman cried at everything that had happened, and bemoaned her young mistress's fate, and the terrible things that might befall her in France. They all realized that she might not survive the trip over, given the minefields and the German submarines lurking at sea. Blanche was well aware that Annabelle didn't care. She had nothing to lose and no one to live for. And at least at the front she might serve some purpose. She was taking all of her medical books with her, thinking that she might need them, and when she left Newport again two days later, they all cried as they waved good-bye, wondering if they'd ever see her again.

Once back in New York, Annabelle went to say good-bye to the doctors and nurses she had worked with at Ellis Island, and some of her favorite long-term patients, especially the children. Everyone was sorry to see her go, and she didn't explain why. She told the head doctor she would be volunteering at a field hospital in France. It broke her heart to say good-bye.

All of her belongings from Josiah's had gone to storage by then, and all she had left were the suitcases she was taking with her and what was in them, the rough clothes she had purchased for the trip, and several warm jackets and coats. She had managed to fit everything into three large valises, and she was planning to stay in her cabin on the ship, so she brought no evening clothes with her. She had taken out her passport and booked passage in her own name and not Josiah's, and on her last day in New York she went for a long walk, past her parents' house. It was the only thing left for her to say good-bye to. She stood there for a long moment, thinking of all that she had lost, and as she did, she saw one of their old neighbors get out of his car, notice her, and give her an evil look. He turned his back on her without greeting her, walked up the steps to his own home, and firmly shut the door. As she walked back to Josiah's apartment, thinking about it, all it did was strengthen her resolve. She had nothing left in New York anymore.

*   *   *

Thomas drove Annabelle to the Cunard dock the next morning, in time to get her three meager suitcases on board. The *Saxonia* was a large fifteen-year-old ship built for passengers and cargo, with four towering masts and a tall funnel. She was built for size and not speed, and would be traveling across the Atlantic at fifteen knots. She was not luxurious, but comfortable, and a moneymaker for the line because of the cargo, which reduced the passenger area considerably. And first class had been eliminated entirely since the outbreak of the war. She was by no means as prestigious as the other ships Annabelle had previously traveled on with her parents, but she didn't care, and had booked one of the larger staterooms in second class.

Two young sailors escorted them to her cabin, and Thomas gave her a warm hug when he said good-bye. He was going to put her father's car up on blocks in a rented garage, and the bank had been instructed to sell it. Thomas was already looking for another job, since Annabelle had no idea when she'd be coming back.

He was still standing on the dock, waving at her, as the ship slowly pulled away from its moorings half an hour later. People on deck were looking serious, knowing the risks they were taking in braving the Atlantic. Those who were going had good reason to do so. No one traveled these waters for pleasure anymore. It was far too dangerous with all of Europe at war.

Annabelle stayed on deck until the Statue of Liberty glided past. She saw Ellis Island and felt her heart ache, and then she went back to her cabin. She took out one of her medical books and began to read it, trying not to think of what would happen if they were torpedoed. It was the first ocean voyage she had taken since her father and brother had gone down on the *Titanic,* and she was tense as she listened to the ship groaning, wondering how close to American waters the submarines might be and if they would attack them. Everyone on the ship was having the same thoughts.

She dined alone in her stateroom, and lay wide awake in her bunk that night, wondering if they'd arrive safely, and what she would encounter when she got to France. She was planning to make her way to the area where she'd been told her services would be most needed. With America not participating in the war in Europe, there had been no way for Annabelle to volunteer from the States, although she knew her Astor cousins had financed a field hospital and one of her Vanderbilt cousins had volunteered. But after news of the divorce had spread, she didn't dare to contact them. She was going to find her own way when she got to France. She had to figure it out there.

Once at the hospital that was her destination, she would do whatever they assigned her. She was willing to undertake the most menial tasks, but from all she'd heard, the trenches were full to overflowing, and the hospitals even more so, with wounded. She felt certain that someone would put her to work, if they managed to survive the trip over.

She had learned a great deal from the doctors and nurses at Ellis Island and was continuing to study her medical books every day. And even if all they let her do was drive an ambulance, at least she knew she would be of greater use than hiding in New York from the gazes of an entire world of once-familiar people from whom she was now excluded.

Although Josiah had meant well, now all her respectability, reputation, propriety, and ability to make a new life had been destroyed by the divorce. He didn't understand. It was like being convicted of a crime, for which she would never be pardoned. Her sentence would be forever, her guilt a certainty to all. And under no circumstances would she ever divulge Josiah's secret. She loved him too much to do so, and what he was hiding was even more shocking than their divorce. The revelation of his longtime love affair with Henry, and the syphilis they now shared would have completely decimated his life. She couldn't do that to him. She still loved him. His secret would die with her. And without meaning to, he had sacrificed her.

It was a relief to be going to France, where no one knew her. At first, she didn't know whether to say that she was a widow, or had never been married. But if anyone knew Josiah, which was possible even in Europe, they would know that he was alive, and she was a liar, to add to the rest. Eventually she decided that she was going to say that she had never been married. It was simpler that way in case she met anyone who knew him. She was Annabelle Worthington again, as though the two years with Josiah had never happened, although they had and she had come to love him deeply. Enough to forgive him for the frailties he couldn't help, and the illness that would ultimately kill him.

Perhaps, she thought to herself, as the ship rolled gently the first night, she would be killed in France, and she wouldn't have to suffer another loss or bereavement. She knew that even after her divorce, when he died, it would break her heart again. All she had wanted was a life with him, a happy marriage, and to bear his children. Hortie didn't know how lucky she was to have a normal husband, and all her babies. And now Annabelle no longer had her either. She'd been shunned and abandoned by all. Hortie's rejection of her cut her the most deeply after Josiah's. And what it all meant to Annabelle was that, as the *Saxonia* made its way cautiously through the Atlantic to France, she was absolutely, totally alone in the world. It was a terrifying thought for a young woman who had been protected all her life, first by her family and then by her husband. And now all of them were gone, along with her good name and reputation. She would be branded as an adulteress forever. As she thought of it again, tears slid from her eyes onto her pillow.

The ship ran into no problems that night. They had doubled all the watches in order to watch for mines. There was no telling where they might turn up, or how close to land the German submarines would dare to come. There had been a lifeboat drill within the hour they left the dock. Everyone knew where their lifeboat station was, and their life jackets were hanging in plain sight in the cabins. In peacetime the life vests were stowed more discreetly, but since the sinking of the *Lusitania* in May, the Cunard Line wasn't taking any chances. Every possible safety precaution was being observed, but that only heightened the atmosphere of tension on the trip.

Annabelle spoke to no one. She had looked at the list of passengers, and saw that there were two acquaintances of her parents on board. Given the tidal wave of scandal her divorce from Josiah had caused in New York, she had absolutely no desire to see them, and risk getting snubbed by them, or worse. She preferred to stay in her cabin for most of the day, and go out for a solitary walk around deck at nightfall, when everyone else was changing for dinner. And she dined alone every night in her stateroom. In spite of the books she had brought along for distraction, her father and brother's deaths on the *Titanic* were much on her mind. And the stories from the sinking of the *Lusitania* had been almost worse. She was tense and anxious much of the time, and barely slept, but she got a lot of studying done during her long waking hours.

The stewardess who took care of her rooms tried to no avail to urge her to go to the dining room for dinner. And the captain had invited her to dinner at his table on the second night out. It was an honor most passengers would have leaped at, but she sent him a polite note and declined, saying she wasn't well. The seas had been a little rough that day, so it was believable if she had been a poor sailor, which she wasn't. She felt fine the entire way.

The steward and stewardess assigned to her wondered if she was recovering from a loss of some kind. She was beautiful and young, but so solemn, and they noted the black she was still wearing in mourning for her mother. They wondered if she was a widow, or had lost a child. It was clear that something had happened to her. She seemed like a tragic, romantic figure as she watched the sunset during her late afternoon walks. She stood looking out to sea, thinking of Josiah, and wondered if she would ever see him again. She tried not to think of Henry, and not to hate him.

Often, when she came back to her stateroom, which comprised both a large sitting room and a bedroom, she looked as though she had been crying. She often wore a veil to hide her face, which was even more shielded by big hats. She had no desire to be recognized, or seen. She was disappearing from her world, shedding the shell of protection she had once enjoyed, and the identity that had been an integral part of her all her life. She was stripping herself of all things safe and familiar, to vanish into a life of service at the front. It was all she wanted now.

It shocked her to realize that other than her parents' summer cottage in Newport, she didn't even have a home. Almost everything she owned was in storage, and the rest of it was in her three bags, all of which she could carry herself. She hadn't brought a single trunk, which was most unusual, the stewardess had commented to the purser, for a woman of her quality. Even without the trappings of furs or jewels or evening gowns, just from her speech and bearing, gentle manner, and poise, it was easy to see that Annabelle was well born. And seeing the look of sorrow in her eyes every day, the young stewardess felt sorry for her. They were nearly the same age, and Annabelle was always kind to her.

On the fourth day out, as they drew closer to Europe, the ship slowed to a startling crawl. They were hardly moving in the water, but the captain of the watch had seen something suspicious, and was concerned that there might be a U-boat nearby. All the passengers were worried, and some were wearing their life vests, although no alarm had sounded. For the first time Annabelle came out in broad daylight herself to see what was going on. One of the officers explained it quietly to her when she asked, and was struck by her beauty, concealed behind her hat and veil. He wondered if she was a famous actress, traveling incognito, or someone well known. She was wearing a well-tailored black suit, and when she took one of her gloves off, he noticed her graceful hands. He reassured her, and staying well away from clusters of people talking or sitting in small groups playing cards, she took a brief walk around the ship, and then went back to her room.

The young officer knocked on her door later that afternoon, and she opened it looking surprised. She had a book in her hand, and her long blond hair was spilling over her shoulders. She looked like a young girl, and he was even more startled by how pretty she was. She had taken off her suit jacket and was wearing a black blouse and long black skirt. Like the stewardess, he suspected she was a young widow, but he had no idea why she was going to Europe. He said he had come to make sure that she was all right, since she'd been concerned earlier that day, and they were still moving at a slow speed. She assured him with a shy smile that she was fine. He glanced down to see what she was reading and was surprised to see what it was. It was a medical book by Dr. Rudolph Virchow, and there were three by Dr. Louis Pasteur and Dr. Claude Bernard, the medical authorities of the time, on a table behind her. They were her bibles.

"Are you studying medicine?" he asked, visibly amazed. It was an unusual book for a woman to be reading, and he wondered if she was a nurse. It seemed unlikely given her obvious station in life.

"Yes...no...well, not really," she said, looking embarrassed. "I just enjoy reading medical books. It's sort of a passion of mine."

"My brother is a doctor," he said proudly. "He's the smart one. My mother is a nurse." He lingered, looking for excuses to talk to her. There was something so mysterious about her, and he couldn't help wondering what was taking her to France. Perhaps she had family there. These days, there were fewer and fewer women doing crossings on the ships. "If there's anything I can do for you, Miss Worthington, please don't hesitate to let me know." She nodded, shocked to hear herself called that for the first time in two years. She wasn't used to it yet. It was like reverting to childhood and traveling back in time. She had been so proud of being Mrs. Millbank. It made her sad to be Worthington again, as though she didn't deserve Josiah's name. They had agreed that she would take back her own. He could have petitioned the court for her to keep his, but they both thought it was best if she didn't. It was easier to start with a clean slate now with her own name, but she still missed his.

"Thank you very much," she said politely. He bowed, and she closed the door and went back to her book, and didn't emerge from her room again until after dark. She was anxious to arrive. Being cooped up in her room all the time made the trip seem very long. And slowing down as they had had cost them a full day, but everyone agreed that it was better to be cautious and safe, even if it meant arriving late.

The following day was even more stressful than the one before. The early morning watch had spotted a minefield in the distance on their starboard side. This time the sirens sounded, and everyone was brought up on deck so the crew could explain what was happening. They all were wearing their life jackets and were told to keep them on all day. Annabelle had left her cabin without her hat and veil, and it was a warm sunny day with a gentle breeze. Her hair was brushed smoothly down her back, and she was wearing a black linen dress. The same officer as the day before approached her again with a smile.

"Nothing to worry about," he told her, "just a precaution. We're staying well out of trouble. Our men are very sharp. They spotted it right off." She was relieved, but it was unnerving anyway.

Without meaning to share it with him, she let a bit of personal information slip out. "My parents and brother were on the *Titanic,*" she said softly, and almost shuddered as she said it and looked up at him with wide eyes.

"I'm so sorry," he said kindly. "Nothing like that is going to happen here. Don't you worry, miss. The captain has everything under control." But the presence of the minefield in the distance meant another day of crawling through the water. And for the next two days they had to be even more vigilant as the *Saxonia* approached France.

In the end the trip took seven days. They reached Le Havre at six in the morning, and the ship was tied up to the dock while most of the passengers still slept. Breakfast was to be served at seven, and disembarking passengers were to take the train at nine. The ship was going on to Liverpool after that, since Southampton had been taken over by the military. And on this voyage, they were stopping in France first, as they had been forced considerably off course by the minefields. Annabelle was on the deck fully dressed when they docked. The familiar young officer saw her and came over. She looked excited and wide awake. It was the happiest he had seen her during the trip, and he wondered if her somber aspect had simply been fear of being on the ship, since her relatives had been on one that went down. And the minefields and U-boats had upset them all. Everyone was happy to arrive safely in France.

"Will you be happy to get to Paris?" he asked her pleasantly. It was obvious that she was, and he suddenly wondered if she had a fiancé there. Her smile was wide as she nodded in the early morning sun. She was wearing a hat, but no veil, and he could look right into her blue eyes.

"Yes. But I'm not staying long," she said simply, and he seemed surprised. No one came to Europe now for a short time, considering the risks involved, and surely not for a brief holiday trip.

"You're going back?"

"No, I'm not. I'm hoping to work at a hospital north of Paris, about thirty miles from the front."

"That's very brave of you," he said, looking impressed. She was so young and pretty he hated to think of her in the carnage of a hospital near the front, but she was visibly excited by the idea. It explained why she had been reading medical books in her cabin when he had stopped by to see her. "Will you be safe there?" he asked, looking worried, and she smiled.

"Safe enough." She would have preferred to be at the front, but she had been told that only trained medical and military personnel were allowed to work there. The hospital that had been set up in the Abbaye de Royaumont in Asnières-sur-Oise was more unusual and far more likely to accept her in their midst.

"Will you be going there today?" he asked with interest, and she shook her head.

"I thought I'd spend a night in Paris, and find a way to get there tomorrow." It was twenty miles north of Paris, and she wasn't sure what kind of transportation she could arrange.

"You're very courageous to be travelling alone," he said admiringly, correctly sensing that she was a woman who had been sheltered and protected all her life, and was not accustomed to fending for herself. But she had no other choice now. Annabelle knew that this was a fresh start for her, or at the very least a time away from the ostracism she had only just begun to taste at home, and could only have gotten worse in time.

The young officer had to tend to his duties then, and Annabelle went back to her stateroom to close her bags. She was ready to go by seven. She thanked the stewardess for her kind attention during the trip, gave her a handsome tip in a discreet envelope, and went to the main dining salon for breakfast. It was the first and only time she had taken a meal in public during the crossing. But everyone was too busy to pay attention to her. They were saying good-bye to new friends, and enjoying a last hearty meal before they left the ship.

Annabelle was one of the first passengers to disembark. And she said good-bye to the young officer when he came to see her off and wish her luck. She boarded the private compartment that had been reserved for her on the train. And she knew these were the last luxuries she would enjoy for a long time. By the next day, with any luck, she would be working hard, and living like all the other medical workers at the Abbey.

She managed her bags herself, and was able to find a cab at the Gare du Nord train station in Paris. She had eaten lunch on the train, and wasn't hungry, so she went straight to her hotel. She had reserved a room at the Hôtel de Hollande in the ninth arrondissement near Montmartre, and as they drove there, she noticed blue-capped men on bicycles, usually in groups of four, patrolling the city. The terraces had been removed from all cafés, which was a big change from the last time she had seen Paris with her parents as a young girl. She hadn't been there since she was sixteen. There was an atmosphere of quiet tension here, and she noticed there were hardly any men in the streets. Most of them had been drafted into the military and were fighting for their country and lives at the front, but the city was still as beautiful as she remembered. The Place de la Concorde was as majestic as ever, as was the Champs Élysées. The weather was beautiful, and it was a splendid autumn day as the cab pulled up in front of her hotel.

Not surprisingly, the clerk at the desk was very old, and showed her to her room on the first floor. It was small, but bright and sunny, looking out over the hotel's garden where chairs had been set up around tables, and a few people were having lunch. She asked him about transportation to Asnières the next day. She wanted to know if it was possible to find her a driver and some sort of vehicle. She spoke to him in the fluent French she had learned from her tutor, as part of a genteel education, which now served her well.

"Why would you want to go there?" he asked with a disapproving frown. It was too close to the front for his taste, but not Annabelle's. She had discreetly tried to suggest, without being vulgar, that she would pay the driver handsomely for the one-way trip, provided the hospital let her stay, which had yet to be seen. But she was optimistic, and she had her letter of reference from the doctor at Ellis Island in her purse.

"I'm going to the Abbey in Asnières," she explained.

"It's not an Abbey anymore," he informed her. "It's a hospital, all run by women."

"I know." She smiled at him. "That's why I'm going."

"You're a nurse?" She shook her head in answer. He couldn't help thinking that it was a fine hotel for a nurse to be staying at, but even in her plain clothes, she looked far more aristocratic.

"No, I'm just a medical worker, or whatever they'll let me do," she said humbly, and he smiled at her, with a look of amazement.

"You came here to help our boys at the hospital?" This time she nodded without hesitation. He sent dinner to her room that night, with a small bottle of wine that he had been saving for himself. "You are a good woman," he said to her the next time he saw her.

"Thank you," she said softly, knowing that all of New York and Newport would have disagreed.

Later, the ancient desk clerk told her that he had asked his nephew to drive her the next day. He had been injured at the front the year before and lost several fingers, but he assured her that Jean-Luc was a good driver, although he apologized that the young man would be driving her to Asnières in a truck. It was the only vehicle they had, and she assured him it would be fine.

She could hardly sleep in her bed at the hotel that night, she was so excited. She had no idea what the next day would have in store for her, or if they'd even let her stay at the Abbey. All she could do was pray that they would.

*

Chapter 14

Annabelle and the desk clerk's nephew, Jean-Luc, set out at six o'clock the next morning, as the sun came up over Paris. It was a staggeringly beautiful day, and he told her that there had been a terrible battle at Champagne the day before, and it was still raging. He said it was the second battle they'd had there, and a hundred and ninety thousand men had been killed and wounded. She listened with silent horror, thinking about the enormous numbers. It was inconceivable.

That was precisely why she was there. To help repair their men, and do what she could to save them, if she was able to help them in some way, or comfort them at least. She was wearing a light black wool dress, boots, and black stockings, had all her medical books in her bags, and was carrying a clean white apron in her purse. It was what she had worn at Ellis Island when she worked there, with slightly brighter skirts and dresses when she wasn't in mourning, as she still was now for her mother. Almost everything she had brought with her to wear was black.

It took them three hours through back roads to get to the hospital. The roads were in bad shape and deeply rutted, with potholes everywhere. No one had time to fix them, and there were no men to do it. Every able-bodied man was in the army, and there was no one left at home to do repairs or maintain the country, except old people, women, children, and the wounded who had been sent home. Annabelle didn't mind the rough roads as they bounced along in Jean-Luc's truck, which he told her he normally used to deliver poultry. She smiled when she saw that there were feathers stuck to her valises. She found herself looking down at her hands for a moment, to make sure her nails were cut short enough, and saw the narrow ridge that her wedding band had left. Her heart ached for a minute. She had taken it off in August and still missed it. She had left it in the bank vault in a jewel box, with her engagement ring, which Josiah had insisted that she keep. But she had no time to think of that now.

It was just after nine when they reached the Abbaye de Royaumont, a thirteenth-century abbey, in slight disrepair. It was a beautiful structure with graceful arches, and a pond behind it. The Abbey was bustling with activity. There were nurses in uniforms pushing men in wheelchairs in the courtyard, others hurrying into the various wings of the building, and men being carried on stretchers out of ambulances driven by women. The stretcher-bearers were female too. There were nothing but women working there, including the doctors. The only men she saw were injured. After a few minutes, she saw one male doctor rushing into a doorway. He was a rarity in a vast population of women. And as she looked around, not sure where to go, Jean-Luc asked if she wanted him to wait for her.

"Yes, if you don't mind," she said, overwhelmed for a minute, but well aware that if they didn't allow her to volunteer, she had no idea where to go or what else to do. And she was determined to stay in France and work there, unless she went to England and volunteered. But whatever happened, she wasn't going home. Not for a long time anyway, or maybe ever. She didn't want to think about that now. "I have to talk to the people in charge and see if they'll keep me," she said softly. And if they did allow her to work, she would need a place to stay. She was willing to sleep in a barracks or a garage if she had to.

Annabelle walked across the courtyard, following signs to various parts of the makeshift hospital set up in the Abbey, and then she saw an arrow pointing toward some offices under the arches, which said "Administration."

When she walked in, there was a fleet of women lined up at a desk, handling paperwork, as female ambulance drivers handed requisition slips to them. They were keeping records on everyone they treated, which wasn't always true at all the field hospitals, where in some cases they were under far more pressure. Here, there was a sense of frenzied activity, but at the same time clarity and order. The women at the desk were French for the most part, although Annabelle could hear that some of them were English. And all of the ambulance drivers were young French women. They were locals who had been trained at the Abbey, and some of them looked about sixteen. Everyone had been pressed into service. At twenty-two, Annabelle was older than many, although she didn't look it. But she was certainly mature enough to handle the work if they let her, and far more experienced than most volunteers.

"Is there someone I should speak to about volunteering?" Annabelle asked in flawless French.

"Yes, me," said a woman of about her own age, smiling at her. She was wearing a nurse's uniform, but was working at the desk. Like everyone else, she was doing double shifts. Sometimes the ambulance drivers, or doctors and nurses in the operating theaters, kept on for twenty-four hours straight. They did what was needed. And the atmosphere was pleasant and cheerful and energetic. Annabelle was impressed so far.

"So what can you do?" the young woman at the desk asked her, looking her over. Annabelle had pinned her apron on, to look more official. In the serious black dress she looked like a cross between a nurse and a nun, and was in fact neither.

"I have a letter," Annabelle said nervously, fishing it out of her purse, worried that they would reject her. What if they only took nurses? "I've done medical work since I was sixteen, volunteering in hospitals. I worked at Ellis Island in New York for the last two years, with immigrants, and I've had quite a lot of experience dealing with infectious diseases. Before that, I worked at the New York Hospital for the Ruptured and Crippled. That might be a little more like what you're doing here," Annabelle said, sounding both breathless and hopeful.

"Medical training?" the woman in the nurse's uniform asked as she read over Annabelle's letter from the doctor on Ellis Island. He had praised her highly, and said that she was the most skilled untrained medical assistant he had ever encountered, better than most nurses and some doctors. Annabelle had blushed herself when she read it.

"Not really," Annabelle said honestly about her lack of training. She didn't want to lie to them, and pretend that she knew things she didn't. "I've read a lot of medical books, particularly about infectious diseases, orthopedic surgery, and gangrenous wounds." The nurse nodded, looking her over carefully. She liked her. She looked anxious to work, and as though it meant a lot to her.

"That's quite a letter," she said admiringly. "I take it you're American?" Annabelle nodded. The young woman was British but spoke perfect French, without a trace of accent, but Annabelle's French was good too.

"Yes," Annabelle said in answer to the question about her nationality. "I arrived yesterday."

"Why did you come over?" the nurse asked, curious, as Annabelle hesitated, and then blushed with a shy smile.

"For you. I heard about this hospital from the doctor on Ellis Island, who wrote the letter. It sounded wonderful to me, so I thought I'd see if you could use some help. I'll do anything you ask me. Bedpans, surgical bowls, whatever."

"Can you drive?"

"Not yet," Annabelle said sheepishly. She had always been driven. "But I can learn."

"You're on," the young British nurse said simply. There was no point putting her through the mill with a letter like that, and she could see that Annabelle was a good one. Her face burst into a broad smile as the woman behind the desk said it. This was exactly what she had come for. It had been worth the long, lonely, frightening trip to get here, despite minefields and U-boats, and her own fears after the *Titanic*. "Report to Ward C at thirteen hundred hours." It was in twenty minutes.

"Do I need a uniform?" Annabelle asked, still beaming.

"You're fine as you are," the woman said, glancing at her apron. And then she thought of something. "Do you have a billet? A place to stay, I mean." They exchanged a smile.

"Not yet. Is there a room I could have here? I can sleep anywhere. On the floor if necessary."

"Don't say that to anyone else," the nurse warned her, "or they'll take you at your word. Beds are in short supply here, and anyone will be happy to take yours. Most of us are hot bunking, we switch off in the same beds with people who work different shifts. There are a few left in the old nuns' cells, and there's a dormitory in the monastery, but it's pretty crowded. I'd grab one of the cells if I were you, or find out if someone will share one. Just go over and ask around. Someone will take you in." She told her what building they were in, and in a daze, Annabelle went out to find Jean-Luc. Her mission was a success, they were going to let her work there. She could hardly believe her good fortune, and she was still smiling when she found Jean-Luc standing next to his poultry truck, as much to protect it as so that she could find him. Vehicles were in short supply, and he was terrified someone would take it from him, and commandeer it as an ambulance.

"Are you staying?" he asked her, as she walked up to him, smiling.

"Yes, they took me," she said, relieved. "I start work in twenty minutes and I still have to find a room." She reached into the back of the truck, brushed the chicken feathers off her valises, and pulled them out. He offered to carry them for her, but she thought she'd best do it herself. She thanked him again, and had already paid him that morning. He gave her a warm hug, kissed her on both cheeks, wished her luck, and got back in his truck and left.

Annabelle walked into the Abbey carrying her bags, and found the area where the nurse had told her the old cells were. There were row upon row of them, dark, small, damp, musty, and they looked miserably uncomfortable, with one lumpy mattress on the floor of each, and a blanket, and in many cases no sheets. Only a few of the cells had sheets, and Annabelle suspected correctly that the women who lived in those cells had provided them themselves. There was one communal bathroom to about fifty of the cells, but she was grateful to have indoor plumbing. The nuns had clearly not lived in any kind of comfort or luxury, in the thirteenth century or since. The Abbey had been purchased from their order many years before, at the end of the last century, and had been privately owned when Elsie Inglis took it over and turned it into a hospital. It was a beautiful old building, and although not in fabulous condition, it suited their purpose to perfection. It was an ideal hospital for them.

As Annabelle looked around, a young woman came out of the cells. She was tall and thin and looked very English, with pale skin, and hair as dark as Annabelle's was blond. She was wearing a nurse's uniform, and she smiled at the new arrival with a rueful expression. She looked like a nice girl. There was an instant affinity between the two women.

"It's not exactly Claridge's," she said with the accent of the upper classes, and she had sensed the same about Annabelle immediately. It was more felt than seen, but neither girl was anxious to advertise her blue blood to anyone else. They had come here to do hard work, and were happy to be there. "I assume you're looking for a room," the girl said and introduced herself. "I'm Edwina Sussex. Do you know your shift?" Annabelle told her her name and said she didn't.

"I'm not sure what they'll have me do. I'm supposed to report to Ward C in ten minutes."

"Good on you. That's one of the surgical wards. Not squeamish, are you?" Annabelle shook her head, while Edwina explained that there were already two other girls sharing her cell, but she pointed to the one next door, and said that the girl who'd lived there had gone home the day before because her mother was sick. None of them was nearly as far from home as she was. The British girls could easily go home, and come back, if need be, although crossing the Channel wasn't easy these days either, but nothing was as dangerous as crossing the Atlantic. Annabelle explained that she had arrived from the States the day before. "Brave of you," Edwina said admiringly. The two young women were exactly the same age. Edwina said she was engaged to a boy who was currently fighting on the Italian border, and she hadn't seen him in six months. As she said it, Annabelle set her bags down in the cell next to hers. It was as small, dark, and ugly as the others, but Annabelle didn't care, and Edwina said they spent no time in their rooms, except to sleep.

Annabelle barely had time to set down her bags, and rush down the stairs again to find Ward C. And as Edwina had suggested, when she got there, she found a huge surgical ward. There was an enormous room that looked as though it had once been a large chapel, filled with about a hundred beds. The room wasn't heated, and the men were covered with blankets to keep them warm. They were in various states of distress, many of them whose limbs had been blown off or surgically severed. Most were moaning, some were crying, and all were very sick. Some were delirious from fevers, and as she went looking for the head nurse to report in, many of the men clutched at her dress. Beyond the big room were two other large rooms being used as operating theaters, and more than once she heard someone scream. It was an impressive scene, and if Annabelle hadn't done the volunteer work she had for the past six years, she would have fainted on the spot. But she looked unruffled as she made her way through the room, past dozens of beds.

She found the head nurse coming out of one of the operating rooms, looking frazzled and holding a basin with a hand in it. Annabelle explained that she was reporting for duty. The head nurse handed her the basin and told her where to get rid of it. Annabelle didn't flinch and when she returned, the head nurse put her to work for the next ten hours. Annabelle never stopped. It was her trial by fire, and by the end of it, she had won the older nurse's respect.

"You'll do," she said with a wintry smile, and someone said she had worked with Dr. Inglis herself, who was back in Scotland by then. She had plans to open another hospital in France.

It was midnight when Annabelle got back to her cell. She was too tired to unpack her suitcases or even undress. She lay down on the mattress, pulled the blanket over herself, and five minutes later she was sound asleep with a peaceful look on her face. Her prayers had been answered. And for now, she was home.

Chapter 15

Annabelle's first days at L'Abbaye de Royaumont were grueling. Casualties from the Second Battle of Champagne were coming in at a rapid rate. She assisted in surgeries, emptying surgical pans and soaking up blood, disposed of shattered limbs, emptied bedpans, held the hands of dying men, and bathed men with raging fevers. Nothing she had ever seen before was even remotely like it. She had never worked so hard in her life, but it was exactly what she had wanted. She felt useful, and was learning more every day.

Annabelle hardly ever saw Edwina. She was working in another part of the hospital, and they were on different shifts. Once in a while they ran into each other in the bathroom or passed in a corridor between wards, and waved at each other. Annabelle had no time to make friends, there was too much work to do, and the hospital was crammed full of wounded and dying men. Every bed was full, and some lay on mattresses on the floor.

She finally got a few minutes one afternoon to go to a local bank, and sent a message to her own bank in New York that she had arrived safely and all was well. There was no one to tell or care. She had been in Asnières for two weeks by then, and she felt as though she'd been there for a year. The English and French had landed in Salonika, in Greece, and Austrian, German, and Bulgarian forces had invaded Serbia and expelled the Serbian army from the country. In France, men were dying like flies in the trenches. Thirty miles from the hospital, the front had hardly shifted, but lives were being lost constantly. There were field hospitals set up in churches closer to the front, but as many men as could be were brought to the Abbey in Asnières, where they could get better care. Annabelle was learning a great deal about surgery. And they were also dealing with everything from dysentery to trench foot, and a number of cases of cholera. Annabelle found all of it terrifying but exciting to be able to help.

On a rare morning off, one of the women in her cell block taught her to drive one of the trucks they used as ambulances, which wasn't so different from Jean-Luc's poultry truck. She had a hard time getting it into gear at first, but she was starting to get the hang of it when she had to report to work again. She was assigned to the operating room more than any of the others, because she was precise, attentive, meticulous, and followed directions to the letter. Several of the doctors had noticed her and commented on her to the head nurse, who agreed that Annabelle's work was excellent. She thought she'd make a terrific nurse, and had suggested to Annabelle that she should train formally after the war, but the head surgeon at the Abbey thought she was better than that. He stopped to chat with her after their final operation late one night. Annabelle didn't even look tired as she scrubbed the room and cleaned up. It had been a particularly exhausting day for all of them, but Annabelle hadn't lagged for a minute.

"You look as though you enjoy the work," he said to her as he wiped his hands on his bloody apron. Hers looked just as bad. She didn't seem to notice, and she had a streak of someone's blood on her face. He handed her a rag to wipe it off with, and she thanked him and smiled. He was a French surgeon who had come from Paris, and was one of the few male doctors they had. Most of the medical personnel were women, which had been Elsie Inglis's intention when she set it up. But they made exceptions, as they needed a lot of help. They were treating so many men that by now they were grateful for all the doctors they could get.

"Yes, I do," Annabelle said honestly, as she put away the rag with the other linens that the girls in the laundry room would pick up later. Some of it just had to be thrown away. "I've always loved this kind of work. I just wish the men didn't have to suffer so much. This war is such a terrible thing." He nodded. He was in his fifties, and he had never seen a carnage such as this himself.

"The head nurse thinks you should go to nursing school," he said tentatively, looking at her as they walked out of the operating room together. It was impossible not to notice what a pretty girl she was, but there was a great deal more to her than that. Everyone had been impressed with her medical skill since she'd arrived. The doctor who had written her reference hadn't exaggerated, she was even better than his glowing praise. "Is that what you'd like to do?" the surgeon inquired. He was impressed by her French as well, and it had improved dramatically in the past two weeks. He had no problem speaking to her in French, or she in responding to him.

She thought for a moment before she answered him. She was no longer married to Josiah, and her parents were gone. She could do anything she wanted now—she answered to no one. If she wanted to go to nursing school, she could, but as she looked up at him, she was as surprised as he by what she said.

"I'd rather be a doctor," she almost whispered, afraid that he would laugh at her. Dr. Inglis, who had established the hospital, was a woman, but it was still unusual for a woman to attend medical school. Some did, but it was very rare. He nodded in response.

"I was thinking that myself. I think you should. You have a talent. I can tell." He had taught at the Faculté de Médecine for years before the war, and had dealt with men far less capable than she. He thought it was an excellent idea. "Is there anything I can do to help?"

"I don't know," she said, looking shocked. She had never allowed herself to think of it as a real possibility before. And now this kind man was taking her seriously and offering to help. It brought tears to her eyes. "Would it be possible?"

"Of course. Anything is possible if you want it badly enough and are willing to work for it. And something tells me you would. Why don't you think about it, and we'll talk about it another time."

His name was Dr. Hugues de Bré, and their paths didn't cross again for another month. She heard that he went to work at one of the field hospitals closer to the front for a while, and came back to the Abbey in November. He smiled the moment he saw Annabelle, and had her administer chloroform to the patient herself. She was gentle and efficient as she put the crying man to sleep, and then a young doctor took over from her after that. Dr. de Bré talked to her that night before he left.

"Have you thought any more about our plan? I thought of another thing," he said cautiously. "Medical school is expensive. Would that be possible for you?" Something about her suggested to him that it would, but he didn't want to assume it. He had been thinking about how to get a scholarship for her. It would have been difficult because she wasn't French.

"I think it would be all right," she said discreetly.

"What about going to Dr. Inglis's medical college in Scotland?" he suggested, and Annabelle shook her head.

"I think I'd rather stay in France." Although the language would be easier in Scotland, she could manage in French, and the prospect of spending years in the dreary weather in Scotland didn't appeal to her as much.

"I could do more to help you here. I was thinking of a small medical school I've always liked in the South of France, near Nice. And I don't think you should wait until the war ends. It would be easier to get in now. Classes are smaller, they need students. Many of the young men are gone, so there is less competition to get in. They would welcome you with open arms. With your permission, I'd like to write to them and see what they say." Annabelle smiled up at him in astonishment and gratitude. It was impossible to believe this was happening. Perhaps it was destiny. Six months before, she'd been married, hoping to have a family one day, in her safe, predictable life in Newport and New York. Now she was alone, in France, talking about going to medical school, and everything in her life had changed. Josiah was with Henry in Mexico, and she had no one to answer to at all. If this was her dream, she could follow it now. There was no one to stop her. The only thing that made her sad was that she had no one to discuss it with except Dr. de Bré.

They were still dealing with waves of wounded coming from the front, as the weather turned colder, and more men died of infections, wounds, and dysentery. She had lost two of the men she'd been caring for only that morning, when Dr. de Bré stopped to talk to her again. It was two weeks before Christmas, and she was homesick for the first time. She'd been thinking that only a year before, her mother had been alive. Dr. de Bré broke into her reverie and told her he had had a letter from the school in Nice. He looked at her portentously, and she held her breath, waiting to hear what he had to say.

"They said they would be very happy to accept you with a recommendation from me. They'll put you on a probationary basis for the first term, and if you do well, you will be accepted as a full student after that." He was smiling at her as her eyes grew wide. "They would like you to begin on January fifteenth, if that appeals to you." Her eyes and mouth flew open in disbelief, and she stared at him.

"Are you serious?" She almost jumped into his arms. She looked like a very young girl as he laughed at her. It had been a pleasure to assist such a talented young woman. In his opinion, the world needed doctors like her. And as much as she was needed here to assist, he thought it far more important for her to train as a physician as soon as possible. She would do the world a lot more good as a doctor.

"I'm afraid I am serious. What are you going to do about it?" he asked, still unsure if she would go. She hadn't been sure herself. His inquiry had been more of an exercise to see what they would say. She hadn't expected it to be so easy, or so quick. But the school needed students desperately, and with a recommendation from Dr. de Bré, they had every confidence that she would justify his faith in her, and so did he.

"Oh my God," she said, staring at him, as they left the ward and walked into the cold night air. "Oh my God . . . I *have* to go!" It was a dream come true, something she had never expected to happen, never dared to dream of, and now the dream was within reach. She didn't have to just read medical books on her own, trying to figure it all out for herself. She could study them, and become exactly who and what she wanted to be. He had given her a gift beyond belief. She had no idea how to thank him as she threw her arms around his neck, and kissed him on the cheek.

"You're going to make a wonderful doctor, my dear. I want you to stay in touch with me, and come to see me when this war is over, and life is normal again, if it ever will be." It was hard to believe that now. The death toll in Europe had reached three million. Far too many lives had been lost already, and nothing had been resolved. All of Europe was at war with each other, and America was still determined not to get involved.

Annabelle hated to leave the Abbey. She knew she was needed there, but Dr. de Bré had made a good point, this was the perfect time for her to go to medical school. In peacetime, with more men applying, they may not have been as willing to accept her. They had told him that in the coming term, she would be the only woman in her class, although they had had female graduates before. Her studies would take six years in all. One mostly in the classroom, and five years thereafter taking classes and working with patients in a hospital near the school. They were affiliated with one of the best hospitals in Nice. She would get a lot of experience, and it was a good place for her to live. In peacetime, it was safer for her than Paris, more provincial and smaller, since she had no one to protect her. He had told her there were dormitories at the school, and they would give her a large private room of her own, since she was the only female student. And he suggested that afterward, she would come back to Paris, and perhaps work for him. He had so much faith in her that she was determined to justify it.

She was floating that night when she went back to her cell, and Dr. de Bré had said he would write to the school to accept the place for her. She had to send them some money by the first of January, which wasn't a problem. She could pay the rest of the tuition for the first year when she got there. Her mind was chock-full of excitement and plans. Her head was spinning, and she was awake most of the night, thinking about it. She remembered telling Josiah once that she wanted to dissect a cadaver, and now she would, and nothing and no one could stop her. She had already learned a great deal more about anatomy after working in the operating room at the Abbey, particularly with Dr. de Bré. He was always careful to teach her as he went along, if the case wasn't too dire. And just watching him operate was an honor.

She told no one her plans until the day before Christmas, when she finally told the head nurse, who was stunned, but thought it an excellent idea.

"Good heavens," she said, smiling at her, "I thought you'd be a nurse. I never thought you'd want to be a doctor. But why not? Dr. Inglis is one of the best. So could you be one day," she said proudly, as though she'd thought of it herself. "What a good thing for Dr. de Bré to do. I heartily approve."

Annabelle had been there for three months by then, and had proven herself in every way. She hadn't really had time to make friends, since she worked all the time, even when she didn't have to. But there were so many wounded, and so much work to do for all of them. She even drove one of the ambulances from time to time when they needed her to. She was willing to do it all. She had driven closer to the front to pick up men from the field hospitals there and brought them back to the Abbey. The sound of the guns nearby had been impressive, and reminded her of how close the fighting was. In a way, she felt guilty leaving them all to go to medical school in Nice, but it was such an exciting prospect there was no way she could resist it. It was more than a little daunting knowing that she would be twenty-eight when she was finished. It seemed like a long time to her, but she had so much to learn in the meantime. She couldn't imagine cramming it all into six years.

She ran into Edwina outside their cells on Christmas morning, they hugged each other, and Annabelle told her she was leaving in three weeks. And Edwina looked instantly disappointed.

"Oh, I'm so sorry. I always want to spend time with you, and chat, but we never get to it, and now you're going." She had hoped they would be friends, but none of them had time. There was always too much work. It made Annabelle think of Hortie then, and the last time they'd met, and her terrible sense of betrayal. Hortie had been all too willing to turn her back on her oldest and dearest friend, and to say that James wouldn't allow her to see Annabelle again. It was all part of why she had decided to come to France. She had lost too many people, and Hortie had been the last straw. It made her look at Edwina with a gentle smile, and the memory of regret, and a beloved friendship lost.

"Maybe I can come back to work here when they give us time off. I don't know if they have holidays in medical school, but they must," Annabelle said hopefully. She wanted to see them all again. In some ways, she didn't want to leave. She had been happy here for three months, as much as one could be among such grievously wounded men, but the camaraderie among the staff had been tremendous.

"You're going to medical school?" Edwina looked stunned. She'd had no idea.

"Dr. de Bré arranged it," Annabelle said with dancing eyes. She got more excited every day. "I never thought something like this could happen to me," she added, with a look of dazed amazement.

"What did your family say?" Edwina asked with interest, as a cloud passed over Annabelle's face, which Edwina didn't understand. "Do they mind your staying over here? They must worry about you, being so close to the front." If the lines shifted and they got overrun, all of them could have been taken prisoner. It was a risk they didn't allow themselves to think about once they were there, but the threat was real. Edwina's parents had been nervous about her coming, particularly her mother, but she had come anyway. Both her brothers were in the war and she wanted to be part of it too.

"I don't have any family," Annabelle said quietly. "I lost them all. My mother died a year ago, and my father and brother on the *Titanic*." She didn't mention Josiah, who had been yet another loss in her life, but no one here knew she had been married, so there was no way to explain it, and she didn't want to anyway. It was a silent loss she bore alone, and always would.

"I'm so sorry," Edwina said softly. "I didn't know." None of them ever had time to share their histories, or much else, just the occasional cup of tea, and a greeting here and there. There was so much else to do, there was rarely time for niceties, or the kind of opportunities that in other circumstances allowed one to build friendships. They just worked side by side until they nearly dropped, and then went to bed on their mattresses on the floor in their tiny old nuns' cells. The most exciting thing they got to do was sneak the occasional cigarette and giggle about it. Annabelle had tried them a few times, just to be sociable, but she didn't like them much.

They chatted for a few more minutes and Edwina wished her a happy Christmas and luck at school. They promised to spend a few minutes together, or meet in the mess hall, before she left, but neither of them knew if it would really happen. And then they went their separate ways to the wards where they worked. Christmas was just another day caring for the sick and wounded. There were no celebrations, no carols, no gifts. There was a cease-fire for the day, but by six o'clock that night the Germans had violated it, and more men came in with missing limbs that night. It was an endless stream of human suffering whatever day of the year.

Annabelle was grateful to work as hard as she did that day. It kept her from thinking of all the people she had loved and lost, two of them only that year. She wouldn't allow herself to think of Christmas Eve at her mother's house the year before. It was just too painful. And soon she would begin a whole new life in Nice. She forced herself to focus on that whenever she had a break that day, which wasn't often. She concentrated on what medical school would be like, but every now and then visions of her mother intruded anyway, or the sound of her voice . . . the last time she had seen her . . . and she thought of it as she lay on her mattress that night, wondering what her mother would think of everything that had happened in the past year. She hoped that wherever she was, watching over her, she would be proud when Annabelle became a doctor. She knew her mother probably wouldn't have approved. But what else did she have now? And who? Becoming a doctor was Annabelle's only dream, her only hope of an entirely new life.

Chapter 16

Annabelle's departure went unnoticed the day she left the hospital at the Abbaye de Royaumont in Asnières. She had gone to say good-bye to Dr. de Bré, and to thank him, the day before, and also made her farewell to the head nurse. Other than that, she had no one to say good-bye to, except Edwina, whom she saw for a few minutes that morning. They wished each other luck, and said they hoped to meet again. And then Annabelle got into the truck that drove her to the station. She was taking the train to Nice, which was a long, drawn-out process. All the routes that went too near the front had been rerouted in circuitous ways, and most of the trains had been commandeered by the army.

It took her a day and a night to get to Nice, and when she finally arrived, she found two taxis at the train station, driven by women. She climbed into one of them, and gave the driver the address of the medical school. It was just outside Nice, on a hill, looking out at the ocean, in a small château that belonged to the family of the school's founder, Dr. Graumont. And with its peaceful gardens and orchards around it, it was hard to believe that there was war or strife anywhere in the world, let alone nerve gas, shattered bodies, or people dying. She felt completely sheltered from the real world here. It was the most tranquil place she had seen since Newport, and in some ways reminded her of it.

A stern-looking housekeeper showed her to her room, handed her the sheets to make her own bed, and told her to be downstairs at eight o'clock for dinner. The first-year medical students lived in a dormitory. The more senior students, all of them men, had individual rooms. Since she was the only woman she had gotten one of their rooms, a comfortable chamber that looked out at the sea. There were forty-four students living at the château, all of whom had been exempted from military service for some reason. There was an Englishman, a Scot, two Italians, and the rest of them were French. Annabelle was the only American. She had been told that she could practice medicine when she went back to the States by taking an exam there, but she wasn't thinking that far ahead yet. For the next six years, she would be here, and it felt like the right place for her to be. She was certain of it as soon as she saw it. She felt safe and protected.

She washed her face and hands, put on a clean black dress, one of the nicer ones she had brought with her, and tied her hair back in a discreet knot. Looking immaculate, she went down to dinner promptly at eight.

The students met in the large drawing room of the château before dinner every night. They talked quietly among themselves, usually about medical matters, and all of them had been there since September. Annabelle was the interloper who had arrived late, and as she entered the room, all eyes turned to her. Then the other students turned away and kept talking and ignored her. She was startled by their cool reception, but she sat quietly by herself until dinner, without trying to break into their conversations. She saw them stealing glances at her, but not one of them came over to talk to her. It was as though she didn't exist, and as though they believed that if they didn't acknowledge her, she'd disappear.

An ancient man in an even more ancient tailcoat called them in to dinner, and the groups then shifted into the dining room and sat down at three long refectory tables that were as old as the château. Everything there was worn and threadbare, but it had a kind of faded grandeur that looked very much Old France.

Dr. Graumont, the head of the school, came to greet her and invited her to sit down next to him. He was extremely polite when he introduced himself, but then spent most of the time speaking to the young man on his other side, who looked to be about thirty. They were conversing about an operation they had both observed that day, and made no attempt to include Annabelle in the conversation. She felt like a ghost, invisible to all.

Later in the meal, Dr. Graumont spoke to her briefly of Dr. de Bré and asked how he was, but he said little more to her than that, and then he bade her good evening, and the others went to their rooms. Not a single one of her fellow students had introduced themselves to her or asked her name. She went up to her room alone, and sat down on her bed, not sure what to make of it, and not nearly as sure as she had been about her decision. It was going to be a long six years if no one ever spoke to her at the château. It was more than obvious that they were not pleased to have a woman in their midst, so they had decided to ignore her. But she wasn't there to socialize, she had come to learn.

She was in the dining room the next morning, at precisely seven o'clock, as she had been told. Breakfast was sparse, due to the war, and she ate very little. The others came and left without a word to her, and she found her classroom in time for her eight o'clock class. The entire château had been dedicated to the school, which had allowed the family to keep it, and support its upkeep. And once the class began, she remembered why she was there. It was fascinating. They were studying diseases of the kidney, and were shown diagrams of surgeries. And they were to go to the hospital in Nice the next day, where they did all their surgical observations and work with patients. She could hardly wait.

She was still excited by the lecture when they went to lunch, and she was more grateful than ever to Dr. de Bré. And forgetting how unfriendly her classmates had been, she broke into conversation with the Englishman, and commented about the lecture. He stared at her as though she had just taken off all her clothes.

"I'm sorry, did I say something wrong?" she asked innocently.

"I don't recall speaking to you," he said rudely, looking down his nose at her in an icy way, which told her in no uncertain terms that he had no interest whatsoever in her comments.

"No, but I spoke to you," she said calmly, refusing to be daunted. She had heard him say that he came from four generations of doctors. He was obviously very full of himself, but like her, he was only a first-year student, although considerably older than she was. He mentioned to someone else that he had gone to Eton and then Cambridge, which explained the discrepancy in their ages. He clearly thought he was a great deal better than she was, and had no desire to waste his time talking to her. The fact that she was also beautiful seemed to have made no impression on him whatsoever. He was far more interested in being unpleasant to her and putting her in her place.

"I'm Annabelle Worthington," she continued pleasantly, refusing to be bested by him. She wanted to hit him over the head with her plate, but she smiled politely and then turned to the student on her other side, and introduced herself to him. He looked at the young man across from him, as though waiting for a cue from the others, and then smiled in spite of himself.

"I'm Marcel Bobigny," he said in French, and with that the others looked at him like a traitor, and stared into their plates as they ate.

Annabelle and Marcel struck up a conversation about the lecture they'd had that morning, and for most of lunch there was silence in the room. She was clearly not welcome, and even the head of the school ignored her. She took her notebook and pen, and went to her next class, after thanking Marcel for chatting with her. He bowed politely, and she could hear his cohorts scolding him for talking to her, as she walked away with her head held high.

"I don't give a damn if she's great-looking," she heard one of them whisper to the others. "She has no business being here." But she had as much right to be there as they did. She had paid her tuition, and was as anxious to be a doctor as they were, possibly more so. But clearly they had made an agreement among themselves to stonewall her.

Their shoddy treatment of her continued through four weeks of classes and three-times-weekly visits to the hospital in Nice, where they heard lectures and saw patients, and she saw that she was being keenly observed by professors and students alike. She sensed that any mistake she made, or incorrect statement she uttered, would be used immediately against her, so she was extremely careful of what she said. So far, she had made no obvious mistakes, and the two papers she had written about diseases of the urinary tract and kidneys had gotten perfect grades.

And it was when visiting patients, and speaking to them, that her jealous classmates hated her most. She had a gentle, compassionate way with them, asked them intelligent questions about their symptoms, and made them feel comfortable with her immediately. The patients much preferred speaking to her, and looking at her certainly, than her colleagues, and those patients who saw her more than once were delighted to see her again. It drove her male classmates insane.

"You're far too familiar with the patients," the Englishman, who was systematically unpleasant to her, criticized her one day.

"That's interesting," Annabelle said calmly. "I think you're very rude to them."

"How would you know? When have you ever been in a hospital before?"

"I just spent three months working near the front in Asnières, and I've worked as a volunteer in hospitals for six years, the last two with newly arrived immigrants at Ellis Island in New York." He said nothing to her after that, and wouldn't have admitted it to her, but he had been impressed by her three months at Asnières. He had heard from others how rough it was. Marcel Bobigny caught up with her after class, and asked what it had been like working at the Abbaye de Royaumont. It was the first real conversation she'd had with anyone there in a month. And she was grateful to have someone to talk to at last.

"It was hard," she said honestly. "We all worked about eighteen hours a day, sometimes more. It's run and staffed by women, which was the original concept, but a few male doctors have come from Paris now. They need all the help they can get."

"What kind of cases did you see there?" he asked with interest. He thought the others were wrong to give her such a hard time. He liked her. She was good-humored, a good sport, worked hard, and lacked their pretensions.

"We saw mostly lost limbs, a lot of gangrene, explosions, nerve gas, dysentery, cholera, pretty much what you'd expect so close to the front." She said it simply and matter-of-factly, with no attempt to impress him or brag about herself.

"What did they let you do?"

"Chloroform in the operating theater, once in a while. Mostly I emptied surgical pans, but the chief surgeon was very nice about showing me things as I went along. The rest of the time I was in the surgical ward, taking care of the men after surgery, and a couple of times I drove an ambulance to pitch in."

"That's pretty good for someone who has no official training." He was impressed.

"They needed the help." He nodded, wishing he was there himself. He said as much to Annabelle, and she smiled. He was the only one of her fellow students who had been civil to her, and even nice. Most of them ignored her.

In February, a month and a half after she'd gotten there, everyone was animated at dinner, discussing the Battle of Verdun, which had begun several days before, and already caused enormous loss of life on both sides. It was a vicious battle that upset them all, and Marcel drew her into the conversation. The others were so involved in the discussion, they even forgot to frown when she spoke, or ignore her.

The Battle of Verdun was the main topic of conversation every night at dinner, until two weeks later, in early March, the Fifth Battle of the Isonzo, in Italy against Austria-Hungary, took precedence. The conversation ricocheted equally between medical issues and the war. It was a cause of deep concern to all.

Eventually the Englishman asked her about when America might join the war. President Wilson was still assuring everyone they wouldn't, but it was an open secret that the United States was supplying both sides, and being criticized heavily for it. Annabelle said clearly that she thought that that was wrong and so did they. She thought the U.S. should get into the war, and come to Europe in aid of their allies. The conversation led to the *Lusitania* then, and everyone's belief that she had been blown up because of war supplies she was secretly carrying, which had never been officially disclosed. Talking about the *Lusitania* somehow led to the *Titanic,* and Annabelle grew quiet and looked pained. Rupert, the Englishman, noticed and made a remark. "It wasn't our finest hour," he conceded with a smile.

"Nor mine," she said quietly. "My parents and brother were on it," she said, as the whole table went quiet and stared at her.

"Did they make it through all right?" one of the French students asked, and she shook her head. "My mother got off in one of the lifeboats, but my father and brother went down with the ship."

There was a chorus of I'm sorry's and Marcel discreetly turned the conversation to other things, trying to make the awkward moment easier for her. He liked her and wanted to protect her from the others. But little by little, they were softening toward her too. Her kindness, simplicity, intelligence, and humility were hard to resist.

Two weeks after that, the French passenger ship *Sussex* was torpedoed, which brought it all up again. By then, the situation at the front had worsened, and almost four million people had died. The toll was mounting day by day. At times, it distracted them all from their studies and they could talk of nothing else. But they were all working hard. There were no slackers in the group, and with their classes so small, every student stood out.

Without actually meaning to, they had all relaxed about Annabelle by April, and by May many of them were actually willing to speak to her, have conversations with her, and even laugh with her. They had come to respect her quietly voiced intelligent questions, and her bedside manner with the patients was much better than theirs. Her professors had all noticed it, and Dr. Graumont had long since written to Dr. de Bré to assure him that he hadn't made a mistake. He told him that Annabelle Worthington was an excellent student, and would make a fine physician one day. And to Annabelle, compared to the Abbey in Asnières, the hospital in Nice was extremely tame, but interesting anyway. And she finally got her wish. They had begun dissecting cadavers, and she found it as fascinating as she always thought she would.

News of the war continued to distract them, as they followed their classes through the summer. On July 1, the Battle of the Somme began, with the highest number of casualties in the war so far. By the time the day was over, there were sixty thousand dead and wounded.

The numbers were horrifying. And as the summer went on, it just got worse. It was hard to concentrate on their studies at times as a result. There was such a shocking loss of life as the war wore on, seemingly with no end in sight. Europe had been at war for two years by then.

In August, she tried not to let herself think of her anniversary with Josiah. It would have been their third, and she had been in Europe for eleven months. It seemed hard to believe. Since she had come to the medical school in Nice, time had flown. They were doing so many things, and trying to learn so much. They were working with patients more frequently now, and spent three full days a week at the hospital in Nice. The war wounded were even finding their way there, as injured men who would not be returning to the front were being transferred closer to home. She even came across two men she had taken care of in Asnières. They were thrilled to see her, and she stopped by to visit them whenever she could.

By then, she and Marcel were good friends. They chatted every night after dinner, and often studied together. And the other students had finally accepted her in their midst. She was well thought of, liked, and respected by her peers. Some of her fellow students even laughed about how unpleasant they had been to her in the beginning, and Rupert, the pompous Englishman who had been the rudest to her, had slowly become her friend. It was hard for any of them to find fault with her work, and she was unfailingly pleasant to all of them. Marcel called her the godmother in their midst.

They were walking through the orchards one day, after classes, when he turned to her with a curious look.

"Why is a beautiful woman like you not married?" he asked her.

She knew he wasn't pursuing her, since he had just gotten engaged to a young woman in Nice. She had been a friend of his family's for years. He was from Beaulieu, not far away, and went home for visits, or even dinner, as often as he could. His fiancée visited him at the school, and Annabelle liked her very much.

"I don't think I can be married and be a doctor. Do you?" she responded, deflecting the question. In her opinion, it was different for a woman than a man. It took so much more sacrifice and commitment for a woman to be a physician.

"Why do I have the feeling that you came to Europe with a broken heart?" He was a wise man, and could see it in her eyes. "I'm not so sure this is so much about sacrificing your personal life for your profession, but perhaps because you're afraid to have a personal life, and are hiding in medicine. I think you can have both," he said gently as he looked into her eyes.

She avoided responding to him for a long moment and took a bite out of an apple. She had turned twenty-three that May. She was beautiful and alive, and terrified of being hurt again. Marcel was right. He knew her well.

"Underneath the laughter and gentle smiles," he went on, "there is something very sad, and I don't think it's about your parents. Women only look that way when their heart is broken by a man." He was sorry that had happened to her. She, more than anyone he knew, deserved a kind and loving man.

"You should have been a fortune-teller instead of a doctor," she teased him with a grateful smile, and laughed. But he knew, even without her confirming it, that he was right. And she had no intention whatsoever of telling him that she was divorced. She wasn't willing to admit that to anyone, not even Marcel, once they became friends. She was too ashamed.

She had had a letter from her bank the month before, advising her that her final divorce papers had come. She and Josiah were now divorced. She had had only one letter from him in the last year, at Christmas, telling her that he and Henry were still in Mexico. She had no idea now if he was still there, and she hoped that he was well. She could deduce from what he had written to her that they were both very ill. She had written back, concerned about him, and hadn't heard from him since. Her letter got no response.

"Am I right?" Marcel persisted. He liked her, and often wished he knew more about her. She never spoke about her early childhood or her history at all. It was as though she didn't have one. All she wanted now was a clean slate and to begin again. He could sense whenever he spoke to her that there were secrets in her past.

"It doesn't matter. I'm here now, broken heart or not."

"Do you think you'll ever go back?" He was always curious about her.

She grew quiet as she thought about it, and answered him honestly. "I don't know. I have nothing there, except a cottage in Rhode Island." Her parents' servants were still there, taking care of the house, and hoping she'd come back. She wrote to Blanche from time to time, and no one else. "My family is gone. I have no reason to go back."

"You must have friends," he said, looking at her sadly. He hated to think of her alone. She was such a warm, gentle, kind person that he couldn't imagine her not having friends, even if she was shy. "You grew up with people. They must still be there." What he said made her think of Hortie, and she shook her head. She had no friends left. However good his intentions, Josiah had seen to that. He had been naïve in thinking he was doing the right thing for her, in freeing her. All he had done was make her an outcast in her own world. The only friend she had now was Marcel.

"No. Everything in my life changed. That's why I came here." But even she wasn't sure if she would stay. She belonged to no one and nowhere now. Her only life was medical school, and would be for the next five years. Her home was the château. Her only city Nice. And the men she was going to school with were the only friends she had, particularly him.

"I'm glad you did," he said simply, not wanting to pry too much or revive old hurts.

"So am I." She smiled at him, and they walked slowly back to the château. Marcel was amazed that none of their classmates had a romantic interest in her. But Annabelle put an unspoken message out that said "Don't come too close." There was a wall around her now. Marcel could sense it, but had no idea why, and he thought it was a shame. Keeping her distance as she did seemed to him the waste of a lovely woman. He thought she deserved to have a man, and hoped she would in time.

It was a long hot summer at the château, studying and visiting the hospital, and finally in August they got two weeks off to go home, or leave on vacation. Annabelle was the only student who stayed. She had nowhere else to go. She went on long walks, and shopped a little in Nice, although there wasn't much in the stores because of the war. She bought a few things to replenish her wardrobe as so much of what she had brought was black, and she was no longer in mourning for her mother. And on an afternoon when she was able to borrow an old truck they kept at the school, she drove to old Antibes and the areas around it, and found an ancient, beautiful eleventh-century church, and stood looking at the view from high above the town. It was a perfect afternoon and a spectacular view.

She stopped and had dinner at a small café, and that night she drove back to the school. Even Dr. Graumont was away, and Annabelle was alone in the château with the two maids. She had a peaceful two weeks, and she was happy when the others came back, particularly Marcel. They all said they'd had a good time, although her English friend who had tormented her in the beginning, Rupert, came back devastated that he had lost his brother to the war. Several of them already had lost brothers, cousins, friends. It was a harsh reminder of the turmoil and anguish that was devouring Europe and never seemed to end.

When they began classes again in September, the Battle of the Somme was still raging on, as it had been for over two months. And the casualties mounted every day. It finally ended in mid-November, which was a huge relief to all. For ten days, there was peace at the end of a terrible battle, with well over a million men dead and wounded in the end. And only ten days after it was over, the Germans attacked Britain with airplanes for the first time. A whole new aspect of the war had been introduced, which terrified them all. By Christmas, they were all demoralized by the losses and constant attacks. Two more of the students had lost brothers. At the end of the month, Dr. Graumont assembled them in the main hall, with a letter from the French government, that he wished to read to them. It was a call to all trained medical personnel to lend their assistance at the front. They were badly needed in field hospitals all over France. He was quiet after he read the letter, and said it was up to them what they chose to do. He said that the school would grant them leave, if they wished it, without prejudice, and would automatically take them back whenever they returned. They had been getting letters from hospitals for months, including a recent one organized by Elsie Inglis again, this time in Villers-Cotterêts, northeast of Paris, closer to the front than Asnières and the Abbaye de Royaumont where Annabelle had been. Once again all of the medical units at Villers-Cotterêts were female, and Annabelle would have been welcome there.

All of the students talked about it that night over dinner, and the conversation was intense. By morning, half of them had made a decision, and went to see Dr. Graumont one by one. They were leaving within the next few days. In addition, it had been a bitter winter at the front, and men were dying of their wounds, illness, and exposure all over Europe. Those who were leaving couldn't resist the plea for help. In the end, all but four students went. Annabelle made her decision on the first day. She was sad to interrupt her medical training, but she felt there was really no other choice. It would have seemed selfish to stay.

"You're leaving us too?" Dr. Graumont asked with a sad smile, but he wasn't surprised. In the past year he had come to like and respect her enormously. She was going to make an excellent physician one day, and in many ways already was.

"I have to go," she said wistfully. She hated to leave the school at the château. "I'll come back."

"I hope so," he said, and meant it. "Where will you go?"

"To the Inglis hospital at Villers-Cotterêts, if they'll have me." With the training the students had, they could all be medics. It was more than she had been able to do in Asnières, and she would be more useful to the men.

"Be careful, Annabelle. Stay safe. We'll be waiting for you here," he reassured her.

"Thank you," she said softly, and gave him a warm hug. She packed her bags that night, left two of them at the château, and planned to take only one valise with her. By the next day, almost all but the remaining four students were gone.

They all hugged each other, wished each other luck, and promised to return as they left. Their good-byes to Annabelle were particularly brotherly and affectionate, and all of them urged her to take good care, and she did the same with them.

Marcel took her to the train before he left. She was carrying her small bag as she walked along beside him. He was her only real friend, and had been kind to her right from the first. She was still grateful to him for that.

"Take care of yourself," Marcel said, as he gave her a last hug and kissed her on both cheeks. "I hope we'll all be back here soon," he said fervently. He was leaving late that afternoon.

"Me too." She waved to him for as long as she could see him, as he stood on the platform waving to her. She watched him until he was out of sight. It was the last time she ever saw him. Two weeks later, he was driving an ambulance that ran over a mine. He was the first casualty of Dr. Graumont's school, and Annabelle had lost another friend.

Chapter 17

Annabelle arrived at the hospital Elsie Inglis had established at Villers-Cotterêts, some thirty miles northeast of Paris. It was roughly fifteen miles from the front. If you listened carefully, you could hear the explosions in the distance. The hospital had just opened, and was a larger and more intense operation than the one where she had worked in Asnières the year before. It was staffed and run by female medical units, as Dr. Inglis intended. Their nationalities represented many of the Allied nations, were almost equally divided between French and English, and Annabelle was one of three Americans there. This time, she had a proper room, although tiny, which she shared with another woman. And their patients were all brought in from the front. The carnage they were seeing was tremendous, shattered bodies, shattered minds, and a shocking number of lives lost.

Female ambulance drivers shuttled constantly back and forth to the front, where men were being dragged out of the trenches maimed, mangled, and dying. In every instance, a medic traveled with the ambulance and its driver, and they had to have enough training and knowledge to perform herculean feats on the way to save the men they were transporting. If too badly injured to move at all, they were left at the field hospitals set up near the trenches. But whenever possible, the injured soldiers were brought back to the hospital at Villers-Cotterêts for surgery and more intensive care.

With a year of medical school under her belt now, and with her years of volunteer work before that, Annabelle was assigned to the ambulance unit, and wore the official uniform of a medic. She worked eighteen hours a day, bumping over rough roads along the way, and sometimes holding the men in her arms, when there was nothing else she could do. She fought valiantly to save them with whatever materials she had on hand, and all the techniques that she had learned. Sometimes in spite of her best efforts, and a breakneck race back to the hospital, the men were just too damaged to survive and died on the road.

She had arrived at Villers-Cotterêts on New Year's Day, which was just another work day to all of them. Over six million men had died in the war by then. In the two and a half years since the hostilities had begun, Europe had been decimated, and was losing its young men to the monster that was war, which devoured them by the thousands. Annabelle felt sometimes as though they were emptying the ocean with a teacup, or worse, a thimble. There were so many bodies to repair, so little left of some of them, so many minds that would never recover from the brutalities they'd seen. It was hard on the medical personnel as well, and all of them were exhausted and looked beaten by the end of every day. But no matter how difficult it was, or how discouraging at times, Annabelle was more confirmed than ever in her decision to be a doctor, and although it broke her heart in so many instances, she loved her work, and did it well.

In January, President Wilson was trying to orchestrate an end to the war, using the United States's neutral status to encourage the Allies to state their objectives in obtaining peace. His efforts had not borne fruit, and he remained determined to keep the country out of the war. No one in Europe could understand how the Americans could not join the Allied forces, and no one believed by January 1917 that they would continue to stay out of the fray for long. And they weren't wrong.

On February 1, Germany resumed unrestricted submarine warfare. Two days later the United States severed diplomatic relations with Germany. Within three weeks the president requested permission from Congress to arm U.S. merchantmen in the event of an attack by German submarines. Congress denied the request, but on March 12, by executive order, Wilson announced that American merchantmen would be armed from then on. Eight days later, on March 20, his war cabinet voted unanimously in favor of declaring war on Germany.

The president delivered his war address to Congress on April 2. And four days later, on April 6, war on Germany was declared by the United States. America was finally entering the war, and the floundering Allies in Europe desperately needed their help. For the next weeks and months, American boys would be leaving home, saying good-bye to families, wives, and girlfriends, and going to be trained. They were to be shipped overseas within two months. Overnight, everything at home changed.

"It's about goddamn time," one of the other American women at

Villers-Cotterêts said to Annabelle, as they met in the dining hall late one night. They had both been working for nineteen hours at their respective jobs. She and the other American women were nurses, and she knew that Annabelle was a medic.

"Were you training to be a nurse before the war?" she asked with interest. She was a pretty young woman from the South and had the heavy accent of Alabama. Her name was Georgianna and she had grown up as a southern belle, which no longer had any meaning here, just as Annabelle's genteel upbringing in her family's elegant mansion in New York no longer had any relationship whatsoever to her daily life. All it had given her was a decent education, good manners, and the ability to speak French. The rest no longer mattered.

"I've been in medical school in the South of France for the last year," Annabelle said, sipping a cup of very thin soup. They tried to stretch their food rations as best they could, to benefit both medical personnel and patients. As a result, none of them had had a truly decent meal in months, but it was good enough. Annabelle had lost a considerable amount of weight in the four months since she had arrived. Even she could hardly believe that it was April 1917, and she had been in France for nineteen months.

Georgianna was impressed that Annabelle had been training to be a doctor, and they talked about it for a few minutes. Both were bone tired. The nurse was a pretty girl with big green eyes and bright red hair, and she laughed when she admitted that after two years here, she spoke execrable French, but Annabelle knew, from what she'd heard of her, that in spite of that she did her job well. She had never known so many conscientious, competent, dedicated people in her life. They gave it their all.

"Do you think you'll finish med school?" Georgianna asked her, and Annabelle nodded, looking pensive.

"I hope so." She couldn't imagine what would stop her, other than being killed.

"Don't you want to go home when this is over?" Georgianna couldn't imagine staying there. She had family in Alabama, three younger sisters, and a brother. Annabelle didn't want to go back to New York. She had nothing there, except punishment and pain.

"Not really. I don't have much there. I think I'm going to stay." She had thought about it a lot recently, and made up her mind. She had five more years of medical school ahead of her, and after that she wanted to go to Paris, and work there. With luck, maybe even with Dr. de Bré. There was nothing she wanted now in New York. And she would have had to train for another year there. She was almost convinced now that her life in the States was history for her. The only future she had was here. It was a whole new life, where no one knew her past, or the shame of her divorce. In France, as far as everyone knew, she had never been married. She was turning twenty-four in a few weeks. And one day, with hard work and some luck, she'd be a doctor. All she would ever be in New York was a disgrace, through no fault of her own.

The two women went their separate ways outside the dining hall and went back to their respective barracks, promising to get together sometime, if they ever got a day off, which even if they did, they never took. Annabelle hadn't taken a day off from her duties as a medic since she'd arrived.

The Third Battle of Champagne ended in disaster for the French in late April and brought them a flood of new patients, which kept them all busy. Annabelle was ferrying men constantly from the front. The only encouragement they had was a Canadian victory at the Battle of Vilmy Ridge. And due to enormous discouragement among their ranks, there were outbreaks of mutiny among the French all through the early weeks of May. There were also ongoing reports of the Russian Revolution—the czar had abdicated in March. But anything that was happening farther than the trenches and the front nearby seemed very remote to all of them at Villers-Cotterêts. They were far too deeply involved in the business at hand to care about much else.

Annabelle forgot about her birthday completely. One day bled into another, and she had no idea what day it was. She only realized a week later, when she saw a newspaper someone had brought from Paris, that she had turned twenty-four. A month later in June, everyone was excited to learn that the first American troops had landed in France.

It was three weeks later, in mid-July, when a battalion of them came to Villers-Cotterêts and set up camp on the outskirts of the city. They were joined within a week by British forces, all of whom were preparing for an offensive at Ypres. It livened up the area considerably to have British and American troops roaming around everywhere. They were happily seducing all the local women, and military police were constantly dragging them out of bars and off the streets drunk, and delivering them back to their camps. If nothing else, it provided a little distraction, and despite the inevitable rowdy soldiers, some of them were very nice. Annabelle saw a group of American soldiers one day, walking along with some very young French girls, as she rode back with the ambulance from a field hospital nearby. She was in no mood to banter with them, as the man they were carrying back to the hospital in Villers-Cotterêts had died on the way. But as the ambulance drove past the Americans, they shouted and waved, having seen two pretty women in the front. And for an aching moment, she had an intense longing to hear American voices. She waved back and smiled. One of the men in uniform ran along beside them, and she couldn't stop herself from saying, "Hi."

"Are you American?" he asked in amazement, and the driver of the ambulance stopped and smiled. She thought he was cute. She was French.

"Yes," Annabelle said, looking tired.

"When did you get here? I thought the nurses weren't coming over till next month." It had taken them longer to organize the women's volunteer units than the conscripted men.

She laughed at the question. There was the sound of Boston in his voice, and she had to admit, it was nice to hear it. It felt like home. "I've been here for two years," she said, smiling broadly. "You guys are late."

"Like hell we are. We're going to kick the Krauts right back to where they came from. They saved the best for last." He looked like a kid and was, and as Boston Irish as they came, and it reminded her of her visits to Boston, and summers in Newport. She was suddenly homesick for only the first or second time in twenty-two months. She couldn't even remember the last time she felt that way.

"Where are you from?" he asked her, as one of his friends chatted up the ambulance driver, on the other side of the truck, but they both knew they had to get back. It wasn't right to hang around talking with them, with a dead man in the back, although others had done worse. At some point, the horrors of war no longer shocked you as they once did.

"New York," Annabelle said quietly.

"I'm from Boston," and as he said it, she could smell the alcohol on his breath. As soon as they left the camps where they were billeted, most of them drank a lot. They had good reason to. They drank, and chased every girl that crossed their path.

"I could tell," she said, referring to his Boston accent, as she gave her colleague the signal to get started again. "Good luck," she said to him and the others.

"Yeah, you too!" he said, and stepped back, and as they drove back to the hospital, a wave of nostalgia for her own country washed over her, and she had never been so homesick in her life. She missed everything familiar that she hadn't seen or allowed herself to think about in two years. She sighed as the two of them carried the dead man on the gurney into the morgue. He would be buried on the hills with countless others, and his family notified. There was no way to send the bodies home. There were just too many of them. And makeshift cemeteries covered the countryside now.

Thinking of the Americans they had seen that afternoon, Annabelle went for a short walk that night, when she got off duty, before she went back to her room. They had lost every man they had driven back from the field hospitals that day. It had been depressing, and although it was a common occurrence, it upset her anyway. The boys were all so young, many of them years younger than she was. Even many of the nurses were younger than she was now. At twenty-four, with a year of medical school behind her, she didn't feel like a young girl anymore. Too many difficult things had happened to her in the past few years, and she had seen far too much pain.

She was wandering along, thinking about her lost life in the States, with her head down, not far from her barracks, on the way back from her walk. It was after midnight, and she had been working since six o'clock that morning. She was tired and not paying attention, and she gave a start when she heard a British voice behind her.

"Hey, pretty girl," he said softly. "What are you doing out alone?" She turned and was startled to see a British officer walking along the same path on his own. He had obviously been drinking, and had left a nearby bar without his companions. He looked very dashing in his uniform, and very drunk. He was a good-looking young man, about her own age, and he didn't scare her, particularly once she saw that he was an officer. She had seen plenty of drunken men in the past two years, and she had never had any trouble keeping them in line.

"Looks like you need a ride," she said with a matter-of-fact smile. "Go that way," she pointed to one of the administration buildings where they often handled matters of that sort, since it was a common occurrence. It was wartime, after all, and they dealt with thousands of men on a daily basis, many of whom caroused at night. "Someone will give you a ride back to camp." Particularly given that he was an officer, there would be no questions asked. Sometimes they gave the enlisted men a slightly rougher time. But officers were always given the respect due their rank. She could see from his uniform that he was a lieutenant, and hear from his accent that he was an aristocrat. It didn't stop him from being as sloppy as anyone else while he was drunk, and he was reeling slightly as he looked at her.

"I don't want to go back to camp," he said stubbornly, "I'd much rather go home with you. What do you say, we stop off and have a drink? What are you anyway? A nurse?" He was looking down his nose at her somewhat haughtily, and trying to focus.

"I'm a medic, and you're going to need one if you don't go lie down somewhere." He looked like he was about to pass out.

"Excellent idea. I suggest we lie down together."

"That's not an option." She looked at him coolly, wondering if she should just walk away and leave him to it on his own. There was no one else on the path, but she wasn't far from the barracks. By then, everyone had gone home for the night, except those who had the late shift and were driving ambulances or working in the wards.

"Who do you think you are anyway?" he asked, as he lurched forward to grab her, and she stepped back. He stumbled and nearly fell, and looked angry as he righted himself. "You're nobody, that's who you are," he continued, looking suddenly nasty. "My father is the Earl of Winshire. And I am Lord Harry Winshire. I'm a viscount," he said grandly, but slurring.

"That's good to know, your lordship," she said politely, responding to his rank and title. "But you need to get back to camp before you get hurt. And I'm going to my barracks. Goodnight."

"Bitch!" he said, spitting the single word at her, as she moved past him. The exchange had gone on long enough, and she didn't want to linger. He was obviously drunk, spoiled, and getting unpleasant from the quantities of alcohol he had consumed. She wasn't afraid of him, she'd dealt with worse before, but she didn't want to press her luck. But before she got more than a step farther on the solitary path, he grabbed her and spun her around hard into his arms and tried to kiss her. She pushed him away firmly and fought hard. He was surprisingly strong even though he was drunk.

"Stop that!" she said loudly. But she was shocked by his strength, and the force of his arms.

Suddenly she realized that she was being overpowered by him. He covered her mouth with one hand, and with the other dragged her to the dark doorway of a nearby barracks. There was no one around, and he was covering her mouth so hard that she couldn't scream. She bit his fingers, but it didn't deter him, and she fought like a cat, as he knocked her to the ground and lay on top of her with his full weight. He had knocked the wind out of her when she fell, and the hand not covering her mouth had yanked up her skirt and was pulling her underwear down. She couldn't believe what was happening, and she used all her strength to fight him, but she was a small woman and he was a large, powerful man. And he was suddenly driven by rage and drink and was determined to have her. She had infuriated him by dismissing him before, and he was going to make her pay for it now. All she could see was the black fury in his eyes as he continued to grab her and press her down. He never took his one hand from her mouth, and all she could make were muffled guttural sounds that no one could hear.

The night was quiet all around them, except for the laughter of women and drunken shouts of men as they left the bars. Whatever sounds she made were far too slight for anyone to hear them, and there was terror in her eyes. By then he had unbuttoned his pants with his free hand, and she could feel him hard against her. What Josiah had never been able to bring himself to do, this drunken stranger was about to take from her by force. She did everything she could to stop him, to no avail. He kicked her legs apart with his own, and in an instant, he was inside her, pumping violently and groaning while she kept trying to fight him, but he pressed her hard to the ground, and each time he drove farther into her, she winced with pain, and he smashed her back against the doorstep where they lay. And in an instant it was over, he released himself with a shout, and then threw her away with such force that she lay huddled in the doorway like a battered doll. She couldn't even scream then, or make a sound. She was too afraid to. She turned over, vomited, and choked on a sob. He stood up, buttoned his pants, and looked down at her with contempt.

"If you tell anyone about this, I'll come back and kill you. I'll find you. And they'll take my word over yours."

She knew that that was probably true, he was an officer and not only a gentleman, supposedly, but a viscount. Whatever she said or did, no one would ever dare to challenge him, much less punish him, for an incident like this. To him, it meant nothing, and for her, the virtue she had kept all her life, and upheld even through two years of marriage to a man she loved, he had taken and disposed of like so much garbage, which was how he had treated her. She pulled her skirt down as he walked away, and she lay on the doorstep sobbing, and then finally got up, feeling dizzy. He had banged her head on the stone step too as he raped her.

She was in a daze as she walked back to her barracks, and stopped again to throw up, grateful that no one saw her. She wanted to hide somewhere and die, and she knew that she would never forget his face or the look of murder in his eyes as he took her. He vanished into the night, and she almost crawled up her barracks steps and went to the bathroom, relieved that no one else was there. She cleaned herself up as best she could, there was blood on her legs and skirt since she had been a virgin, which mattered nothing to him, she was just another whore he had taken after a lively night in the bars. And there was a terrible throbbing ache between her legs, to match the pain in her back and head from where he had banged her into the stone step, but all of it was nothing compared to the ache in her heart.

And he was right, if she tried to tell anyone, no one would listen or care. Girls claimed that soldiers raped them every day, and no one did anything about it. If they persisted with the authorities or a military tribunal, they were humiliated and disgraced, and no one believed them. They were instantly accused of being whores who had encouraged their attackers. And with a British lord being accused of having perpetrated the crime, she would have been laughed out of any official office. Worse yet, this was wartime, and a medic getting raped by a British officer was the least of anyone's problems. All she could do now was pray that she didn't get pregnant. She couldn't imagine that fate could be as cruel as that. All Annabelle could think, as she crawled into her bed that night, running her mind over what had happened, was that nothing and no one could have been as cruel as the viscount. And as she lay there and sobbed, all she could think about was Josiah. All she had ever wanted was to share a life with him and have his babies. And instead this bastard had turned an act of love into a travesty and raped her. And there was absolutely nothing she could do about it, except try to forget.

Chapter 18

In September, the Germans were soundly beating the Russians. And in Villers-Cotterêts, Annabelle was throwing up every day. The worst had happened. She hadn't had her period since July, and she knew that she was pregnant. She had no idea what to do about it. There was no one she could tell, no way to stop it. Her back and head and other parts of her had taken weeks to heal, but the effects of what he'd done would last forever. She thought about finding an abortionist somewhere, but she didn't know whom to ask, and she knew how dangerous it was. Two of the nurses had died of abortions since she'd been at the hospital. Annabelle didn't dare risk it. She would have preferred to just kill herself, but she didn't have the courage to do that either. And she didn't want that monster's baby. As best she could figure it, the child was due in late April, and she would have to leave the hospital as soon as it began to show. Fortunately, so far it didn't. And she was working harder than ever, carrying men and heavy equipment, bumping along the rutted roads in the ambulance. She was praying that nature would be kind to her and she'd have a miscarriage, but as time went on, it became increasingly obvious that she wouldn't. And as her waist and body began to thicken, she stole strips of linen from the surgery, and bound herself as tightly as she could. She could hardly breathe, but she was determined to work as long as she was able. And she had no idea where to go once she couldn't.

At Christmas, it still didn't show, but by then she could feel the baby moving gently inside her. She tried to resist it, and told herself she had every reason to hate it, but she couldn't. The baby was as innocent as she was, even if she loathed its father. She thought of contacting him to tell him what had happened and force him to take responsibility, but she knew that given what she'd seen that night, he would only deny it. And who knew how many women he had raped before, or since? She was just a piece of flotsam that had drifted past him on the sea of war, and he would cast her away just as he had that night, and his baby with her. She had no recourse whatsoever, she was only a woman carrying an illegitimate baby in wartime, and no one would care for an instant that she had been raped.

In January she was still working. She was six months pregnant, and she covered her thickened midsection with her apron. There was no bulge because she was still binding herself so tightly, and from worry and the poor food anyway, she ate very little. She had gained no weight, if anything she had lost some. She had been deeply depressed since July when it happened. And she told no one.

It was a bitter cold, rainy day later that month when she was working in the men's surgical ward one afternoon, to fill in for someone else, when she heard two of the men talking. Both were British, one an officer, the other a sergeant. Both had lost limbs in the most recent awful battle in the trenches. And she stopped in her tracks when she heard them mention Harry. She didn't know why, it could have been anyone, but a moment later the officer said that it was a terrible loss that Harry Winshire had died. They talked about what a good man he was and how they would miss him. She wanted to turn and scream at them that he wasn't a good man, but a monster. She stumbled from the ward, and stood trembling outside in the cold, gulping air, and feeling as though she were strangling. Not only had he raped her, but now he was dead. Her baby would have no father and never had. She knew it was probably better this way, and he deserved it, and as the enormity of what was happening to her hit her again, she was suddenly so overcome by a feeling of raw terror that she staggered slowly like a willow in the breeze, and fainted into the mud around her. Two nurses saw her fall and came running toward her, as one of the surgeons leaving the building stopped and knelt beside her. As always, everyone was terrified of cholera, but when they touched her, they saw that she had no fever. They suspected it was too much work and too little food or sleep, a condition from which they had all been suffering for years.

The doctor helped carry her inside, and she regained consciousness as they put her on a gurney. She was soaking wet, her hair was matted to her head from the rain, and her apron was plastered to her. She was apologizing profusely for causing so much trouble, and tried to get up and escape them. But the moment she did, she fainted again, and this time the doctor pushed the gurney into a small room and closed the door. He didn't know her well, but had seen her often.

He quietly asked her if she had dysentery, and she insisted she was fine, and said she had been working since early that morning and hadn't eaten since the day before. She tried to smile brightly at him, but he wasn't fooled. Her face was the same color as her apron. He asked her name, and she told him.

"Miss Worthington, I believe you are suffering from battle fatigue. Perhaps you need to go away for a few days, and try to recover." None of them had taken a break in months, and she didn't want to, but she also knew that her days at the hospital were numbered. Her belly was growing exponentially now and was harder and harder to conceal, no matter how tight her binding. "Is there anything else about your health you haven't told me?" he asked with a look of concern. The last thing they wanted was their medical personnel spreading infectious diseases or starting an epidemic, or simply dying from overwork and illnesses they had concealed. They were all so conscientious about their work that many of the nurses and doctors hid it when they were sick. He was afraid that was the case with her. She looked awful.

She started to shake her head, and then he saw the tears in her eyes. "No, I'm fine," she insisted.

"So fine that you just fainted twice," he said gently. He had the feeling there was something else, but she was determined not to tell him, and she looked as malnourished as many others. He asked her to lie down so he could feel her body through her clothes, and as soon as she lay down, he saw the gentle bulge of her belly and met her eyes. He ever so gently put his hands on it, and could feel the swelling she had concealed with such determination for so long, and he understood instantly what it was. She wasn't the first young woman to get pregnant by a soldier during wartime. As he looked at her, she began to sob.

"I think that's the problem," he said as she sat up, took out a handkerchief, and blew her nose. She looked mortally embarrassed and desperately unhappy. "When are you expecting?"

She nearly choked on the words, and wanted to explain how it had happened, but didn't dare. The truth was so awful, and surely he and everyone else would blame her, and never believe her. She was certain of it, she had seen it happen to others before. Women who said they had been raped, when in fact they had simply had an affair out of wedlock. Why should he believe her? So, like Josiah's secret that she had safeguarded for him to protect him when he left her, now she was keeping Viscount Winshire's. And the one who paid the price for all of it was her. "In April," she said, with a look of despair.

"You've managed to keep it secret for a long time." He loosened her apron, undid her waistband, and lifted up her blouse, and was horrified when he saw how tightly she had bound herself, and obviously had for months. "It's a wonder you can breathe." It was far tighter than any corset, and a cruelty to mother and child.

"I can't," she said through her tears.

"You'll have to stop work soon," he said, telling her what she already knew. "And the father?" he inquired kindly.

"Dead," she whispered. "I just found out today." She didn't tell him that she hated Harry and was glad that he was dead. He deserved it. She knew the doctor would have been shocked if she said it.

"I see. Will you be going home?"

"I can't," she said simply, for reasons he couldn't begin to understand. She was no longer welcome in New York and Newport, and being pregnant would finish her forever.

"You're going to have to find a place to live. Would you like me to try and help you find a family where you can stay? Perhaps you could help take care of their children." Annabelle shook her head. She had been thinking about it recently as her belly grew. She couldn't go back to the medical school either, at least not for now. But the one place she could think of was the area above Antibes near the ancient church, where she had gone occasionally when she got a break from medical school. If she could find a small house there, she could hide until after the baby was born, and then either come back to the front or go back to school. It was hard to imagine coming back to the front with a baby, and she had no one to leave it with. She had much to figure out, but she declined his help. She wanted to sort it out for herself. And he couldn't know that she could make her own financial arrangements, and was capable of renting or buying a house if she chose.

"Thank you, I'll manage," she said sadly, as he helped her off the gurney.

"Don't wait too long," he advised her. It amazed him that she had been able to conceal her pregnancy for six months.

"I won't," she promised. "Thank you," she said with tears in her eyes again, as he patted her shoulder to reassure her, and they left the room. The two young nurses were still waiting outside to see how she was.

"She's fine," he told them with a smile. "You all work much too hard here. I told her she needs to take some time off, before she comes down with cholera and starts an epidemic." He smiled at them all reassuringly, gave Annabelle a knowing look, and left. The other two women escorted her to her room, and she took the rest of the afternoon off.

She lay on her bed, thinking. He was right. She had to leave soon, she knew. Before everyone found out, and she was once again disgraced through no fault of her own.

Annabelle managed to stay in Villers-Cotterêts until the first of February, and then regretfully, she said she had to leave. She told her supervisor that she was going back to medical school in Nice. But no one could complain. She had been there for fourteen months, and she felt like a traitor leaving now, but she had no other choice.

It was a sad day for her when she left the hospital and the people she had worked with. She took the train to Nice, and it took her two days to get there, with sidetracked trains, and long waits in many stations, to allow military transports to pass them by, carrying supplies to the front.

The first thing she did when she reached Nice was go to a small jeweler and buy a gold wedding band. She slipped it on her finger, as the jeweler congratulated her. He was a kind old man, and said he hoped she would be very happy. She left the shop in silent tears. The story she had concocted for herself was that she was a war widow and her husband had been killed at Ypres. There was no reason for anyone not to believe her. She looked respectable, and the country was full of widows by then, many of whose babies had been born after their husbands' deaths. Annabelle was just one more in a sea of casualties and tragedies caused by the war.

She checked into a small hotel in Nice, and bought herself several black dresses in larger sizes, and was shocked to note that once she no longer wore the restrictive bindings, her stomach was surprisingly large. Not in Hortie's league, but it was obvious that she was having a baby, and there was no reason to conceal it now. With a wedding band on her finger, and the black dress of a widow, she looked like the respectable woman she was, and the sadness anyone could have seen in her eyes was real.

She would have liked to visit Dr. Graumont at the medical school, but she didn't feel she could. Later, she would reappear with the baby, with her story of the man she had married and who was then killed. But it was all too new for now. She didn't feel ready to face anyone until after the baby. And she was not yet sure how to explain that she would not change her name. She would figure it out later. For now, she had to find a place to live, and one day she went back to Antibes, and the little church she loved so much. It was a sailors' chapel and had a full view of the port and the Maritime Alps. She was leaving the church when she asked the guardian if she knew of any houses in the area, preferably to rent. And the woman shook her head, and then cocked her head to one side with a pensive look.

"I don't think so," she said, in the heavy accent of the South. Annabelle's French was so smooth by then that no one would have suspected she wasn't from Paris, or any of the northern cities in France. "There's a family that lived here before the war. They moved back to Lyon, and both their sons were killed. They haven't been here since, and I don't think they'll ever come back. Their boys loved it here. It would break their hearts." She told Annabelle where the house was. It was in walking distance from the church, and was a small, pretty villa that looked like it had been a summer home. There was an old man tending the grounds, and he nodded when Annabelle spoke to him, and asked if there was a possibility that the house was for rent. He said he didn't think it was, but was willing to write to the owners for her. He said all the furniture and their belongings were still there, if that was a problem for her. And she assured him that it wasn't, and in fact she would prefer it.

He could see that she was heavy with child, seven months pregnant by then, and she said she was a widow. She told him she would be grateful to rent it for as long as they wanted, till the end of the year perhaps. She was hoping to go back to school for the fall term, or January at the latest. In September, the baby would be five months old, and she could go back to medical school, if she could make some arrangement for the baby. She might even be able to travel back and forth from this house, if she could find a vehicle to get there. She left the name of her hotel, and the caretaker said he would contact her when he heard from the owners, one way or the other. She hoped he'd feel sorry for her, and press the owners to rent her the house.

And on the way back to Nice, she thought to herself that she could stay at the hotel if she had to, although it wasn't an ideal set-up for a baby, but it was neat and clean. A house would have been better for her, but if she couldn't find one, she could stay where she was.

For the next several weeks, she went walking every day in Nice. She walked on the beach, ate as decently as possible, and slept long hours. She found a local doctor through the hospital, and went to see him, telling him the same fabricated tale that she was a war widow. He was kind and sympathetic, and she told him she wanted to give birth at home. She didn't want to run the risk of running into any of the doctors she knew at the hospital, through her medical school. She didn't tell the doctor why, but he was willing to deliver her at home.

In March she came back from a walk one day, and found a message from Gaston, the caretaker of the house in Antibes. He asked her to come and see him, which she did. He had good news for her. The owners were sympathetic to her, and happy to rent her the house. They might even be willing to sell it to her eventually, although they hadn't decided yet. As he had suspected, they said they had too many memories of their children there, and it would be too sad for them to return. For now, they were willing to rent it to her for six months and decide the rest later. He offered to show her around, and she was delighted by what she saw. There was a sunny master bedroom of cozy proportions, and two smaller bedrooms close to it. The three bedrooms shared a single bathroom, which didn't bother her. The bathroom was old and tiled, and had an enormous bathtub, which appealed to her. And downstairs there was a living room and dining room, and a small glassed-in sunroom that gave onto a porch. It was the perfect size for her and a baby, and maybe a young girl to help take care of the baby later. For now, all she wanted was to be alone.

She penned a letter of agreement to the owners, and said she would have her bank handle the transfer of funds. Gaston was very pleased and congratulated her, he said it would be nice to have life in the house again, and his wife would be happy to come and clean for her and even help her with the baby when it was born. She thanked him and left and went to a bank in Nice that afternoon. She introduced herself to the manager, and had him send a wire to her bank at home, informing them where she was. All they needed to know was where to send her money, since she had closed her account in Villers-Cotterêts when she left. They had no idea why she was in Nice or what was about to happen to her there, and she couldn't help wondering how many babies Hortie had had since she left. She still missed her old friend. However badly Hortie had betrayed her, she had done it out of weakness. It didn't stop Annabelle from caring about her, although they would never be friends again. Even if she went back one day, too much had happened since.

Annabelle moved into the house above Cap d'Antibes on the fourth of April. The doctor said the baby would come soon, although he had no idea when. Annabelle was large by then, and she walked slowly in the hills every day, and went to the church she loved and admired the view. Florine, Gaston's wife, was cleaning house for her, and cooked occasionally. And Annabelle spent her nights reading her old medical books. She still had mixed emotions about the child. It had been conceived in such violence and anguish, it was hard to imagine not remembering that each time she saw it. But destiny had given them to each other. She had thought of contacting the viscount's family to advise them of it, but she owed them nothing, and if they were as wayward and dishonorable as their son, she wanted nothing to do with them. She and the baby would have each other, and needed no one else.

In the third week of April, Annabelle went for a long walk, stopped at the church as she always did, and sat down heavily on a bench to admire the view. She had lit a candle for her mother, and prayed for Josiah. She had heard nothing from him now in more than two years, and had no idea where he and Henry were, whether still in Mexico or back in New York. He had let her go, and kept no contact with her. He wanted her to be free to find a new life, but he could never have remotely imagined the twists and turns of fate she had endured.

She walked slowly back to the house in the dappled sunlight that afternoon, thinking about all of them, Josiah, Hortie, her mother, father, Robert. It was as though she felt them all near her, and when she got back to the house, she went to her bedroom and lay down. Florine had left, and Annabelle fell into a gentle sleep. Much to her surprise, it was after midnight when she woke. She had a cramp in her back that woke her, and suddenly she felt a stabbing pain low in her belly, and knew instantly what it was. There was no one to fetch the doctor for her, and she had no telephone, but she wasn't frightened as she lay there. She was sure that it was a simple process and she could do it alone. But as the night deepened and the pains worsened, she wasn't as sure. It seemed cruel beyond belief that she had suffered when she conceived the child, and now she would have to suffer again, for a child with no father, whom she didn't want. All those years she had longed for Josiah's baby, it had never occurred to her that a child would come into her life like this.

She writhed with each contraction, clutching at the sheets. She saw the sun come up at dawn, and was bleeding heavily by then. The pains were agonizing, and she was beginning to feel as though she were drowning and might die. It made her think of the horror stories Hortie had told her, and the terrible births she had endured. She was just beginning to panic when Florine appeared in her bedroom doorway. She had heard her from downstairs, and ran up the stairs. Annabelle was lying in bed looking wild-eyed, unable to speak with the pain that had gone on all night. She had been in labor for eight hours.

Florine walked quickly into the room, and gently lifted the covers from her, and spread old sheets under her that they had put aside for this purpose. She made gentle cooing sounds to Annabelle and told her things were going well. She looked and said she could see the baby's head.

"I don't care," Annabelle said miserably. "I want it to come out..."
She let out a scream then, as the baby seemed to move forward for an instant, and then back. Florine ran downstairs to find Gaston, and told him to bring the doctor quickly. But nothing she was seeing alarmed her, it was going well. And she knew from other births she'd seen that it could go on for a long time. The worst was yet to come, and the spot of the baby's head she saw was no bigger than a small coin.

Annabelle lay in bed crying, as Florine bathed her forehead in lavender-scented cool cloths, and then finally Annabelle wouldn't even let her do that. She wanted no one to touch her, and she was crying out in pain. It seemed a lifetime before the doctor came. He had been at another birth, with a woman having twins. He came to Annabelle at two in the afternoon, and nothing had progressed, although the pains were getting worse.

He looked very pleased when he checked her, after he washed his hands. "We're doing very well," he said, encouraging his patient, who was screaming with every pain. "I think we're going to have a baby here by dinnertime." She looked at him in utter panic, knowing she couldn't stand another minute of the agony she was in. And finally, as she sobbed miserably, he asked Florine to prop her up on pillows and then brace her feet. Annabelle was fighting them every inch of the way and calling for her mother, and the doctor spoke to her sternly then and told her she must work. The top of the baby's head was much bigger now, and again and again he told Annabelle to push. She finally fell back on her pillows, too exhausted to do it again, and with that he told her to push even harder than before and not stop. Her face turned beet red as suddenly the top of the baby's head came through, with a tiny wrinkled face, as Annabelle screamed, and looked down at the child emerging from her womb.

She pushed with all her might, and finally there was a long thin wail in the room, and a tiny face with bright eyes looking at them, as Annabelle laughed and cried, and Florine exclaimed in excitement. The baby lay in a tangle of tiny arms and legs amid the cord, as the doctor cut it, and Florine wrapped the baby in a blanket and handed her to her mother. It was a girl.

"Oh . . . she's so beautiful! . . ." Annabelle said with tears streaming down her cheeks. The tiny little being was perfect, with exquisite little features, graceful limbs, and tiny hands and feet. The doctor had been right, and it was just after six o'clock, which he said was very quick for a first child. Annabelle couldn't stop looking at her, and talking to her as the doctor finished his work. Florine would clean Annabelle up later, and for now they covered her with a blanket. And with infinite tenderness, Annabelle put the baby to her breast, with perfect maternal instinct. The tiny angel in her arms was the only relative she had in the world, and had been worth every instant of pain, which seemed insignificant now.

"What are you going to call her?" the doctor asked her, smiling at them, sorry for her that she was a widow, but at least she had this child.

"Consuelo," Annabelle said softly, "after my mother," and then she gently bent down and kissed the top of her daughter's head.

Chapter 19

The baby was perfect in every way. She was healthy, happy, easy for her mother to manage. She was like a little angel fallen to earth that had landed in her mother's arms. Annabelle had never expected to love this baby so much. Any ties to the father who had spawned her vanished at the moment of her birth. She belonged to Annabelle and no one else.

Annabelle went to visit Dr. Graumont at the medical school in July, just after the Second Battle of the Marne began. The death toll had continued to mount shockingly since Annabelle had left Villers-Cotterêts. And once Consuelo was born, she realized that she couldn't go back to the front. She didn't want to take the baby with her, be away from her so much, or risk her exposure to illnesses or epidemics. Although she felt guilty for no longer helping the war effort, Annabelle knew her place was with her baby now. Florine had offered to keep her for Annabelle if she did go to the front, but she couldn't bear to be away from the baby for an hour, let alone leave her for months with someone else. So she had decided to stay in Antibes, for the time being.

She still wanted to go to medical school, and hoped she could arrange to return. She had her story firmly in place when she went to see Dr. Graumont. She told him she had married a British officer shortly after she got to Villers-Cotterêts. They had kept it secret from his family until they could go to England to announce it, and before they could, he had been killed. And because no one knew of the marriage, she had decided to keep her own name, particularly as her family had no heirs now, so she didn't want to give up the Worthington name, to honor them. It was a stretch, but he appeared to believe her, or was willing to accept whatever story she told. He said the baby was beautiful, and agreed to let her use a small cottage on the grounds for the baby and herself when she returned for the beginning of the next term in September. There were nine students at the medical college, and three new ones who were starting in September. Sadly, he told her that seven of her original classmates had died since they all left. He was relieved to find Annabelle healthy and hearty, and more beautiful since the birth. She looked even more womanly now, and had turned twenty-five that spring. She was clearly prepared to undertake her studies again, and undaunted that she would be thirty by the time she graduated and was fully a doctor. All she wanted now was to get started. The beginning of the term was only six weeks away.

She decided to keep the house in Antibes to go to whenever possible. But she needed someone to take care of Consuelo when she was in class, so she hired a young girl, Brigitte, to stay with them. The three of them would live in the cottage Dr. Graumont had assigned her, for a nominal fee. Everything was falling into place.

And on the appointed day in September, Annabelle, the baby, and Brigitte arrived at the château. They settled into the cottage, and

Annabelle began classes the next day. It was more exciting than ever for her, and she was happier than she had ever been. She had Consuelo, whom she loved so dearly, and she was steeped in her studies of medicine again. And working at the hospital in Nice was easier for her now. After all she had learned at the Abbey, and at the hospital in Villers-Cotterêts, as a medic, she was far advanced from where she had been when she left.

The war raged on through September, and at the same time, a fearsome epidemic of influenza began that raged in both Europe and the States, decimating civilians and military personnel alike. Thousands, especially children and old people, were dying.

And finally, at the end of the month, French and American troops began the Meuse-Argonne offensive. Within days General Douglas Haig's forces stormed the Hindenburg Line and broke through it. Six days later Austria and Germany contacted President Wilson to request an armistice, as British, American, and French forces continued to crush the opposition and turn the tide. The fighting continued for five more weeks, during which Annabelle and her classmates at the medical college could talk of nothing else.

At last, on November 11, at eleven A.M., the fighting stopped. The war that had ravaged Europe for more than four years and cost fifteen million lives was over.

Annabelle stood holding her baby when she heard the news, tears streaming down her cheeks.

Chapter 20

With the war over, people began to drift back to their normal lives. Soldiers returned to their hometowns, married the women they had left there, or new ones they had met in the years since. They returned to their former lives and jobs. The maimed and injured were seen everywhere on the streets, on crutches, in wheelchairs, with missing or artificial limbs. It sometimes seemed as though half the men in Europe were crippled now, but at least they were alive. And those who didn't return were mourned and remembered. Annabelle often thought of her old classmates who hadn't come back. She missed Marcel every day, and even Rupert, who had tormented her so mercilessly in her first months at the château, and had become such a kind friend in the end.

New arrivals appeared regularly, and there were sixty students at the château by spring, earnest, determined, wanting to become doctors and serve the world. Annabelle remained the only woman student, and everyone was in love with Consuelo. She had a first birthday party shared by sixty-one adoring medical students, and walked for the first time the next day. She was everyone's darling, and even touched the heart of the sometimes stern Dr. Graumont. She was seventeen months old as her mother began her third year of medical studies. Annabelle was particularly careful to keep her away from strangers, as the fierce worldwide influenza epidemic raged on. By then several million people had already died.

The medical school became the perfect home for both Annabelle and Consuelo, with sixty loving uncles fussing over her every chance they got. They brought her little presents, played with her, and one or the other of them was always holding her or bouncing her on their knee. It was a happy life for her.

Annabelle eventually had to give up the house in Antibes, when the owners decided to sell it, and she was sad to say good-bye to Gaston and Florine. But Brigitte stayed with them, and the cottage on the château grounds was comfortable enough for them.

Once in a while, as she watched Consuelo flourish, Annabelle thought of contacting the viscount's family. Now that she had her own child, she wondered if his parents would want some sort of last link to their son through his daughter. But she couldn't bring herself to do it. She didn't want to share Consuelo with anyone. The baby looked exactly like her, as though no one else had contributed to her birth. Everyone who saw her said that she was the portrait of Annabelle in every way.

The years of Annabelle's medical studies drifted past her at lightning speed. She was so busy and engaged in what she was doing that it felt as though in the blink of an eye it was over, although she had worked so hard to get there.

Annabelle turned thirty the month she graduated from Dr. Graumont's medical college as a physician. And Consuelo had just turned five in April. Leaving the college, and the cottage where they had lived, was like leaving home again. It was both exciting and painful. Annabelle had decided to go to Paris, and had applied for an association with the Hôtel-Dieu de Paris Hospital near Notre Dame on the Île de la Cité. It was the oldest hospital in the city. She was planning to open an office of general medicine. She had always hoped to work for Dr. de Bré, but he had died the previous spring. And her last tie with home had been severed a month before she graduated. She got a letter from the president of her father's bank, to tell her that Josiah had died in Mexico in February, and Henry Orson shortly afterward. The man who handled her affairs at the bank thought she would want to know and had enclosed a letter Josiah had left for her. Josiah had been forty-nine years old.

His death, and his letter, brought a flood of memories back to her, and a tidal wave of sadness. It had been eight years since he had left her, and she had come to Europe, seven since their divorce. The letter from him was tender and nostalgic. He had written it close to the end. He said he had been happy in Mexico with Henry, but that he always thought of her with love, and regret for the terrible things he had done to her, and that he hoped she had found happiness too and would one day forgive him. As she read it, she felt as though the world she had grown up in and shared with him no longer existed. She had no ties to any of it anymore. Her life was in France, with her baby, and her profession. Her bridges had long since been burned. The only thing she had left in the States was the house in Newport, which had stood empty for eight years, still tended by her parents' loving servants. She doubted she would ever see it again, but hadn't had the heart to sell it yet, and she didn't have to. Her parents had left her more than enough to live on and assure Consuelo's future and her own. One day, when she got up the courage, she would sell their old summer cottage. She just couldn't bring herself to do it yet. Just as she couldn't bring herself to contact the errant viscount's parents. She and Consuelo existed in their own world alone.

It was painful leaving the medical college and the friends she'd made there. All of her fellow graduates were dispersing to various parts of France. Many were staying in the South, and she had never been close to the only one going to Paris. For all the years she'd been in Europe, she had made no romantic alliance. She was too busy working for the war effort, and then with her studies and her daughter. She was a dignified young widow, and now she would be a dedicated doctor. There was no room in her life for anything else, and she wanted it that way. Josiah had broken her heart, and Consuelo's father had destroyed the rest. She wanted no man in her life, and no one other than her daughter. Consuelo, and her work, were all she needed.

Annabelle and Consuelo took the train to Paris in June with Brigitte, who was thrilled to go to the city with them. Annabelle hadn't been to Paris in years, and it was a bustling city now. They arrived at the Gare de Lyon station, and took a taxi to the hotel on the Left Bank where Annabelle had made a reservation. It was a small establishment Dr. Graumont had recommended to her, which was suitable for two women and a child. He had cautioned her about the dangers of Paris. Annabelle noticed that their cab driver was Russian, and had a distinguished look. Many of the noble White Russians were in Paris now, driving taxis, and working at menial jobs, after the Bolshevik Revolution and the murder of the czar's family.

It was a thrill when she signed herself into the hotel as *Docteur*

Worthington. Her eyes lit up like a child's. She was still the beautiful young woman she had been when she arrived in Europe, and when she played with Consuelo, she looked like a girl again. But beneath the youthful spirit was a responsible, serious woman, someone others could confide in, and entrust their health and lives to. Her manner with patients had been the envy of her fellow students and colleagues and had won all her professors' respect. Dr. Graumont knew that she would make an excellent physician, and be a tribute to his school.

They settled into the hotel. Dr. Graumont was going to send their things later, once they found a house. Annabelle wanted a place where she could establish her medical practice and see patients.

The day after they got to Paris, she went to the Hôtel-Dieu de Paris Hospital, to see about their permission to allow her to put patients there, while Brigitte took Consuelo to the Luxembourg Gardens. The beautiful blond child clapped her hands in excitement when she met her mother back at the hotel.

"We saw a camel, Mama!" Consuelo said, describing it to her, as Brigitte and her mother laughed. "I wanted to ride it, but they wouldn't let me," she pouted, and then burst into delighted giggles again. She was an enchanting child.

The Hôtel-Dieu Hospital's permission had been granted with Dr. Graumont's recommendation. It was an important step for Annabelle. She took Consuelo and Brigitte to dinner at the Hôtel Meurice as a special treat, and one of the Russian taxi drivers drove them all around Paris to see the sights of the city at night all lit up. It was a far cry from when Annabelle had arrived there during the war, brokenhearted and freshly shunned in New York. This was the beginning of a whole new life that she had worked hard for.

They finally went back to the hotel at ten o'clock. Consuelo had fallen asleep in the taxi, and Annabelle carried her upstairs and set her gently down on the bed. And then she went back to her own room and looked out the window into the Paris night. She hadn't felt this young and excited in years. She could hardly wait to begin work, but she had to find a house first.

For the next three weeks Annabelle felt as though she were seeing every house in Paris, on the Right Bank and the Left, while Brigitte took Consuelo to every park in Paris—Bagatelle, the Luxembourg Gardens, the Bois de Boulogne, and rode the carousel. The three of them went out to dinner every night. It was the most fun Annabelle had had in years, and was a whole new grown-up life for her.

Between seeing houses, Annabelle went shopping for a new wardrobe, serious enough for a doctor, but stylish enough for a Parisian woman. It reminded her of when she had shopped with her mother for her trousseau, and she told her own Consuelo about it. The little girl loved hearing stories of her grandmother and grandfather and Uncle Robert. It gave her a sense of belonging to more people than just her mother, and always made Annabelle's heart ache a little for the family she couldn't give her. But they had each other, and she always reminded Consuelo that it was all they needed. Consuelo commented solemnly that they needed a dog as well. Everyone in Paris had one, and Annabelle promised that when they found a house, they'd get a dog too. They were happy days for all of them, and Brigitte was enjoying herself, flirting with one of the bellboys at the hotel. She had just turned twenty-one and was a very pretty girl.

By the end of July, Annabelle was getting seriously discouraged. They still hadn't found a house. Everything they saw was either too big or too small, and didn't have the right set-up for her medical practice. It felt like she was never going to find what they needed. And then, finally, she found the perfect place on a narrow street in the sixteenth arrondissement. It was a small but elegant little house with a front courtyard and a back garden, and a unit with a separate entrance where she could see patients. It was in excellent condition, and was an estate being sold by the bank. And Annabelle liked the fact that it had a dignified look. It seemed wonderfully suitable for a doctor. And there was a small park nearby where Consuelo could play with other children.

Annabelle made an offer on the house immediately, met the asking price established by the bank, and took possession of it at the end of August. In the meantime, she ordered furniture, linens, china, some adorable children's antiques for Consuelo's room, and some lovely things for her own rooms and some simple furniture for Brigitte. She bought some serious-looking furniture for her office, and spent September purchasing the medical equipment she needed to run an office. She went to the printers and ordered stationery, and hired a medical secretary who said she had worked at the Abbaye de Royaumont as well, although Annabelle had never met her. Hélène was a quiet older woman, who had worked for several doctors before the war, and was delighted to help Annabelle start her practice.

By early October, Annabelle was ready to open her office. It had taken longer than expected, but she wanted everything to be just right. With trembling hands she hung out her shingle, and waited for something to happen. All she needed was for one person to walk through the door, and after that things would get started by word of mouth. If Dr. de Bré had still been alive, he could have referred patients to her, but he wasn't. Dr. Graumont had written to several physicians he knew in Paris, and had asked them to refer a few patients to her, but that hadn't borne fruit yet.

For the first three weeks, absolutely nothing happened. Annabelle and Hélène, her secretary, sat looking at each other with nothing but time on their hands. She went up to the main part of the house and had lunch with Consuelo every day. Then finally, at the very beginning of November, a woman walked into her office with a sprained wrist, and a man with a badly cut finger. From then on, as though by magic, there was a steady stream of patients in Annabelle's waiting room. One patient referred another. They weren't difficult cases, they were all small things that were easy for her to handle. But her seriousness and competence and gentleness with her patients won them over immediately. Soon people were switching from other doctors, sending friends, bringing their children, and consulting her on minor and major problems. By January, she had a constantly full office. She was doing what she had trained for, and loving every minute of it. She was careful to thank other physicians for their referrals, and always respectful of their earlier opinions, so as not to make them look like fools to their patients, although some would have deserved it. Annabelle was meticulous, skilled, and had a lovely bedside manner. Despite her beauty, and look of youth, she was clearly serious about her profession, and her patients trusted her completely.

In February, she hospitalized the son of one of her patients. The boy was only twelve and had a severe case of pneumonia. Annabelle visited him at the hospital twice a day, and was gravely worried about him at one point, but the boy pulled through, and his mother was forever grateful. Annabelle had tried some new techniques they had used at the hospital at Villers-Cotterêts with the soldiers, and she was always creative about mixing new methods with old ones. She still read and studied devotedly at night to learn about new research. Her openness to new ideas stood her in good stead, and she read about everything in all the medical journals. She stayed up reading them late at night, often while cuddling Consuelo in her bed, who had begun saying she wanted to be a doctor too. Other little girls wanted to be nurses, but in Annabelle's family they set a high standard. Annabelle couldn't help asking herself at times what her mother would have thought of it. She knew it wasn't what she had wanted for her, but she hoped she would have been proud of her anyway. She knew how devastated Consuelo would have been about Josiah divorcing her, and she wondered if he would have, if her mother hadn't died. But it was all water over the dam now. And what good would it have been to stay married to him if he was in love with Henry all his life? She had never had a chance. She wasn't bitter about it, but she was sad. Whenever she thought of it, it pained her with a dull ache she suspected she would carry all her life.

The one thing that never made her sad was Consuelo. She was the happiest, sunniest, funniest child, and she adored her mother. She thought the sun rose and set on her, and Annabelle had created a fantasy father for her, so the little girl didn't feel deprived. She told her that her father had been English, a wonderful person, from a lovely family, and that he had died as a very brave war hero before she was born. It never seemed to occur to the child to ask why she didn't see her father's family. She knew that all her mother's relatives were dead, but Annabelle had never said that Harry's were. Consuelo never mentioned it, she only listened with interest, and then one day Consuelo turned to her over lunch and asked if her "other" grandmother could visit her sometime, the one from England. Annabelle stared at her across the table as though a bomb had exploded, and didn't know what to tell her. It had never dawned on Annabelle that this day might come, and she wasn't prepared for it. Consuelo was six, and her friends in the park all had grandmothers. So why couldn't hers visit too?

"I . . . uh . . . well, she's in England. And I haven't talked to her in a long time . . . well, actually"—she hated lying to her child—"ever . . . I never met her. Your daddy and I fell in love and married during the war, and then he died, so I never knew them." She was fumbling with her words as Consuelo watched her.

"Doesn't she want to see me?" Consuelo looked disappointed, and Annabelle felt her heart sink. She had created her own mess, and other than telling her daughter that her grandparents didn't know she existed, she had no idea what to say. But she didn't want to be forced into contact with them either. It was a terrible dilemma for her.

"I'm sure she would want to meet you, if she can . . . that is, if she's not sick or anything . . . she might be very old." And then with a sigh and a heavy heart, Annabelle promised, "I'll write to her, and we'll see what she says."

"Good." Consuelo beamed at her across the table, and as Annabelle went back to her office she was cursing Harry Winshire as she hadn't in years.

Chapter 21

T rue to her promise to Consuelo, Annabelle sat down to write
Lady Winshire a letter. She had no idea what to say or how to introduce the subject. The truth that her son had raped her, and she'd
later had an illegitimate daughter, hardly seemed like an appealing
introduction, and wasn't likely to be to Lady Winshire either. But she
didn't want to lie to her. In the end, she wrote an extremely pared-
down and simplified, sanitized version. She really didn't want to see
Lady Winshire, or even to have Consuelo meet her, but at least she
wanted to tell the child she had tried.

She wrote to her that she and Harry had met during the war at
Villers-Cotterêts, at a hospital where she had been working. That
much was true at least, although saying that he had knocked her
down on some stone steps and raped her would have been more accu-
rate. She then said that they did not know each other well and were
not friends, which was also true, and that an unfortunate incident
had happened, extremely true, as a result of which, she had had a
child, a little girl, six years before. She said that she had not contacted

them until then because she wanted nothing from them. She explained that she was American, had come over as a volunteer, and her encounter with Harry, and the pregnancy that had resulted from it, was one of those extremely unhappy outcomes of war, but that her daughter was a wonderful little human being and had recently inquired about her paternal grandmother, which was extremely difficult for Annabelle too. She said she didn't want to flat-out lie any more than she already had. She said the child believed that her parents had been married, which was not the case. And Annabelle then suggested that if Lady Winshire was so inclined, perhaps a letter or a short note to Consuelo, maybe even with a photograph, would do. They could let it go at that. She signed the letter "Dr. Annabelle Worthington" so the woman would know at least that she was a respectable person, not that it really mattered. It was her son who had been anything but respectable and should have been put in prison, but instead he had fathered the most enchanting child on earth, and Annabelle couldn't hate him for it. In her own way, she was grateful to him forever, but he was not a happy memory for her.

After she mailed the letter, Annabelle put it out of her mind. She had a busy month of May, with her waiting room constantly full. She'd had no answer from Lady Winshire, and for the moment, Consuelo seemed to have forgotten about it. She had started school that winter and went there every day, which gave Brigitte time to help them in the office.

Annabelle had just come back from seeing a patient in the hospital when Hélène told her there was a woman waiting for her. She had been there for two hours and refused to say what it was about.

Annabelle assumed she probably had some kind of embarrassing problem. She put her white coat on, sat down at her desk, and told Hélène to let her in.

Two minutes later, Hélène was escorting in a dowager of impressive proportions. She was a large woman with a big voice, wearing an enormous hat, about six long strands of huge pearls, and she was carrying a silver cane. She looked as though she were going to hit someone with it as she marched into the office. Annabelle stood up to greet her, and had to force herself not to smile. The woman ignored Annabelle's extended hand and stood glaring at her. She did not look sick and Annabelle had no idea what she was doing there. She got right to the point.

"What is all this nonsense about a granddaughter?" she barked at Annabelle in English. "My son had no children, no encumbrances, no important women in his life when he died. And if you're claiming that you had a child by him, why exactly have you waited six years to write to me about it?" As she said it, she sat down in the chair at the other side of Annabelle's desk and glared at her some more. She was as pleasant as her son, and Annabelle was not amused once she realized what this was about, and that instead of responding to her letter, his mother had just shown up and barged in.

"I waited six years to contact you," Annabelle said coldly, "because I didn't want to contact you at all." She could be just as blunt as Lady Winshire was herself. She looked to be about seventy years old, which seemed roughly the right age, since Harry would have been in his early thirties by then. She had guessed him to be about her own age the night that she was raped. "I wrote to you because my daughter was upset about not having a grandmother. She couldn't understand why we'd never met you. And I said her father and I were married for a short time, at the front, and then he was killed. So you and I never had time to meet. This is very awkward for me too."

"Were you married to my son?" Lady Winshire looked appalled.

Annabelle quietly shook her head. "No, we were not. I only met him once." Saying that gave his mother a very poor impression of her, but she didn't think that the woman, however disagreeable, needed to know that her son was a rapist. It seemed to Annabelle that she and Consuelo both deserved to keep their illusions, so she was leaving Lady Winshire's intact, at her own expense. "I'd rather my daughter continue to believe that we were married. I'd like to at least give her that."

"Were you a doctor then?" Lady Winshire asked with sudden interest.

Annabelle shook her head again. "No, I wasn't. I was a medic, attached to the ambulance corps."

"How did you meet him?" Something in her eyes softened. She'd lost both her sons in the war and was no stranger to loss or pain.

"It's not important," Annabelle answered quietly, wishing she hadn't come. "We never really knew each other. My daughter was an accident."

"What kind of accident?" She was like a dog with a bone. And Annabelle was the bone.

Annabelle sighed before she answered, trying to figure out how much to say. Surely not the truth. "He had a lot to drink."

Lady Winshire didn't look surprised. "He always did. Harry always drank too much, and did a lot of stupid things when he did." Her eyes bored into Annabelle's. "How stupid was he with you?"

Annabelle smiled, wondering if his mother thought she was trying to blackmail her, and decided to reassure her again. "I don't want anything from you."

"That's not the point. If that's the case, then I have a right to know how badly my son behaved."

"Why? What difference does it make?" Annabelle spoke with quiet dignity.

"You're a very generous woman," Lady Winshire said calmly, sitting back in the chair. She looked like she was there to stay, until she had the truth. "But I also knew my son. My son Edward was nearly a saint. Harry was the devil in our lives. Adorable as a child, and badly behaved as a man. Sometimes *very* badly behaved. It didn't improve when he drank. I think I know most of the stories about him." She sighed then. "I wanted to come and see you, because no one has ever said to me that there was a child. I was very suspicious of you when I read your letter. I thought you wanted something. I can see now that you're an honest woman, and you're as suspicious of me now, as I was of you." The old woman smiled a wintry smile and ran a hand down her many pearls. "I hesitated to come," she admitted. "I didn't want to get embroiled with some dreadful vulgar woman, who has some gutter brat she pretends was spawned by my son. But clearly, that's not the case with you, and I have the strong feeling that your entire encounter with my son was unpleasant, or worse, and I don't want to be a reminder of that for you."

"Thank you," Annabelle said, appreciating everything she'd just heard. And then Lady Winshire stunned her with what she said.

"Did he rape you?" she asked bluntly. Apparently, she knew her son well. There was an endless hesitation in the room, and finally Annabelle nodded, sorry to tell her the truth.

"Yes."

"I'm sorry," the older woman said more gently. "It's not the first time I've heard that," she continued, with motherly regret. "I don't know what went wrong." Her eyes were filled with sorrow as she and Annabelle looked at each other. "What do we do now? I have to admit, I was afraid of what I would find here, but I also couldn't resist seeing my own grandchild, if there truly was one. Both my sons are dead. My husband died of pneumonia last spring. And neither of my sons ever married, nor had children. Until you." There were tears in her eyes, as Annabelle looked at her with compassion.

"Would you like to meet Consuelo?" She warned her then, though it didn't matter, since she was making no claims on his estate, "She doesn't look like him. She looks like me."

"I'd say that could prove to be a great blessing," the old woman said, smiling. She stood up with some difficulty and used her cane.

Annabelle rose too, came around her desk, and led Lady Winshire out of the office, after telling Hélène where they were going. Fortunately, she had a break in her scheduled patients. The two women walked through the courtyard toward the main part of the house. She knew that Consuelo would be home from school by then, and she let herself in with her key, still wearing her doctor's coat. Lady Winshire marched up the steps, outside the house, and stood looking around the front hall as they walked in.

"You have a very pretty home," she said politely. She was impressed by everything she saw. Annabelle had good taste, and an obvious history with fine things.

"Thank you," Annabelle said, and led her into the main living room. She then ran up the stairs to get her daughter. She told her they had a guest and she wanted her to say hello. But she didn't want to say more.

As Annabelle and Consuelo came down the stairs, they were chatting animatedly with each other, and holding hands. At the bottom Consuelo stopped, smiled shyly at their guest, curtsied, and went to shake her hand. The child was obviously extremely polite and well behaved, and Lady Winshire glanced approvingly at Annabelle over Consuelo's head.

"How do you do, Consuelo," she said, as the child took in the huge hat and many strands of pearls.

"Your hat is very pretty," the little girl said, staring at it as the older woman smiled.

"That's a very nice thing to say. It's a bit of a silly old hat, but I like it. And you're a very pretty girl." She had never had a grandchild before, and hadn't spoken to a child in years. "I came all the way from England to see you," she went on as Consuelo stared. "Do you know who I am?" she asked gently, and Consuelo shook her head. "I'm the grandma you've never met. I'm your father's mother." Consuelo's eyes grew wide as she looked over her shoulder at her mother and then back at her grandmother. "I'm sorry we've never met before. That won't happen anymore," Lady Winshire said solemnly. She had never seen such an enchanting child, and her manners were exquisite. "I brought some photographs with me of your father when he was a little boy. Would you like to see them?" Consuelo nodded and sat down next to her on the couch, as Lady Winshire took a stack of faded photographs out of her bag, while Annabelle quietly went to ask Brigitte to make tea.

Lady Winshire stayed with them for over an hour, and when

Consuelo went back upstairs with Brigitte, she congratulated Annabelle for having such a lovely child.

"She's a wonderful little girl," her mother agreed.

"My son didn't know how lucky he was to run into someone like you, and leave such a sweet little girl in the world." She was looking at Annabelle with gratitude and compassion. She had fallen in love with Consuelo at first sight. It would have been hard not to, and for the first time Annabelle was glad she'd come, instead of just writing back. It had been a lovely gift for Consuelo too. "I'm sorry he was so bad to you. There was a sweet side of him. I'm sorry you never knew it. This must have been very hard for you at first."

Annabelle nodded. "I stayed at the hospital as long as I could, and then I went to Antibes. Consuelo was born there."

"And your family is in the States?" It seemed odd to her that Annabelle was practicing medicine in Paris instead of at home, although the child had obviously complicated things for her.

"My family is gone," Annabelle said simply. "They all died before I came here. It's just Consuelo and I." Lady Winshire was alone in the world now too. And in an odd way, now they had each other.

She finally stood up, and took Annabelle's hand in her own. "Thank you for this most extraordinary gift," she said with tears in her eyes. "It's a little piece of Harry I can hang on to, and Consuelo is a very special child on her own." And with that, she hugged Annabelle and kissed her on the cheek. Annabelle helped her down the stairs to the car and driver waiting for her outside. She suddenly looked even older than she had when she arrived. And she smiled at Annabelle again before she left, and gently slipped something into her hand. "This is for you, my dear. You've earned it. It's a very small thing." Annabelle tried to resist, without even looking at it, but Lady Winshire insisted. The two women hugged again, and Annabelle felt as though they had a new friend, a kind of wonderful old eccentric aunt. She was glad she'd written to her now. It had been the right thing to do, for them all.

She waved as Lady Winshire drove away, and only after she had left did Annabelle look at the object in the palm of her hand. She had sensed that it was a ring, but she was in no way prepared for the kind of ring it was. It was a beautiful old emerald of enormous proportions, in an antique diamond setting. Annabelle was stunned. It looked like the rings her own grandmother had worn, which were still in the vault at the bank in New York. But she slipped the ring on her finger with the wedding ring she had bought herself. She was deeply touched by the gesture. She would give it to Consuelo one day, but in the meantime she was going to wear it. And as she walked back into her office she thought to herself that they had a grandmother now. She and Consuelo were no longer alone in the world.

Chapter 22

There was a mild outbreak of influenza in Paris that summer, some thought from the heat, and Annabelle had several patients in the hospital. She visited them twice a day, but she was hoping to go away with Consuelo and Brigitte in August. She couldn't decide between Dordogne, Brittany, or the South of France. As it turned out, they never got to any of those places. She had too many sick people to tend to. They went to Deauville, at the seashore in Normandy, instead for a few days, when her patients recovered.

And after they got back, two more of her patients were hospitalized with pneumonia. She was leaving the hospital late one afternoon, thinking about the patient she'd just visited, an elderly woman who wasn't doing well. Annabelle was trying to come up with some new solutions for her many problems, when she bumped into someone on the steps of the hospital, coming up as she was going down. They hit each other with such force that he almost knocked her over, and made a quick save to grab her before she fell down the stairs.

"Oh, I'm so sorry," she said apologetically. "I wasn't looking where I was going."

"Neither was I." He was equally apologetic and had a dazzling smile. "Were you visiting a friend?" It was an honest mistake and she laughed.

"No, I'm a doctor." At least he hadn't asked if she was a nurse.

"What a happy coincidence," he said, laughing back at her. "So am I. Why have I never been fortunate enough to meet you before?" He was very charming, and she wasn't used to bantering with men that way. For years now, she had hidden behind her role as a doctor, widow, or Consuelo's mother. Men never flirted with her, but he seemed full of mischief and fun and was undeniably very good-looking. "What's your specialty?" he asked with interest, not in the least bothered that they had had no formal introduction. He told her his name was Antoine de St. Gris, and asked for hers, which she gave him. He refused to believe she was American, since she spoke such flawless French.

"I'm in general medicine," she said simply, embarrassed to be talking to a stranger.

"I'm an orthopedic surgeon," he said with visible panache. She knew that most of the orthopedic surgeons had big egos, except during the war when they had been humbled, like everyone else, by what they saw, and how little of the damage they could repair.

He walked her back down the steps of the hospital, to ensure that she didn't fall, he said, and saw her to the car that she drove herself.

"Will I be fortunate enough to see you again?" he asked with a twinkle in his eye, and she laughed.

"If I break my leg, I'll call you."

"Don't wait until then. Or I'll have to develop pneumonia and call you. And it would be such a shame. I would much prefer to see you while we're both healthy." He waved as she drove away and hurried back up the hospital steps. It had put a little spark in her day to have a man chat with her. It happened to her so rarely, almost never.

She spent a quiet evening reading to Consuelo and put her to bed. And the next day in the office, she was in the midst of seeing patients when Hélène told her that there was a doctor in the waiting room, demanding to see her immediately. He said he had to consult her about a case. She finished with her patient, and walked out, puzzled. She couldn't imagine who it was. And there was Antoine de St. Gris in a handsome blue topcoat, creating havoc in her waiting room, entertaining the patients, most of whom were laughing. He had been telling them jokes, and she took him into her office for a moment.

"What are you doing here?" she asked with an embarrassed smile. It pleased her to see him again, but she was working. "I'm seeing patients."

"I'm very impressed. I think I caught a severe cold last night. I have a very bad sore throat." He stuck his tongue out for her to look at when he said it. And she laughed at him. He was outrageous, irreverent, and embarrassingly charming.

"It looks fine to me."

"How's your leg?" he asked.

"My leg? Fine. Why?"

"It looks broken to me. Let me have a look at it." He made as though to reach for the hem of her skirt, and she stepped away from him, laughing.

"Doctor, I must ask you to leave. I have to see my patients."

"Fine, if you're going to be that way. Then see me tonight for dinner."

"Uh...I don't...I can't..."

"You can't even think of a decent excuse." He laughed at her. "That's truly pathetic. I'll pick you up at eight." And with that, he went back to the waiting room, waved at her patients, and left. He was completely overwhelming, very improper, and in spite of that, or maybe because of it, very appealing, almost irresistible in fact.

"Who was that?" Hélène asked with a look of disapproval, before ushering the next patient in.

"He's an orthopedic surgeon."

"That explains everything," Hélène growled, and noticed the girlish expression on her employer's face. She had never seen her look that way before. "He's a lunatic," Hélène added, and then smiled in spite of herself. "A good-looking lunatic though. Are you going to see him again?"

Annabelle blushed. "Tonight. For dinner."

"Uh-oh. Watch out for him," Hélène warned.

"I will," Annabelle reassured her, and then went back to seeing patients.

She got to the house after seven that night, after her last patient and closing the office. Consuelo was in the bathtub, laughing with Brigitte. Annabelle looked at her watch and realized that she had less than an hour to dress for dinner with the slightly outrageous Dr. St. Gris. She went in to kiss Consuelo, who wanted to play cards with her mother after the bath.

"I can't," Annabelle said apologetically. "I'm going out."

"You are?" Consuelo looked shocked. It was a most unusual occurrence. In fact, it never happened, except once in a great while if Annabelle went to a meeting of physicians, or a conference for women doctors. Other than that, she never went out, and had no social life, not since leaving New York nine years before. So her announcement had the effect of a bomb dropped in their midst. "Where are you going?"

"To dinner with a doctor," she said innocently.

"Oh. Where?" Consuelo wanted to know everything, and her mother looked slightly embarrassed.

"I don't know. He's picking me up at eight."

"He is? What does he look like?"

"Just a person," Annabelle said vaguely. She didn't want to say that he was very good-looking. She left the bathroom then, and went to get dressed. It was a warm night. She wore a white linen suit she had bought in Deauville, and a very pretty hat she had found with it. She felt a little silly getting all dressed up, but it wasn't every day she got invited out to dinner, and she couldn't have worn the suit or hat for work.

Antoine de St. Gris arrived promptly at eight, and Brigitte let him in. She seated him in the drawing room, and having been unattended for five minutes, Consuelo came bouncing down the stairs in her nightgown and dressing gown. She walked into the living room and smiled at him, as Brigitte attempted unsuccessfully to shoo her back upstairs.

"Hello," she said cheerfully. "Are you the doctor having dinner with my mother?" She was missing her two front teeth currently, which made her look particularly cute.

"Yes, I am. What happened to your teeth?" Antoine asked, looking right at her.

"I lost them," she said proudly.

"I'm sorry to hear that," he said seriously. "I hope you find them soon. It could be very annoying to grow up without teeth. How would you ever eat an apple?"

She giggled at what he said. "No, I won't find them. A fairy took them and left me candy instead. I'm going to get new ones soon. I can already feel them . . . see?" She turned her head at a funny angle, half upside down, and showed him the little white edges peeking through her gums.

"Oh, I'm so glad," he said with a broad grin as Annabelle walked into the room, and saw her daughter conversing happily with the doctor.

"Have you two met?" she asked, looking a little nervous.

"Not officially," he confessed, and then bowed elegantly to Consuelo. "Antoine de St. Gris," he said formally. "I am honored to meet you, particularly now that I know you're going to get new teeth." She giggled again. Annabelle introduced her daughter, who curtsied properly to Antoine. "Ready?" he asked Annabelle, and she nodded. She kissed Consuelo, told her to go upstairs and get ready for bed, since she had had dinner before her bath. Consuelo scampered up the stairs with a wave at their guest, as Annabelle followed him out of the house. "I'm sorry," he said seriously, as he led her to the beautiful blue Ballot Open Tourer he had left outside. It was a very elegant car and suited him to perfection. Everything about him was stylish, smooth, and assured. "I shouldn't be taking you out at all. I'm spoken for. I've just fallen madly in love with your daughter. She must be the most adorable child I've ever seen." Annabelle smiled at what he'd said.

"You have a nice way with children."

"I was one, a long time ago. My mother insists I still am and never grew up." Annabelle could see why she would say that, but his boyishness was part of his charm. She wondered how old he was, and guessed him to be around thirty-five, which would make him four years older than she was. They were very close in age, but Annabelle had a far more serious, reserved demeanor. He was a little bit of a handsome, charming clown. She liked how lighthearted he was, and he had a nice sense of humor. The patients in her waiting room had loved it too. So did his.

They chatted easily as he drove her to Maxim's. She had never been there, and knew that it was one of the best restaurants in Paris, and a very fashionable place. It had been there forever.

When they arrived, it was obvious that he was well known to them. The headwaiter acknowledged him, and he was well acquainted with people at several tables and introduced Annabelle to them proudly. He introduced her as Dr. Worthington, which always made her feel important. She had worked hard for her title.

He suggested what she might like to eat, and ordered dinner for them, with a bottle of champagne. She very rarely drank, but the champagne made the evening feel like a celebration. She hadn't been out with a man for an evening like this since Josiah, ten years before. Her life had been entirely different here in France, at the front, in medical school, and now as Consuelo's mother, and suddenly here she was at Maxim's with Antoine. It was entirely unexpected and a treat.

"How long have you been widowed?" he asked her gently over dinner.

"Since before Consuelo was born," she said simply.

"That's a long time to be alone, assuming you have been," he asked, prying a little. He was curious about her. She was an unusual woman—beautiful, distinguished, clearly well born, and a doctor. He had never met anyone quite like her, and was very attracted to her.

"I have been," she confirmed, and in fact, she had been alone for a lot longer. Nine years, since Josiah had left her, but she couldn't tell him that.

"You couldn't have been married for long," he said, looking thoughtful.

"Only a few months. He was killed at the front, right after we were married. We met where I was working at Villers-Cotterêts, at the hospital Elsie Inglis set up, with female medical units."

"Were you already a physician then?" He looked confused, as that would have made her older than she looked. She appeared very young to him.

"No." She smiled. "Just a medic. I left medical school to work there. I worked at L'Abbaye de Royaumont before that, in Asnières. I went back to medical school after Consuelo was born."

"You're a very enterprising woman, and very brave," he said, sounding impressed, as they ate dinner, which was delicious. He had ordered lobster, and she was having a delicate veal dish. "What made you want to become a doctor?" He wanted to know everything about her.

"Same thing as you probably. I've loved science and medicine since I was a child. I just never thought I'd get the chance to do it. What about you?"

"My father and both my brothers are physicians. And my mother should have been. She tells us all what we do wrong. And I hate to admit it, but sometimes she's right." He laughed. "She's been helping my father in his office for years. But why are you practicing here and not in the States?" He still couldn't get over the fact that she wasn't French, she spoke the language like a native. He would never have suspected she was American.

"I don't know. It didn't happen there. I came here to volunteer for the war effort. And then I just fell into a series of circumstances. One of the surgeons in Asnières helped me get into medical school in Nice. And I could never have done it while my parents were alive. My mother was never happy about my fascination with medicine. She thought I'd wind up catching a disease. I worked with immigrants in New York."

"Well, lucky for me that you came over here. Do you think you'll go back to the States one day?"

She shook her head solemnly. "I have no one left there. All my family are gone."

"That's very sad," he said sympathetically. "I'm very close to mine. I would be lost without them. We're something of a tribe." She liked that about him. It seemed warm and friendly, and if they were all as much fun as he was, they must have been a lively group. "What about your late husband's family? Do you see them?"

"Very little. They're in England. Although Consuelo's grandmother came over recently. She's a very nice woman." But she didn't tell him it had been the first time they'd ever met.

There was so much about her history that she couldn't tell him. That her real husband had left her and was in love with a man. That she was divorced because of that. That she'd been raped and never married to Consuelo's father. The truth was far more shocking than the version she told. The worst of it was that she was paying for sins she hadn't committed, and would all her life. He was so easygoing that she could almost imagine he wouldn't be as shocked by the truth as some might be. But she wouldn't tell him anyway. The history she told was one of complete respectability, and he had no reason to suspect otherwise. Everything she said was eminently believable, and she looked so proper that no one would ever expect anything less of her.

He commented during dinner that he had never been married. Specializing in orthopedic surgery had kept him in medical school for a long time, which he had attended in Paris at the Faculté de Médecine. He had trained at the Pitié-Salpêtrière Hospital, and the war had interrupted his studies for a while. He somehow let it slip out that he had been decorated twice during the war. Despite his joking style, he was an impressive person, and it was obvious that he thought the same of her. As she talked to him over dinner, she felt as though he had been dropped into her life like a gift from heaven. She was glad he had almost knocked her down the stairs at the hospital, otherwise she would never have met him. And he seemed equally pleased to have found her.

When he drove her home he asked when he could see her again. She had no other conflicting engagements, for the rest of her life in fact, except dinner and evenings with Consuelo, and he promised to call the next day and make a plan. And much to her amazement, he did.

She was sitting at her desk, filling out files on the patients she had seen that morning, when Hélène told her he was on the line. He invited her to dinner the coming Saturday, in two days. He was suddenly an unexpected pleasure in her life. And he asked if on Sunday, she and Consuelo would like to have lunch with his two brothers and their children, at his parents' home. It was a very appealing invitation. And she mentioned it to Consuelo that night. She was delighted. Consuelo thought he had been very funny about her teeth. She looked at her mother thoughtfully then and volunteered that he was nice. Annabelle agreed that he was.

On Saturday, he took her to La Tour d'Argent for dinner, which was even more elegant than Maxim's. She wore a very simple well-cut black dress, and Lady Winshire's emerald ring. Annabelle had no other jewelry in France, but she looked very stylish nonetheless. Her natural beauty was more striking than anything she wore. And they had a wonderful time again, talking until almost midnight about a great many things—the war, surgery, medicine, the reconstruction of Europe. He was a fascinating dinner partner and fun to be with.

The day they spent with him on Sunday was even better. As it turned out, his parents' home was only a few blocks from her house. His brothers were as entertaining as he was, and their wives were very sweet. Their children were around the same age as Consuelo, and the whole family talked medicine constantly, which Annabelle loved. His mother was a benevolent tyrant who ruled them all. She scolded Antoine frequently, and rolled her eyes in disgust that he still wasn't married, and said so. She seemed to approve of Annabelle, and refused to believe that she wasn't French and had grown up in New York. She let Consuelo sit on her lap, and all the others, and then chased them all out into the garden to play. By the time he took Annabelle and Consuelo home, they were all pleasantly exhausted and had had a wonderful day.

"Thank you for putting up with my mother," he said with a smile. "I don't usually take people home for Sunday lunch. Most women would run screaming out the door."

"I loved it," Annabelle said honestly. She missed her own family so much that she found his an enormous blessing, and it was wonderful for Consuelo to be around families like that, with aunts, uncles, cousins, grandparents. It was everything they lacked. And Consuelo had enjoyed every minute of it, even more than her mother did. "Thank you for taking us."

"We'll do it again," he promised. "I'll call you and we'll organize some dinners for this week." Not just one. Several. Suddenly, Antoine had become a major feature in her life, and she had to admit, he made her very happy. And his family was an added bonus in her eyes.

He called her on Tuesday, and invited her to dinner on Friday night, and he suggested that they have lunch at La Cascade, one of the oldest and nicest restaurants in Paris, on Saturday, and with his family on Sunday again if she could stand it. He was giving her a major rush.

And every one of their dates was absolute perfection. Dinner on Friday at the Ritz was exquisite, just as the two previous dinners had been. Lunch at La Cascade was sumptuous and relaxing, and they went for a walk in the gardens of Bagatelle afterward and admired the peacocks. When he brought her home later, she invited him to stay for an early dinner with her and Consuelo in their kitchen. And after that, he played cards with Consuelo, and she screamed with glee when she beat him, which Annabelle suspected was fixed.

Their Sunday with his family was even better than the first one. His family was a classic example of the French bourgeoisie, with all its opinions, political views, unspoken rules and etiquette, and solid family values, all of which she loved. She was as traditional as they were, and enjoyed talking to both his sisters-in-law before lunch, chatting about their children.

After lunch she fell into medical discussions with his brothers, one of whom had been a surgeon in Asnières, although they had never met, since she was already in medical school when he was assigned there. They all seemed to have a great deal in common, and Annabelle fit right in.

The following weekend, Antoine invited her to Deauville with Consuelo. He had booked separate rooms for them, and there was no question of anything being less than circumspect. Consuelo was over the moon at the prospect, and so was she. They stayed at a wonderful hotel, walked on the boardwalk together, gathered seashells, looked in all the shops, and had delicious meals of seafood. Annabelle said she didn't know how to thank him when they got back. Consuelo went upstairs sleepily with Brigitte after the long drive, and Antoine and Annabelle stood in her courtyard as he looked tenderly at her. He gently touched her face with his long surgeon's fingers, and then he kissed her, and afterward pulled her into his arms.

"I've fallen in love with you, Annabelle," he said softly, sounding shocked himself, and she was equally shaken by what he said. But she felt the same way. She had never known anyone as wonderful as he was, or as kind to her and her daughter. She hadn't felt this way about anyone, not even Josiah, who had always been more of a friend, and was less romantic. Antoine had totally swept her off her feet, and she was as madly in love as he was. And it had all happened so quickly. He kissed her again then, and felt that she was shaking. "Don't be afraid, my darling," he reassured her. And then he added, "Now I know why I've never married." He looked down at her with a long, slow smile. He was the happiest man on earth, and she the happiest woman. "I was waiting for you," he whispered as he held her.

"So was I," she said, melting in his arms. She felt totally, completely safe with him. The one thing she already knew about Antoine, and trusted completely, was that he would never hurt her. She had never been as sure of anyone in her life.

Chapter 23

The ensuing weeks and months with Antoine were like a dream for both of them. He spent time on the weekends with her and Consuelo. He let Annabelle watch some of his surgeries. She consulted him on several of her patients, and respected his diagnostic skill and opinions, sometimes even more than her own. He invited her to all the best restaurants in Paris, and took her dancing afterward. As the weather got colder, they went for long walks in the park. He took her to the gardens of Versailles, and they were there holding hands and kissing as the first snow came down. Every moment they shared was magical, and no man had ever been as kind and loving to her in her life, not even Josiah. Her relationship with Antoine was more mature, far more romantic, and they had their profession in common. He made constant thoughtful gestures, showed up with flowers for her, and he gave Consuelo the most beautiful doll she'd ever seen. He couldn't do enough for them. And they spent every Sunday with his family. Annabelle felt as though she and Consuelo had been adopted and embraced in every way.

She prepared a real Thanksgiving dinner for him, with all the trimmings, and tried to explain the holiday to him, which he said he found touching. They spent Christmas Eve with his family, and everyone gave them presents. She had picked a gift for each of them as well, a warm cashmere shawl for his mother, handsome gold pens for both his brothers, a rare first-edition book on surgery for his father, pretty sweaters for both his sisters-in-law, and toys for all their children. And they had been equally generous with her.

On Christmas Day she invited them all to her house, to thank them for the many Sundays she and Consuelo had shared with them. Antoine hadn't said anything official yet, but it was obvious that he was thinking long term. He was already making plans with her for the following summer. And Hélène teased her about it all the time.

"I hear wedding bells!" she said, smiling. She had decided that she liked him, and he was so good for Annabelle. She looked blissfully happy.

On New Year's Eve he took her dancing at the Hôtel de Crillon. He kissed her tenderly at midnight, and looked into her eyes. And then, without warning, he got down on one knee and gazed imploringly at her as she stood there in a white satin evening gown embroidered with silver beading, and looked down at him in amazement. He spoke solemnly, with great emotion in his voice.

"Annabelle, will you do me the honor of marrying me?" There was no one else to ask for her hand, and with tears in her eyes, she nodded and then said yes. He stood up and swept her into his arms, and people around them in the nightclub cheered. They were the golden couple everywhere they went, beautiful people who were talented, intelligent, stylish, dignified. They had never disagreed on a single thing, and he was always loving and kind.

They announced their engagement to his family on New Year's Day. His mother cried and kissed them both, and everyone drank champagne. They told Consuelo that night. He was going to move into the house with them when they married, and they had already talked about having children. It was what he wanted most, and so did she. And this time, it would be right, and she wouldn't be alone. It was the marriage she always should have had, but had been cheated of till now. This time, everything about it was perfect. They hadn't slept with each other but he was so sensual and passionate with her, that she had no concern about it.

The only thing that bothered her was that Antoine still did not know about her past. She had never told him about Josiah, their marriage, why he had divorced her, or the reason she had left New York, that if she hadn't she would have been shunned and run out of town on a rail for being a disgrace, since no one knew Josiah's dark secrets, and she had never told, and never would.

He knew nothing about Consuelo's conception, the rape at Villers-Cotterêts by Harry Winshire. At first she had seen no reason to share it all with him. As they grew closer, she wanted him to know all of it, and thought he should. But there had never been a right time. And now that he had asked her to marry him and she'd accepted, it felt awkward explaining it to him and seemed almost too late. But Annabelle was a woman of honor and thought she should tell him. There was a good chance that he would never know, but even if he never found out, she still felt she owed him the truth. She had been married to one man, and raped by another. And the truth that he couldn't have imagined was that other than the rape, she had been a virgin all her life. She was thirty-one years old, had been married for two years, and had never been made love to by a man, only brutalized for a few minutes on stone steps in the dark. And somehow, it seemed important to Annabelle that he should know it. What she had lived and experienced was part of who she was. And although both stories were upsetting, she had no doubt that he would be compassionate about it.

The day after New Year's they talked about their wedding. Since he had never been married, he wanted a big wedding, and he had many friends. She would have preferred a small one, since she was officially a "widow," and she had very few friends, and no family of her own except Consuelo. But she wanted to do what made him happy, and whatever he thought best.

They were talking about guest lists and locations, and how many children they wanted, while finishing lunch at Le Pré Catalan in the Bois de Boulogne, and afterward they went for a walk. The day was crisp and clear. And suddenly, as she walked with her hand tucked into his arm, she knew that it was the right time, whether she liked it or not. They couldn't talk about the details of their wedding, and how many babies they wanted, without his knowing the details of her life. She knew it wouldn't change anything between them, but she felt honor-bound to tell him.

There was a moment of peaceful silence as they walked, and she turned to him with a serious expression.

"There are some things I have to tell you," she said softly. There was a small butterfly fluttering in her stomach, but she wanted to get it over with, and get the butterfly out.

"What about?" he asked, smiling at her. He was the happiest man on earth.

"My past."

"Ah, yes. Of course. To pay your way through medical school, you were a dancer at the Folies Bergère. Correct?"

"Not quite." She smiled. It was nice to know that he would make her laugh for the rest of her life.

They walked past a bench, and she suggested that they sit down. They did, and he put an arm around her shoulders and pulled her close. She loved it when he did that. For the first time in years, she felt loved, protected, and safe.

"There are some things about my past I haven't told you," she said honestly. "I'm not sure if they're important, but I still think you ought to know." She took a breath and started. It was harder than she thought. "I was married once before."

He smiled broadly. "Yes, my love, I know."

"Well, not exactly the way you think, or to whom."

"That sounds mysterious."

"In some ways, it is. Or it was to me. For a long time. I was married to a man named Josiah Millbank, when I was nineteen. In New York. He worked for my father's bank. I think in retrospect, he probably felt sorry for me when my father and Robert died. He was really more of a friend, nineteen years older than I was. And a year after they died, he asked me to marry him. He's from a very respected family or rather he was. At the time, it all made sense. We got married and nothing ever happened.

"To be blunt, we never made love. I always thought there was something wrong with me. It never happened, he always put it off. He said that we 'had lots of time.'" Antoine was not saying a word, and Annabelle had tears in her eyes at the memories of her long-forgotten disappointment and grief. She went on. "Two years after we were married, he told me that he had thought he could be married to me and lead a double life. As it turned out, he couldn't. He was in love with a man, a very dear old friend of his who was always with us. I never suspected anything. And finally, Josiah told me he was in love with him, and had been for twenty years. They were going to go to Mexico together, and he was leaving me. What finally made the decision for him was that he had discovered they both had syphilis. I never saw him again. He died earlier this year. And I was never at risk, because he had never slept with me. I was a virgin at the end of our marriage, just as I had been when it began. To be honest, I wanted to stay married to him anyway. I loved him, and I was willing to give up any kind of life or future for myself. But he refused. He said he owed it to me to free me, and that I deserved better than that—a real husband, and children, and everything he promised me and couldn't give." There were tears running down her cheeks by then at the memory.

"He filed for divorce, because I refused to. He thought he was doing the right thing for me. And in New York, the only grounds he could do it under were adultery. So he divorced me for adultery. Someone sold the story to the newspapers, and I became a pariah overnight. No one would speak to me, not even my best friend. If I had stayed, I would have been shunned by everyone I had ever known in New York. I was an outcast and a disgrace. So I left and came to France. I felt I had no other choice. And I went to work at the Abbaye de Royaumont. That's how I wound up there."

"And then you married again?" Antoine was looking stunned. The only reaction on his face that she could read was astonishment.

She shook her head. "No, I didn't marry again. I never got involved with another man. I was too shell-shocked by everything that had happened in New York. I just worked, day and night. I never looked at another man."

"And Consuelo was a virgin birth?" he asked, looking confused.

"More or less," she admitted, took a deep breath and said the rest. "I was raped one night at Villers-Cotterêts. By a drunken British officer, who turned out to be from a decent family, though he was a very, very black sheep. I only saw him for those few minutes, and never again. He was killed shortly afterward. I found out I was pregnant. I worked until I was almost seven months pregnant, by binding myself." They were painful details too, and hard to admit to him. But she had no other choice. Once he knew all of it, she would never have secrets from him again. And this was all there was. "I was never married to him. I didn't even know him. All I knew was his name. And he left me with Consuelo. I never contacted his family until this year. His mother came over to see us, and she was very kind. She was very sweet to both of us. Apparently he had done things like it before. She wasn't surprised." She turned to look at Antoine then, her face awash with tears. "So I was married, but not to him. Technically, Consuelo is illegitimate. I gave her my name. And I'm not a widow. I'm a divorcée, from a marriage to another man. That's it," she said, finally relieved.

"That's all?" he said, looking tense. "You haven't done time in prison or killed a man?" She smiled at the question and shook her head.

"No." She looked lovingly at him and wiped her eyes. It had been hard to tell him but she was glad she had. She wanted to be completely honest with him. And as she looked at him, he sprang to his feet and began to pace. He looked upset and as though he were in shock. And even Annabelle had to admit that the story was shocking.

"Let me get this straight. You were married to a man with syphilis, but you claim you never slept with him."

"That's right," she confirmed in a small voice, worried about the tone of his.

"He divorced you for adultery, which you claim you never committed, although he never slept with you. You became an outcast in New York society, for the adultery you did not commit, but he divorced you for, because you refused to divorce him, although he cheated on you with a man. So you ran away after the divorce. And once here, you became pregnant out of wedlock, by a man you claim raped you. You never married him. You never saw him again. You gave birth to his bastard, while pretending to be a widow, instead of a divorcée, cast off by her husband for sleeping with another man. And then you brought your bastard to my parents' house to let her play with my nephews and nieces, while pretending to be a widow to my parents and me, which is also a lie. For God's sake, Annabelle, has anything you've said since the beginning been the truth? And on top of it, you claim that other than the convenient rape, which led to your bastard, you're nearly a virgin now. How big a fool do you think I am?" His eyes were blazing at her, and his words were stabbing her in the heart. She had never in her life seen anyone so upset, but so was she. She started crying again as she huddled miserably on the bench, and he paced more and more furiously. She didn't even dare reach out to touch him—he looked as though he might have hit her. What he had said to her was unforgivable.

A Good Woman

"You'll have to admit," he said icily, "it's all a little hard to believe. Your saintly innocence in all of it, your lack of responsibility, when in fact I suspect you cheated on your husband, probably have syphilis, and thank God I haven't slept with you. I wonder when you were planning to let that little secret out. You were treated like the whore you obviously were in New York, and then you have a bastard child with someone you've claimed is British nobility, and who gives a damn for God's sake? You've behaved like a trollop from beginning to end. And spare me the story of your virginity," he raged on. "Given the risk of syphilis, I don't plan to put it to the test." If he had beaten her with his fists, he couldn't have caused her more pain. She stood up to face him then, trembling from head to foot. He had just proven everything she had feared most, that she was branded forever with other people's sins and no one would ever accept her innocence, not even a man who claimed to love her, and didn't believe her when she told him the truth.

"Everything I've just said to you is true," she said miserably, "from beginning to end. And don't *ever* call my daughter a bastard. It's not her fault that I was raped, nor mine. I could have gotten an abortion, but I was too afraid, so I decided to have her anyway, and cover it as best I could, so people didn't say about her what you just did. Syphilis may be contagious, but illegitimacy isn't. You don't need to worry about your nieces and nephews catching it from her. I can assure you there's absolutely no risk."

She was angry now, and hurt by the cruelty of his words.

"I can't say the same about you!" He spat angrily at her again, his eyes like fire on ice. "How dare you think that you could trick me into marrying you by pretending to be a widow, and failing to mention all this to me. Everything from syphilis to adultery and bastard children.

273

How could you present yourself to my family as something you're not? And try to convince me now of all these outrageous lies. At least have the guts to admit what you are." He was in a white rage. He felt as though she had stolen something from him, his faith, his trust, and the sanctity of his family. What she had told him was unthinkable, and he would never believe another word she said, and he certainly didn't believe the way she was trying to clean it up now.

"And what is it that you think I am, Antoine? A whore? What happened to love and faith in me if you love me? I didn't have to tell you any of this. You would probably never have found out. But I wanted to tell you the truth because I love you, and you have the right to know everything about me. The bad things that have happened to me were mostly done to me by others, and I've paid a high price. I was left by a husband I loved in a marriage that was a fraud, and was then shunned by the only world I knew as a result. I lost everyone I loved and came here alone at twenty-two. I got raped when I was still a virgin. And I had a baby I didn't want, alone. How much worse does it have to get for you to be a human being and have a little compassion and faith in me?"

"You're a loose woman, and a liar, Annabelle. It's written all over you."

"Then why didn't you see it before?" she said, crying through her words. They were shouting at each other in the Bois de Boulogne, but there was no one else around.

"I didn't see it before because you're a damn good liar. The best I've ever known. You had me totally convinced. You've contaminated my family and violated everything I hold dear," he said, looking pompous and sounding cruel. "I have nothing more to say to you," he said, standing as far away from her as he could get. "I'm going home, and

I'm not driving you. Maybe you can pick up a soldier or a sailor, and have a little fun on the way back. I wouldn't get near you with the toe of my boot." He turned away from her then and strode off, as she stood and stared at him and shook from head to foot, unable to believe what she'd just heard or what he'd done. A moment later, she heard his car drive off, and she walked slowly out of the Bois de Boulogne. She felt as though her world had ended, and she knew she would never trust anyone again. Not Hortic. Not Antoine. Not anyone she knew. From now on, her secrets were her own, and she and Consuelo didn't need anyone. She was so devastated she was almost hit by a car when she finally reached the street.

She hailed a cab and gave the driver her address. She was frozen to the bone, and sat sobbing in the back seat. The kindly Russian who was driving her finally asked her if there was anything he could do to help. And all she did was shake her head. Antoine had just proven all her worst fears, that no one would ever believe her innocence, and she would be condemned forever for what everyone else had done. Whatever had been left of her heart was in a million pieces at her feet. He had just proven to her that there was no such thing as love, or forgiveness. And the idea that Consuelo could contaminate anyone's family, or be accused of it, made her feel sick.

When they reached her house in the sixteenth arrondissement, the gentle old White Russian refused to take the fare from her. He just shook his head and put it back in her hand.

"Nothing can be as bad as that," he said. He had had hard times of his own in recent years.

"Yes, it is," she said, choking on a sob. And then she thanked him, and ran into the house.

Chapter 24

Annabelle roamed her house like a ghost for the next three days. She canceled her appointments, didn't go to her office, and told everyone she was sick. She was. She was heartsick over everything Antoine had said to her, and all that he had utterly destroyed. If he had stoned her in the street or spat on her, it wouldn't have hurt as much. And in fact, he had done both. And worse. He had broken her heart.

She had Brigitte take Consuelo to school, and to the park, and she told them she was sick as well. Only Hélène at her office didn't believe her. She could sense that something terrible had happened, and she was afraid it involved Antoine.

Annabelle was lying in bed thinking about all of it, and everything he had said, when the doorbell rang. She didn't want to get up to answer it, and Brigitte was out. There was no one she wanted to see, and after everything Antoine had said to her she had nothing left to say to anyone, especially to him. She hadn't heard a word from him since he walked out on her in the park. And she didn't plan to ever speak to him again. She doubted she'd hear from him in any case.

The doorbell persisted for at least ten minutes, and finally, she put on her dressing gown and went downstairs. Maybe it was an emergency and someone in the neighborhood needed a doctor. She pulled the door open without even bothering to look to see who it was and found herself staring up at Antoine. She had no idea what to say. And for the fraction of an instant, neither did he.

"May I come in?" he asked solemnly. She hesitated, not sure if she wanted him in her house again, and then slowly she stepped aside. She took a moment to close the door, and didn't invite him to sit down. She stood looking at him standing near the front door. "Could we sit down for a minute?" he asked cautiously. Fortunately, he hadn't given her an engagement ring yet, so she had nothing to return to him.

"I'd rather not," she said in a dead voice. "I think you said more than enough the other day. I don't think there's much point saying any more." He was startled by the look in her eyes. She looked as though something in her had died.

"Annabelle, I realize I reacted severely. But what you said to me was extremely hard to swallow. You've had marriages you never told me about, babies out of wedlock. You lied about being a widow. You owed me better than that. You've even been exposed to a fatal disease you could have transmitted to me once we were married." What he said to her was yet another slap in the face, and proved yet again that he hadn't believed a word she'd said. His words tore at her already battered heart again.

"I told you I was never exposed. If I had been, I would never even have had dinner with you. I wouldn't have taken the risk of falling in love with you, if I had been exposed to a disease that could kill you. I love you, Antoine. Or I did. I told you. I never slept with Josiah."

"That's a little hard to believe. You were married to the man for two years."

"He was sleeping with his best friend," she said in a dead voice. "I just didn't know it. I thought there was something wrong with me. As it turns out, there was a lot wrong with him. And all you did is prove to me that I shouldn't have told you at all." She was devastated as she met his eyes.

"Would you rather have continued to lie to me, as you did from the beginning? You would have been marrying me under false pretenses. I might remind you that that's fraud."

"That's why I told you. What I meant just now was that I shouldn't have bothered to tell you. I should never have gotten involved with you at all."

"How can you say such a thing? I love you," he said, looking pompous. She wasn't charmed by him anymore.

"That's no longer believable, given everything you said to me the other day. You don't treat someone you love that way."

"I was upset." She didn't comment, and looked away. He didn't go near her. He was afraid that if he did, she might hit him. There was murder in her eyes.

"What you said about Consuelo is unforgivable. I would never let you near her again. It's not her fault that she's illegitimate. It's mine because I gave birth to her, and chose to, in spite of everything. And it's not even my fault. It's the fault of some drunken lunatic who threw me on the ground and raped me. And you would blame me for it forever, instead of believing me." Her eyes were wounded and cold.

"That's why I came to talk to you. I've been thinking about it," he said cautiously. "I'll admit, this isn't what I expected. And it's not really what I wanted in a wife. But I love you, and I'm willing to overlook and forgive you for your past mistakes. All I'd want from you is that you take a syphilis test and prove to me that you're not carrying the disease."

"That won't be necessary," she said, pulling the door open again, and shivering in the chill wind of the January afternoon. "You don't need to forgive me for my mistakes or anyone else's, or even overlook them. Consuelo won't contaminate your nieces and nephews or family gatherings, because we won't be there. And I don't need to take a test, because you won't ever be getting that close to me."

"That means you have it then," he said, narrowing his eyes at her.

"May I remind you that you told me you wouldn't touch me with the toe of your boot. I remember that distinctly. In fact, I remember everything you said, and I always will. You may be able to forgive me, but I won't be able to forgive you."

"With everything you've done, how dare you?" He suddenly raged at her again. "You're damn lucky I'd be willing to put up with you at all. A woman like you, who's had God knows how many men in your life, syphilitic husbands, illegitimate children, and who can even guess or know who else you've been with between the two and since." She wanted to slap him, but he wasn't worth it. Not anymore.

"I heard everything you said, Antoine. I'll never forget it. Now get out of my house." They were both shivering in the chill breeze, and he stared at her in disbelief.

"You must be joking. Who else do you think would have you after everything you've done?" He looked very grand as he stood there, and very handsome. But what she didn't like anymore was the man inside the well-cut suit.

"Maybe no one," she said, answering his question. "And I don't really care. I've been alone since Josiah left me nine years ago, nearly ten. I have Consuelo, my 'bastard,' as you put it. I don't need anyone else. And I don't want you." She pointed to the open door again. "Thank you for your generous offer, doctor, which I am graciously declining. Now please leave." She had drawn herself up to her full height, and he could see in her eyes that she meant it. It was impossible for him to believe.

He stood inches away from her then and looked down at her in contempt. "You're a fool. No one will ever want you if you tell them the truth."

"I don't plan to be in that position again. You taught me that lesson. Thank you very much for that. I'm sorry this has been a disappointment to us both, and that the truth was so hard for you to believe, and to accept, once I told it to you."

"I told you," he said again, "I would be willing to forgive you, or tolerate it at least, as long as you have the test I require. You have to admit that's only fair."

"Nothing about this is fair. It never was, not before you, or now. And I don't want to be tolerated. I wanted to be loved. I thought I was. Apparently, we both made an enormous mistake." He stood there staring at her, shook his head, and without another word, he walked out. She shut the door behind him, leaned against it, and trembled from head to foot. No man had ever been as kind to her as he had been in the beginning, or as cruel at the end.

She went to sit in the living room all by herself, staring into space.

She still couldn't believe the things he had said to her about Consuelo being a bastard and contaminating his family, or his insistence that she was some kind of trollop because she'd been divorced, and his refusal to believe that she'd been raped.

She was still sitting there, when Brigitte and Consuelo came back from the park. Consuelo climbed onto her lap, looking worried about her, and put her arms around her mother's neck. That was all Annabelle needed now. Her daughter was the only person she could trust, or ever would again.

"I love you, Mama," she said as tears filled her mother's eyes. "I love you too, sweetheart," she said, holding the child close.

And even though she still felt terrible, and looked like she'd been beaten up, and felt it, Annabelle went back to work the next day. There was no other choice. She had to go on with her life. She had learned a terrible lesson with Antoine about how small-minded people were, and the assumptions they made. She had learned that lesson in New York, when everyone believed the worst about her. Antoine had violated her trust and destroyed her faith in the human race once and for all.

Hélène looked worried about her at work, and she was concerned about her for weeks. Annabelle never heard from Antoine again. He had thought Annabelle a fool for not being willing to be "tolerated," and "forgiven" for sins she claimed she didn't commit. He had been entirely willing to believe only the worst.

Annabelle went back to concentrating on her patients and her daughter, and forgot about men. She looked grim for the next few months, but by March she was feeling better. She was actually smiling again, and spending Sunday afternoons in the park with Consuelo.

The little girl had been disappointed at first not to go to the de St. Gris Sunday lunches anymore—she had had fun with Antoine's nephews and nieces. Her mother told her that she and Antoine felt they'd made a mistake and weren't friends anymore. And every time Annabelle thought about what he had said about Consuelo contaminating them, and being unworthy of them, she remembered why she was alone, and intended to stay that way for good. All he had done in the end, other than disappoint her and shatter any hope she had left in the decency of humanity, was convince her of what she already knew—that she would never escape the fate that Josiah had condemned her to, and Harry Winshire had confirmed. All anyone would ever see of her were the labels others had put on her, and what they assumed was her guilt. She was convinced now that no one would ever believe her innocence, trust her, or love her, no matter what she said. Antoine had confirmed every one of her worst fears.

Chapter 25

Annabelle received two letters in the early days of spring. Both gave her food for thought. One was from Lady Winshire, who was inviting her and Consuelo to come for a visit for a few days. She said that she thought it would be good for Consuelo to see where the other half of her family came from and how they lived, that it was part of her ancestry. She was hoping that they would come over as soon as they could. Annabelle thought about it, but wasn't sure. Harry Winshire was a terrible memory for her, and yet what his mother said was true. This wasn't about Harry, it was about Consuelo and the grandmother she had finally met. And she had a feeling that Consuelo would enjoy visiting her.

The other letter was from the man at her father's bank who still managed her affairs. She always had money sent over to live on in France, but the bulk of her fortune had remained in the States. He was asking her, for the first time in a long time, what she wanted to do about the house in Newport. She hadn't been there in ten years, but she had never had the heart to part with it. She had too many memories in that house, and yet she couldn't see herself going back, even for a visit. And that was part of Consuelo's heritage too, far more than Lady Winshire's estates, since Consuelo's father had never been part of their lives.

The man at the bank had written to tell her that he had had a very reasonable offer for the cottage. Blanche, William, and the other servants were still there, maintaining it, and they had lost all hope of seeing her again. She couldn't say that they were wrong. She had had no desire to go back in all these years. She missed it occasionally, but she also knew the miseries of ostracism that she would experience if she went back, even for a visit. There was no one left for her to see. And she was afraid that if she went back, it would open all the old wounds of missing her family again, and all that she had lost, even Josiah. She didn't want to relive that pain. But she didn't feel ready to sell it either, although her banker was right, the offer they had in hand was good. She didn't know what she wanted to do.

She thought about Lady Winshire's offer first, and talked to Consuelo about it at dinner that night. The little girl was instantly enthusiastic and said she wanted to go. And in an odd way, Annabelle did too. She thought it might do them good to get away. Consuelo had been begging to go back to Deauville again, but Annabelle didn't want to go there, after her bitter experience with Antoine. It seemed as though she had bad memories everywhere, and was constantly hiding from her own ghosts.

She answered Lady Winshire's letter the next day, and said they would like to come. Lady Winshire wrote back immediately, offering a choice of dates. In the end, they chose Consuelo's birthday weekend. She would be seven years old. The weather would be a little better by then. Annabelle had Hélène at her office get the tickets and make the plans. They would take the train to Calais, cross the Channel to Dover, and Lady Winshire said she would have someone meet them there. It was only a two-hour drive to their estate.

When the appointed weekend came, Consuelo was so excited she could hardly sit still. They were leaving Brigitte in Paris, where she was planning to spend time with her new boyfriend. Annabelle boarded the train, carrying their two suitcases, and guiding Consuelo along, and they settled into the first-class compartment Hélène had reserved for them. It was the biggest adventure Consuelo had had since they came to Paris two years before, and the weekend in Deauville with Antoine. They no longer spoke about him. Even at her tender age, Consuelo had understood that the subject was painful for her mother and stayed away from it. Annabelle had seen him at the hospital once, and the moment she caught a glimpse of him she had turned away and run up the back staircase to see her patient. She never wanted to speak to him again. His betrayal had been too great.

As the train pulled out of Gare du Nord station, Consuelo was looking at everything with fascination, and Annabelle smiled. They had lunch in the dining car, "like big ladies," as Consuelo said, and then they watched the scenery drift by, until the child finally fell asleep on her mother's lap. Annabelle lay her head back against the seat, thinking of the past few months. They had been hard. It was as though Antoine had taken back not only the dream he had offered her but her hope that things would ever be different in her life.

It seemed now as though she would always be punished for the past. She had been a victim of other people's decisions, weaknesses, and lies. It was depressing to come away from that feeling as though the truth would never come to light and she would never clear her name. No matter how much she had done since, or what she had achieved, what seemed to linger on forever, like a tattoo she could never remove, were the sins she had been branded with, even though they were someone else's. She was a good mother and a fine doctor, a decent person, and in spite of that, she would be labeled by her past, and Consuelo worse than that, forever. Only Antoine had dared to say the word. It was a cruel label for an innocent child.

Just over three hours later, they reached Calais, and boarded the boat. Annabelle was dreading it. She was a decent sailor, but the Channel was always rough and she was afraid that Consuelo would be seasick. As it turned out, it was indeed a rough trip, and Consuelo loved every minute of it. The more the ferry pitched and rolled in the bouncing seas, the more she giggled and squealed and was totally delighted. By the time they reached Dover on the other side, Annabelle was beginning to feel ill, and Consuelo was happier than ever. She bounced right off the boat, holding her mother's hand, and her favorite doll in the other.

Lady Winshire's chauffeur and ancient Rolls were waiting for them on the dock, as promised. The two-hour drive was through gently rolling countryside, with farms and cows and enormous estates, and the occasional ancient castle. As far as Consuelo was concerned, it was a great adventure. And now that they were off the boat, Annabelle was enjoying it too.

But neither of them was prepared for the magnificence of the Winshire estate, and the splendor of the enormous house. There were huge ancient trees bordering the long driveway, and due to Lady Winshire's fortune, independent of the late earl's, the house itself, built in the sixteenth century, was in impeccable condition. The stables were bigger, cleaner, and more beautiful than most homes. Lady Winshire had been a notable horsewoman in her youth, and still liked keeping a stable of fine horses, which half a dozen grooms rode every day.

She came out to greet them on the front steps, looking grander than ever, wearing a deep blue dress, stout walking shoes, the familiar pearls, and another enormous hat. She brandished her silver cane like a sword, pointing it at their suitcases and asking her driver to see to it that the bags got to their rooms. And with a broad smile, after she had hugged both Annabelle and Consuelo, who was looking wide-eyed at everything she saw, she motioned them to follow her inside.

There was an endless gallery lined with serious-looking family portraits, a gigantic living room with a magnificent chandelier, a library lined with miles of ancient books, a music room with two harps and a grand piano, a dining room with a table long enough to seat forty people for the dinner parties they used to give. The reception rooms seemed to go on forever, until they finally reached a small, cozy drawing room where her ladyship liked to sit and gaze out at the gardens. As Annabelle looked at the surroundings, and the splendor of the home, it was hard to believe that anyone who had grown up here could rape a woman, and then threaten to kill her if she told. There were photographs of both the Winshire sons on the mantelpiece in the room where they were sitting. And after they had tea with scones and clotted cream and jam, Lady Winshire asked one of the maids to show Consuelo the stables. She had arranged for a pony to be brought around, if she wanted to try and ride it, and Annabelle thanked her for her kindness to them, and her warm welcome as Consuelo disappeared to see the pony.

"I have a lot to make up for," the older woman said simply, and Annabelle smiled. She didn't hold her responsible for her son's crimes. And how could they be considered crimes when they had resulted in Consuelo, no matter how she had happened. She said as much to Lady Winshire, who thanked Annabelle for her generosity of spirit, and said her son didn't deserve it, much as she had loved him. She confessed sadly that he had been wild and spoiled.

They chatted for a while and strolled in the gardens, and in a little while, one of the grooms appeared, leading Consuelo on the pony. She looked ecstatic. It was clear that the child was having a ball, thanks to her newfound grandmother. Lady Winshire asked if Annabelle would like to ride too. She said she hadn't in years, but might do so the next morning. All of those luxuries and indulgences had gone out of her life when she left the States. It would be fun, Annabelle thought, to ride again. She had done a lot of it in her youth, mostly in Newport in the summer.

After Consuelo and the groom went back to the stables, Annabelle mentioned that she was thinking of selling her house in Newport.

"Why would you sell it?" the older woman asked, with a look of disapproval. "You said it had been in your family for generations. You need to preserve it, if it's part of your history. Not sell it."

"I'm not sure I'll ever go back. I've been gone for ten years. It's just sitting there, unloved and empty, with five servants."

"You should go back," Lady Winshire said firmly. "That's part of Consuelo's history too. She has a right to that, yours, ours, it's all part of who she is, and who she'll become one day. Just as it's a part of you." Clearly, all of that hadn't helped Harry, Annabelle thought to herself, but she wouldn't have said it to his mother, who knew it anyway, and had said as much herself. "You can't run away from who you are, Annabelle. You can't deny it. And Consuelo should see it. You should take her back to visit sometime."

"That's all over for me," Annabelle said, looking stubborn as Lady Winshire shook her head.

"It's only beginning for her. She needs more than Paris in her life, just as you do. She needs all our histories blended together, and offered to her like a bouquet."

"I've had a very good offer. I could always buy a property in France." She never had, though. All she had was her very modest house in the sixteenth arrondissement. She had nothing in the country, and she had to agree, seeing Consuelo here, it was doing her good.

"I suspect you can do that anyway," her ladyship guessed correctly. Annabelle had inherited a very large fortune from her father, and an only slightly smaller one from her mother, and she had hardly spent anything in years. It was no longer in keeping with her lifestyle, or her life as a doctor, and she had been careful not to let any of that show for the past ten years. It spoke well of her, but now, at almost thirty-two, she was old enough to enjoy it.

Lady Winshire turned to her with a smile then. "I hope you'll both come to visit often. I still go to London once in a while, but most of the time I'm here." It had been her late husband's family seat, which had brought her to another thought she had wanted to mention to Annabelle, when Consuelo wasn't around. She wasn't sure if it was too soon to mention it, but it had been much on her mind. "I've been thinking a great deal about Consuelo's situation, because you and her father were never married. That could be a heavy burden for her to carry in a few years, as she gets older. You can't lie to her forever, and one day someone may figure it out. I spoke to our attorneys, and it makes no sense for me to adopt her, and she's your daughter. Harry can't marry you posthumously, which is unfortunate. But I can officially recognize her, which would improve things somewhat, and she could add our name to yours, if that would be acceptable to you," she said cautiously. She didn't want to offend the child's mother, who had been so brave about shouldering all her responsibilities alone. But Annabelle was smiling at her. She had become more sensitive to it herself, ever since Antoine's outrageous insults, especially calling Consuelo a bastard. The thought of it still hurt her now.

"I think that's a lovely idea," Annabelle said gratefully. "It might make things easier for her one day."

"You wouldn't mind?" Lady Winshire looked hopeful.

"I'd like it very much." She associated Lady Winshire with the name, and not her evil son. "That would make her Consuelo Worthington Winshire, or the reverse, whatever you prefer."

"I think Worthington-Winshire would do very well. I can have our attorneys draw up the papers whenever you like." She beamed at Annabelle, who leaned over and hugged her.

"You've been very kind to us," Annabelle said gratefully.

"Why wouldn't I be?" she said gruffly. "You're a good woman. I can see what a wonderful mother you've been to her. Somehow, in spite of everything, you've managed to become a doctor. And from what I've been told, you're a good one." Her own physician had discreetly checked, through connections he had in France. "In spite of what my son did to you, you've recovered, and you don't hold it against the child, or even against me. I'm not even sure you hold it against him, and I'm not sure I could have done that in your place. You're respectable, re-sponsible, decent, hard-working. You worked like a Trojan during the war. You have no family behind you. You've done it all on your own, with no one to help you. You were brave enough to have a child out of wedlock and make the best of it. I can't think of a single thing about you not to respect or like. In fact, I think you're quite remarkable, and I'm proud to know you." What she said brought tears to Annabelle's eyes. It was the antidote to everything Antoine had said.

"I wish I could see it the way you do," Annabelle said sadly. "All I see are my mistakes. And all people seem to see, except for you, are the labels others have put on me." She confessed one of her darkest secrets then, and told her she had been divorced before she left the States, and told her why. It only made Lady Winshire admire her more.

"That's quite an amazing story," she said, thinking about it for a moment. She wasn't easily shocked, and the story of Annabelle's mar-riage to Josiah only made her feel sorry for Annabelle. "It was foolish of him to think he could pull it off."

"I think he believed he could, and then found he couldn't. And his friend was always close at hand. It must have made it even more diffi-cult for him."

"People are such fools sometimes," Lady Winshire said, shaking her head. "And it was even more foolhardy of him to think that divorcing you wouldn't blacken your name. It's all very nice to say he was trying to free you up for someone else. Divorcing you for adultery in order to do it only threw you to the wolves. He might as well have burned you at the stake in a public place. Really, men can be so ignorant and selfish at times. I don't suppose you can undo that very easily now." Annabelle shook her head. "You just have to tell yourself that you don't care. You know the truth. That's all that matters."

"It won't stop people from slamming their doors in my face," Annabelle said wistfully. "And Consuelo's."

"Do you really care about those people?" Lady Winshire asked honestly. "If they're mean-spirited enough to do that to you, and to her, then they're not good enough for either of you, rather than the reverse." Annabelle told her about her recent experience with Antoine then, and she was outraged. "How dare he say things like that to you? There is nothing more small-minded and downright vicious than the self-righteousness of the so-called bourgeoisie. He would have made you miserable, my dear. You were quite right not to let him come back. He wasn't worthy of you." Annabelle smiled at what she said, and had to agree. She was sad about what had happened, but once she had discovered who Antoine was, she didn't miss him. She just missed the dream of what she had hoped they would have, but clearly never would. It had been an illusion. A beautiful dream that turned into a nightmare with his ugly words and assumptions. He was far too willing to believe the worst of her, whether true or not.

Consuelo came bounding into the room then, excited about all the horses she had seen in the barn, and the ride on the pony. And she was even more so when she saw her room. It was a big, sunny chamber, decorated in flowered silks and chintz, and it adjoined her mother's room, which was more of the same. And that night at dinner, they told her about her new double name.

"It sounds hard to spell," Consuelo said practically, and both her mother and grandmother laughed.

"You'll get used to it," her mother said. She was more grateful than ever for Lady Winshire's legal acknowledgment of her child. It might avoid her ever being called a bastard again, by someone as cruel as Antoine.

They played cards after dinner, and eventually all three of them went up to bed. Consuelo was already half asleep and leaning against her mother. In the end, she slept in Annabelle's bed. And she headed straight out to the barn again the next morning as soon as she was dressed.

The two women talked easily all day, about assorted topics, everything from politics to medicine to novels. Her ladyship was intelligent and extremely well read. Their exchanges reminded Annabelle of the ones she had shared with her own mother, and she had given Annabelle much to think about with their conversation on the first day, about Annabelle not being daunted by the labels people had put on her unfairly. She kept reminding her throughout the weekend that she was a good woman. It made Annabelle feel proud of herself, and not like the pariah she had been when she left New York. Antoine's words had just been more of the same, and worse because they came from someone she loved, and whom she had believed loved her.

On the last day, at lunch in the garden, Consuelo's grandmother had a surprise for her. She had one of the grooms join them at dessert, when they served Consuelo's birthday cake, and he was holding a hatbox tied with a big pink bow. Both Consuelo and her mother thought she was being given a riding hat to wear when she came back. And then Annabelle saw the box shake slightly and began to suspect what was in it. The groom held the box firmly while Consuelo undid the bow and cautiously took off the lid. And as soon as she did, a small black face was peering at her and leaped out of the box into her hands. It was a little black and fawn pug puppy, just like Lady Winshire's own dogs, and Consuelo was so excited she could hardly speak as the little dog licked her face. Both women were smiling at her, and Consuelo turned to her grandmother and threw her arms around her neck.

"Thank you! She's so wonderful! What shall I name her?"

"That's up to you, my dear." Lady Winshire was beaming. This unexpected grandchild had become a great joy in her life.

They were all sad to leave each other when Consuelo and her mother got back in the car to return to Dover, for the long boat and train trip back to Paris. Lady Winshire reminded them to come back soon. Consuelo thanked her again for the puppy, who still didn't have a name, but was very excited to be going on the trip. And Lady Winshire reminded Annabelle discreetly that she'd be sending her the papers about Consuelo as soon as they were drawn up.

She stood on the front steps waving as they drove away, and Consuelo played with the puppy all the way back to Paris. She told her mother it was the best birthday she had ever had, and it had been good for Annabelle too.

The day after they got home, Annabelle wrote to the attorneys and told them not to sell the cottage in Newport. And in her office the next morning, she asked Hélène to book passage on a ship to New York in June, with a return to Paris in July. She had taken all of Lady Winshire's advice to heart.

Chapter 26

In the third week of June, Annabelle, Consuelo, and Brigitte set sail on the *Mauretania.* It was the same ship her parents and Robert had sailed on, going to Europe, on their final, fateful voyage. Knowing that was poignant for Annabelle. They left Le Havre on a brilliantly sunny warm day, and had two beautiful staterooms side by side on an upper deck.

The *Mauretania* was one of the largest, fastest, most luxurious ships afloat. Annabelle had also sailed on her sixteen years before with her parents. And she had reserved two of the magnificent ship's largest staterooms. Frequent travelers loved her for her spacious cabins, even in second class, which was rare, and particularly in first.

Consuelo was beside herself with excitement. Brigitte was nervous about the crossing. She had had a distant relative in steerage on the *Titanic,* who didn't survive. And she started crying and crossing herself almost the moment they came on board, talking about the earlier disaster, which annoyed her employer. Annabelle didn't want her frightening Consuelo, and reminding her of how her grandfather and uncle had died. Brigitte was sparing them no details, of all she'd heard and read about at the time, including the screams from dying people in the water.

"Is that true, Mama?" The child looked up at her with wide eyes. She couldn't even imagine a ship this big going down. Consuelo knew the story, but not the details.

"Some of it," Annabelle said honestly. "Sometimes bad things happen, but not very often. That was a long, long time ago, and many, many, many ships have gone back and forth across the ocean since then without a problem. This one has been traveling safely for eighteen years, and there won't be icebergs in our path on this trip. Look how beautiful and sunny it is, and how big the ship is. I promise you, we will be fine," she said gently, and flashed a warning look at Brigitte over the child's head.

"The *Titanic* was bigger . . . and what about the *Lusitania?*" Brigitte insisted, and Annabelle wanted to strangle her for frightening her child.

"What's the loofamania?" Consuelo asked, getting the name garbled.

"Brigitte is just scared and being silly. I promise you, we're going to have a fantastic trip. And we're going to do lots of fun things in New York, and see my old house in Newport." For different reasons, she was as nervous as Brigitte. She wasn't worried about the ship sinking this time, particularly in peacetime, but it was going to be her first time back in New York in ten years, and she was anxious about what it would feel like, and about facing the ghosts and traumas she had left there. But she agreed with Lady Winshire. It was all part of Consuelo's ancestry, and she had a right to see it, and learn more about it, just as she did about the Winshire side. And Annabelle couldn't hide from it forever. It had taken her a long time to go back. The war had been a good excuse not to for a long time, and medical school later. But the war had been over for nearly seven years, Consuelo's entire lifetime. It was long enough. But she didn't need to hear the details of the sinking of the *Titanic,* courtesy of Brigitte, complete with dying screams from the water, thank you very much. And she told her so in no uncertain terms when Consuelo stepped away to pet someone's dog. There were many traveling on the ship. And children for Consuelo to play with.

She asked Brigitte to start unpacking, to keep her busy, and Annabelle took Consuelo to see the swimming pool, the spectacular dining room, the game rooms, and the dog kennels on another deck. They had left her pug at home with Hélène, who adored her. Consuelo had named her Coco.

As the ship pulled out of the harbor, all three women stood on deck and watched France disappear slowly behind them. Consuelo was begging to go play shuffleboard, and Annabelle had promised her they would that afternoon. And that night, she and her mother dined in the stately dining room. This was a very different trip from the one Annabelle had made coming to Europe ten years before, when she had rarely left her stateroom, and she had no idea what lay in store for her when she reached her destination. All Annabelle had wanted then was to flee the people who had blackballed her in New York. And now, at last, ten years later, she was going back.

Everything went pleasantly, until on the third day out, Annabelle saw an older couple standing near the shuffleboard game, with a younger couple who were obviously their married children. They were staring at her, but she pretended not to recognize them, as she and Consuelo drifted past. Annabelle instantly began an animated conversation with her daughter, so she didn't have to acknowledge the people she had recognized at once. They had been acquaintances of her parents. As she and Consuelo walked past them, she heard the older woman speak to her husband in an undervoice that carried clearly across the deck.

"...married to Josiah Millbank...don't you remember...Arthur Worthington's daughter...some dreadful scandal...she had an affair and he divorced her...she ran off with the other man to France..." So that was what they thought, Annabelle realized with a shudder. And they still remembered. She wondered if they all did. It had truly been a life sentence, and she was never to be paroled or pardoned. She was an adulteress forever.

It shocked her to realize that some people thought she had gone to France with a man. Just hearing it made her want to run to her room and hide. And then she thought of Lady Winshire's words to her. "Hold your head high, Annabelle. You're a good woman. You don't care about them." And as she listened to her words echo in her head, she realized that Lady Winshire was right, to some extent. She did care, she didn't want to be a pariah, she hated the labels they used on her...adulteress being the worst of all...but she wasn't an adulteress and never had been. She had been faithful to her husband, she had been a good woman then, and still was now. Nothing had changed, divorced or not. And after all these years, what did they care about why she had gone to Europe, or with whom? None of them had been there for her, to support her, console her, or embrace her in the losses she had sustained. Her life might have been different if they had. But if so, she would never have gone to Europe, become a doctor, or had Consuelo at her side. So she was the winner in the end.

On their way back from another visit to the dog kennels, to visit with a sweet black pug, Annabelle strolled past them again, holding Consuelo's hand. And this time she looked the woman in the eye, and acknowledged her with a nod. Annabelle was wearing a chic cloche hat that matched the gray silk suit she had purchased for the trip, and she looked very stylish, and no longer American, but French. The moment Annabelle nodded at her, the woman rushed forward with a broad, false smile, gushing words of greeting.

"My goodness, Annabelle, is that you? After all these years! How are you, and what a beautiful little girl. She must be yours, she looks just like you ... is your husband on board?"

"No," Annabelle said, shaking hands politely with both of them, "I'm a widow. And this is my daughter, Consuelo Worthington-Winshire." Consuelo curtsied politely in the pretty dress she'd chosen to wear that day, with white gloves and a hat.

"Ahh ... how dear ... you've named her for your mother. Such a wonderful woman. Are you still living in France?"

"Yes, in Paris," Annabelle said coolly.

"Do you never come to New York? We haven't seen you there in dogs' years."

"This is my first time back, since I left," because of two-faced people like you, she wanted to say, who kept the rumors going forever and ever, had slapped the labels on her, and would never let anyone forget.

"That's hard to believe. And the cottage in Newport?"

"We're going up in a few weeks. I want Consuelo to see it." The child spoke English with just a hint of a French accent, which was very sweet. "And we have lots to see in New York," she said, smiling at her daughter, as they were about to walk away. At least the woman had talked to her. That was something of an improvement. Ten years before, she wouldn't have. She would simply have turned her back, and not spoken to her at all. At least now she pretended to be pleasant, no matter what she thought of her or said behind her back.

"Perhaps we'll see you in Newport," the older woman said, still curious about her, as she looked at Annabelle's expensive suit and hat and Consuelo's pretty dress. "What do you do to keep busy in Paris?" she asked nosily, clearly wanting more details about Annabelle's life, so she could gossip about her when she went back. It was written all over her. She had also noticed Lady Winshire's handsome emerald along with the wedding band Annabelle still wore. It was the one she had bought herself, before Consuelo was born, and never taken off, just a narrow gold band.

"I'm a physician," Annabelle said, smiling at her, remembering Lady Winshire's words again, and this time she almost laughed. These people were so small and unimportant, so petty, like scavengers, looking for things that sparkled in the rubbish so they could carry them to others, or trade them for the reputations of good people, who were worth ten of them.

"You *are*? How *amazing!*" The woman's eyes almost fell out of her head. "How ever did you do that?"

Annabelle smiled benevolently at her. "I went to medical school in France, after my husband died."

"Was he a doctor as well?"

"No," she said simply. The husband who had died did not exist. "Consuelo's father was the Viscount Winshire. He was killed in the war, at Ypres." All of that was true. She had not told a lie about

Consuelo's father. And it was none of her business, and never would be, that they hadn't been married. It didn't diminish her accomplishments, or the good she had done in the world.

"Of course," the woman said with a sniff, far more impressed than she wanted to admit, but she could hardly wait for Annabelle to leave so she could tell her daughter, whom Annabelle scarcely recognized she had gotten so fat, and had hardly known before she left. She was playing shuffleboard with friends.

And a moment later, Annabelle and Consuelo walked on.

"Who was that?" Consuelo asked with interest.

"Just someone my parents knew in New York," she said, feeling better than she had in a long time. Antoine had struck hard. And those who had come before him had taken their toll as well. But suddenly all of them seemed to be losing their effect on her.

"She has mean eyes," Consuelo said wisely, and her mother laughed.

"Yes, she does. And a mean mouth. I used to know a lot of people like that."

"Is everyone in New York like that?" Consuelo looked worried.

"I hope not," Annabelle said brightly. "But we're not going there for them. We're going there for us." And she was no longer willing to stay away and hide from them either. They didn't own Newport and New York. She had her own world now, with her life in Paris, her patients, her practice, and her child. The only thing missing in her life was a man, but if she had to be belittled, humiliated, and "forgiven" by men like Antoine, who didn't believe or respect her, then she preferred to be alone. She was fine.

The crossing passed uneventfully. They had a lovely time. Annabelle and Consuelo ate in the dining room together every night, and when the captain invited her to join his table one night, Annabelle politely declined. She preferred to dine with her daughter, than amid the nonsense and hypocrisies of people like the friends of her parents she had met on board.

As they steamed into New York harbor, assisted by tugs, Annabelle felt a lump in her throat as she saw the Statue of Liberty, standing proudly with her torch aloft. It was a moving moment, as though she had been waiting just for them. She pointed out Ellis Island to her daughter, and explained what she had done there, before she was a doctor, and that it had been an impossible dream for her then.

"Why, Mama? Why couldn't you be a doctor here?" She didn't understand. Her mother being a doctor seemed the most natural thing in the world to her, and she wanted to be one too, and might well be one day.

"Because women didn't do that very often. They still don't. People think they should be married and have babies and stay home."

"Can't you do both?" Consuelo looked at her with a puzzled expression.

"I think you can," she said, looking at the Statue of Liberty again. It was a reminder to all that the light of freedom never dimmed. Even if you closed your eyes, she was still there, lighting the way for all, men, women, rich, and poor. Freedom belonged to everyone, and to Annabelle now too.

Consuelo was looking pensive then. "If we were married, like to Antoine or someone like him, would you stop being a doctor?"

"No, I wouldn't." She offered no comment about Antoine, who had called her child a bastard. She would never forgive him for that. And hadn't been able to forgive him for the rest.

When they tied up at the dock and cleared customs, they found two cabs to take them and their luggage to the Plaza Hotel. It had a lovely view of the park, and was in walking distance of her old house. Annabelle was shocked at how New York had changed, how many new buildings had appeared, how much more crowded it seemed. Consuelo was fascinated by it, and as soon as they settled in and had lunch, she and her mother set out on foot to explore the city.

It was inevitable that they went to her old house first. Annabelle couldn't help herself. She had to see it. It was in good repair, although the shutters were closed and it looked unoccupied. She supposed that the new owners were away for the summer. Annabelle stood staring at it for a long time as Consuelo held her hand.

"That's where I lived as a little girl." She was about to say "until I was married" but stopped herself. She had never told Consuelo about Josiah, although she knew she would one day.

"It must have been very sad when your papa and brother died," Consuelo said solemnly, as though visiting their grave, which in a way it was. And her mother's. She had died in that house. And Annabelle had been born there.

"Your Grandmother Consuelo lived there too."

"Was she nice?" Consuelo asked with interest as her mother smiled.

"Very. And she was beautiful, just like you. She was a wonderful, kind person. And I loved her very much."

"You must miss her very much too," Consuelo said softly.

"Yes, I do." Standing there, Annabelle remembered the morning she learned that the *Titanic* had gone down, and the day her mother died. But she remembered the happy memories too. The days of her childhood when everything had been so simple and easy for her. She had had a golden life among loving people who protected her from all harm. And in the years after, she had paid her dues for everything she had now.

They walked away slowly, and Annabelle took Consuelo to see other landmarks in her life. She told her about her debut ball. And they visited her grandfather's bank, where Annabelle introduced Consuelo to the manager and several employees she still knew. Consuelo politely curtsied and shook hands. At the end of the afternoon, they came back to the Palm Court at the Plaza for tea. It was very impressive, and they saw beautifully dressed, stylish women wearing extravagant hats and jewels, chatting and enjoying teatime under the enormous skylight.

Consuelo loved New York, and Annabelle was happier than she had expected to be. It was nice to come back, and fun to show it all to her daughter. Lady Winshire had been so right, it was a piece of her own history and her daughter's, and it was important for Consuelo to see where her mother had grown up. They stayed for a week, and Annabelle saw no one she knew. There wasn't a soul she wanted to see. By the end of the week, she was anxious to get to Newport and the cottage. She knew Consuelo would love it there, just as she had as a child. Independent of the social life that was so essential to the residents, the ocean and the beach and all the natural beauty were even more appealing than the cottages that were so vital to their owners and all who knew them.

They checked out of the Plaza and took the train to Boston, and her parents' old butler William was waiting at the station for them with one of her parents' old cars that they still kept in Newport. He began to cry the moment he saw her, and bowed when he met Consuelo, who was very impressed by how old he was, and how respectful to her. And she felt so sorry for him when he cried that she stood on tiptoe to kiss him. He and Annabelle both had damp eyes when they greeted each other. The staff knew about Consuelo from Annabelle's letters to Blanche, but they were not entirely clear on who her father was or when the marriage had happened. From what they could gather, he had been killed shortly after he and Annabelle were married. William looked at Consuelo with misty eyes and a nostalgic expression.

"She looks just like you at her age. And there's a little bit of your mother." He helped them settle into the car, and they set off on the seven-hour drive to Newport, with Consuelo observing and commenting on everything along the way. William explained it all to her. And here again, Annabelle found that much had changed, though not in Newport itself. As they drove into town, it looked as venerable as ever. And Consuelo's eyes grew wide when she saw the cottage and the vast expanse of land it sat on. It was an imposing estate, and they had kept it in perfect condition.

"It's almost as big as Grandmother's house in England," Consuelo said, in awe of the enormous home, and her mother smiled. It looked just as she had remembered, and brought her back to her own childhood with a sudden pang.

"Not quite," Annabelle assured Consuelo. "Your grandmother's house is bigger. But I had some wonderful summers here." Until the last one. Coming back here brought up so many memories of Josiah, and the terrible end to their marriage. But it made her think of their happier beginnings as well, when she was young and all was hopeful. She was thirty-two years old now, and so much had changed. But it still felt like home to her.

As soon as the car stopped, Blanche and the others came running out of the cottage. She wrapped her arms around Annabelle and couldn't stop crying. She looked much older, and when she saw Consuelo, she hugged her too. And like William, she told Annabelle that her daughter looked just like her.

"And you're a doctor now!" Blanche still couldn't believe it. She could believe even less that she had finally come home. They had thought she never would. And they had been deathly afraid she would sell the house. It was their home too. And they had kept everything in pristine condition for her. It looked as though she had left the day before, not ten years ago. Those ten years seemed like an entire lifetime, and yet when she saw the house again, the time since she'd last seen it melted away to nothing.

It made Annabelle miss her mother again, as she walked past her bedroom. She was staying in one of the guest rooms and had given Consuelo and Brigitte her old nursery for Consuelo to play in. But most of the time, she would be outdoors, as Annabelle had been at her age. She couldn't wait to take Consuelo swimming, which they did that afternoon.

Annabelle told her that she had learned to swim here, just as Consuelo had learned in Nice and Antibes.

"The water is colder here," Consuelo commented, but she liked it. She loved playing in the waves, and walking down the beach.

Later that afternoon, when they went back to the house from the beach, Annabelle left her with Brigitte. She wanted to go for a walk by herself. There were some memories she didn't want to share. She was just leaving the house, when Consuelo came running down the stairs to join her, and Annabelle didn't have the heart to tell her she couldn't come. She was so happy there, discovering her mother's old world, which was so different from the one they lived in now, with their tiny, comfortable house in the sixteenth arrondissement. Everything in her old world seemed huge to her now, and to her child.

The house she had wanted to see was not far, and when she got there she saw that the trees were overgrown, the shutters closed, and it was in disrepair. Blanche had told her it had been sold in the past two years, but it looked like no one lived there, and it hadn't been used in a decade. It appeared deserted. It was Josiah's old house, where she had spent her married summers, and where he and Henry had continued their affair, but she didn't think about that now. She only thought of him. And Consuelo could see that this house had been important to her mother too, although it was small and dark, and looked sad.

"Did you know the people who lived here, Mama?"

"Yes, I did," Annabelle said softly. She could almost feel him near her as she said the words, and she hoped he was peaceful now. She had long since forgiven him. There was nothing left to forgive. He had done the best he could, and loved her in his own way. And she had loved him too. There was none of the raw disappointment and betrayal she still felt at Antoine's hands, more recently. The scars of what had happened with Josiah had faded years before.

"Did the people die?" Consuelo asked sadly. It looked that way, judging by the condition of the house.

"Yes, they did."

"A nice friend?" Consuelo was curious why her mother looked so far away and shaken by being there. And Annabelle hesitated for a long moment. Maybe it was time. She didn't want to lie about her history to her forever. The lie that she'd been married to Consuelo's father was enough, and one day she would tell her the truth about that too, not that she'd been raped, but that they hadn't been married. Now that Lady Winshire had acknowledged her, it wouldn't be quite as onerous, though still hard to explain.

"This house belonged to a man named Josiah Millbank," she said quietly, as they peeked into the garden. It was completely overgrown, and looked entirely deserted, which it was. "I was married to him. We got married here in Newport when I was nineteen." Consuelo looked at her with wide eyes, as they sat down on an old log. "I was married to him for two years, and he was a wonderful man. I loved him very much." She wanted her to know that part too, not just that it had gone wrong.

"What happened to him?" Consuelo asked in a small voice. So many people had died in her mother's life. Everyone was gone.

"He got very sick, and he decided that he didn't want to be married to me anymore. He didn't think it would be fair to me, because he was so sick. So he went to Mexico, and he divorced me, which means that he ended our marriage."

"But didn't you want to be with him even though he was so sick, to take care of him?" She looked shocked, and Annabelle smiled as she nodded.

"Yes, I did. But that wasn't what he wanted. He thought he was doing a good thing for me, because I was very young. He was a lot older.

Old enough to be my father. And he thought I should marry someone else who wasn't sick and have lots of children."

"Like my father," she said proudly, and then a cloud passed her eyes. "But then he died too." It was all very sad, and made her realize, even at seven, all that her mother had been through, and come out the other end, whole, and alive, and even a doctor.

"Anyway, he divorced me, and went to Mexico." She didn't tell her about Henry. She didn't need to know. "And everyone here was very shocked. They thought he divorced me because I did something wrong. He never told anyone he was sick, and neither did I. So they thought I had done something terrible, and I was very sad. I went to France, and went to work in the war. And then I met your father, and had you. And everyone lived happily ever after," she said with a smile, as she took Consuelo's hand in her own. It was a highly edited version, but it was all Consuelo needed to know. And her marriage to Josiah was no longer a secret. It seemed better that way. She didn't want to keep secrets, or tell lies to cover them anymore. And she had been fair to Josiah in the story. She always had been.

"But why was everyone so mean to you when he went away?" That seemed horrible to Consuelo, and so unfair to her mother.

"Because they didn't understand. They didn't know what had really happened. So they told bad stories about it, and about me."

"Why didn't you tell them the truth?" That part made no sense to her at all.

"He didn't want me to. He didn't want anyone to know he was sick." Nor why, which was far more understandable. Not to mention the part about Henry Orson.

"That was silly of him," Consuelo said, glancing over her shoulder at the empty house.

"Yes, it was."

"Did you ever see him again?"

Annabelle shook her head. "No. He died in Mexico. I was in France by then."

"Do people know the truth now?" Consuelo asked, still looking pensive. She didn't like that part of the story at all, when they'd been mean to her mother. She must have been very sad at the time. She even looked sad talking about it now.

"No, they don't. It's been a long time," Annabelle answered.

"Thank you for telling me, Mama," Consuelo said proudly.

"I was always going to tell you one day, when you were older."

"I'm sorry they were mean to you," she said softly. "I hope they won't be anymore." The only one who had been recently was Antoine. Not just mean, but cruel. It had been the worst betrayal of all, and had reopened all her old wounds. Talking to Lady Winshire about it had helped her. She saw now what a small, petty person Antoine really was, if he couldn't love her, even with her past. She wouldn't have done the same to him. She was a far bigger person.

"It doesn't matter now. I have you," Annabelle reassured her, and it was true. Consuelo was all she needed.

They got up and walked back to their cottage then, and for the next three weeks they played and swam and did all the things Annabelle had done as a child and loved there so much.

It was during their last week there that Annabelle took Consuelo to the Newport Country Club for lunch. It was one of the few grown-up things they had done. Other than that, Annabelle had avoided all the places where she might run into old friends. They had stayed mainly on their own grounds, which were large enough. But this one time, they had decided to go out, which was brave of Annabelle.

And just as they were leaving after lunch, Annabelle saw a portly woman walk toward the restaurant. She looked flustered, red-faced, there was a nanny with her, and she was leading six young children and had a baby on her hip. She was snapping at one of them, the baby was crying, and her hat was askew. And it was only when they were inches from each other that Annabelle saw that it was her old friend Hortie. Both of them were shocked and stopped walking, and stood staring at each other.

"Oh . . . what are *you* doing here?" Hortie said as though Annabelle didn't belong there. And then she tried to cover the awkward moment with a nervous smile. Consuelo was frowning, looking at her. Hortie hadn't even noticed her, she was just staring at her mother as if she'd seen a ghost.

"I'm here with my daughter for a visit." Annabelle smiled at Hortie, feeling sorry for her. "I see the baby factory is still producing," she teased her. Hortie rolled her eyes and groaned, and for an instant looked like the friend Annabelle had loved so dearly, and would never have abandoned.

"You're remarried?" Hortie asked with interest, and then glanced at Consuelo.

"Widowed."

"And she's a doctor," Consuelo piped up proudly, as both women laughed.

"Is that true?" Hortie looked at Annabelle, impressed if it was, but she knew that Annabelle had loved medical things as a young girl.

"It is. We live in Paris."

"So I heard. I was told you were some kind of hero during the war."

Annabelle laughed. "Hardly. I was a medic, riding ambulances to field hospitals to pick up wounded men. Nothing very heroic about that."

"It sounds heroic to me," Hortie said as her gaggle of children swirled around her, and the nanny tried to keep them in control with little success. Hortie didn't apologize for the betrayal or say she'd missed her, but you could see it in her eyes. "Will you be here long?" she asked wistfully.

"A few more days."

But Hortie didn't ask her to come over, or say she would drop by the Worthington cottage. She knew that James would never have allowed it. He thought Annabelle would be a bad influence on her. Divorcées and adulteresses were not welcome in his home, although the stories about him had been far worse.

For a minute, Annabelle wanted to tell her that she'd missed her, but she didn't dare. It was too late for both of them. And seeing her had made her sad. Hortie looked blowsy, tired, and overwhelmed, and wasn't aging well. The pretty young girl she'd been years before was gone. She had become a middle-aged woman with a flock of children, and had turned on her best friend. Annabelle would miss her always. Running into her was like seeing a ghost. They said good-bye without embracing, and Annabelle was quiet as they left the restaurant.

Consuelo didn't speak until they were driving home and then turned to her mother and spoke in a soft voice. "Is that one of the people who said mean things about you?"

"Sort of. She was my best friend when we were growing up, and

314

until then. People do silly things sometimes," Annabelle said, smiling at her. "We were like sisters when we were your age, and even when we grew up."

"She's ugly," Consuelo said, crossing her arms and frowning. She was angry in her mother's defense. "And fat." Annabelle laughed and made no comment.

"She was very pretty as a young girl. She's had a lot of children."

"They're ugly too, and they make a lot of noise," Consuelo said in disapproval and snuggled up to her mother.

"That they do," Annabelle commented. Hortie had never been able to control her children, even when she only had one or two. It looked like James had kept her pregnant ever since.

The rest of their stay in Newport was everything they had both hoped it would be. It was a real homecoming for Annabelle and warmed her heart. And as they packed to leave, Consuelo asked her mother if they could come back again. Annabelle had been thinking the same thing, and was glad she hadn't sold the house. Once again, Lady Winshire had been right. She was, about many things. And her emerald never left Annabelle's hand. It was a gift she cherished, particularly now that they were friends.

"I was thinking that it might be nice to come back every summer for a few weeks. Maybe even a month. What do you think?" Annabelle asked Consuelo, as Brigitte closed her charge's bags.

"I'd like that." Consuelo beamed at her mother.

"So would I." It would keep her connection to the States, and would establish one for her daughter. With time, all things healed. She had felt it while she was there. Even if they still talked about her, and remembered the scandal of years before, if you held your ground for long enough, people forgot. Or at least the ugly labels faded so people didn't bother to read them quite as often anymore. It didn't matter as much to her now. And so much had happened since. She had a whole life of her own somewhere else, a home, a profession, and a child she loved. But she also felt that an old part of her had been returned to her. And it was a part of an old life that she had missed.

William drove them back to Boston, and they took the train to New York. They were only planning to spend two days there this time, and do the few things they had missed when they arrived.

"Take good care of yourself, Miss Annabelle," William said with tears in his eyes again. "Will you be back soon?" They could all see what a good time she'd had. There had been times, at the beach, or running on the lawn with Consuelo, when she looked like a girl again herself.

"Next summer. I promise." The farewells with Blanche had been tearful too, but she had made her the same vow.

William hugged and kissed Consuelo and Annabelle, and stood waving from the platform for as long as they could see him.

And then mother and daughter settled into their compartment for the trip to New York. They had had a wonderful time in Newport. It had exceeded all of Annabelle's hopes.

Chapter 27

Their last two days in New York were hectic but fun. Annabelle took Consuelo to the theater to see a musical and she loved it. They had dinner at Sardi's and the Waldorf Astoria, in grand style. They took a ferry around Manhattan, and Annabelle pointed out Ellis Island to her again, and told her more about it. And on the last afternoon they walked past her old house again, just to say good-bye. Annabelle stood there for a long moment, paying tribute to it, and all of those who had lived there, even the innocent part of herself that had been lost. She no longer had anything in common with the girl she had been then. She had grown up.

She and Consuelo walked away quietly hand in hand. Consuelo had learned much about her mother during this trip, and her grandparents, her uncle Robert, and even some of her mother's friends. She hadn't liked her friend in Newport, the one with all the children. She hated knowing that she had been mean to her mother and made her sad. And she was sorry about the man who had died in Mexico. She could tell that her mother loved him.

This time, Brigitte was slightly less nervous as they boarded the *Mauretania* to go back. The ship had been so comfortable and luxurious on the way over that she had calmed down considerably. It was an odd feeling for Annabelle as they slipped past the old White Star piers, and Cunard. It reminded her suddenly of when she had gone to pick up her mother thirteen years before, after the *Titanic* sank. But she didn't mention it to her daughter, and surely not to Brigitte, who managed to bring it up anyway. Annabelle scowled at her and she stopped.

Annabelle felt herself leaving a piece of her heart behind as they glided past the Statue of Liberty again. She hadn't felt this tied to her own country for a long time and it was a comfort knowing that they'd be back next summer. Consuelo had talked of it constantly in New York. She loved the cottage and couldn't wait to return.

There was no one they knew on the ship this time; Annabelle had checked the passenger list. But she wouldn't have cared. She had nothing to fear. She had braved Newport and New York without incident, and had no more secrets to protect. And even if someone found out about her past, what could they do to her? They couldn't take away her house, her life, her work, her child. All they could do was talk about her, and she had lived through it before. They had nothing that she wanted. Even Hortie's painful betrayal had shrunk in size on this trip when she saw her. All the people who had once hurt her so badly were gone, and they had nothing she wanted anymore. They could take nothing from her. She had her own life, and it was a good one.

Annabelle and Consuelo visited the dog kennels again, as they had on the last trip. There was no pug this time but several Pekingese and poodles. Consuelo had missed Coco, her pug, and couldn't wait to get back to her. Her mother had promised her a weekend in Deauville when they were home. Even Antoine's impact on Annabelle had faded during this trip. He was a nasty little small-minded man, who lived in a tiny world full of people with narrow ideas. There was no room for her in that world. And no place for him in hers.

They were walking back from the dog kennel, and stopped at the rail to look out at the sea. Consuelo's long blond hair was blowing in the breeze, and Annabelle's hat blew off her head and rolled like a wheel down the deck as they chased it, laughing. Annabelle's hair was still as blond as her child's, and the hat stopped finally at the feet of a man who picked it up and handed it to them with a broad grin.

"Thank you," Annabelle said breathlessly, with a girlish smile. The hat had led them a merry chase. Her face was brown from the sun in Rhode Island. She put the hat on again, at a slightly cockeyed angle.

"I think it will blow off again," the man warned her. She agreed and took it off, as Consuelo struck up a conversation with him.

"My grandfather and uncle died on the *Titanic*," she announced, to open the conversation, and he looked at her soberly.

"I'm very sorry to hear that. So did my grandparents. Maybe they met each other." It was an intriguing idea. "That was a very long time ago. Before you were born, I think."

"I'm seven," she said, which confirmed it. "And I'm named after my mother's mother. She's dead too." He tried not to smile at the conversation, and it sounded as though their family had been decimated. "So's my father," she added for good measure. "He died before I was born, in the war."

"Consuelo!" Annabelle scolded her, startled. She had never heard her give out so much information, and she hoped she didn't do it often. "I'm sorry," she turned to the man who had retrieved her hat.

"We didn't mean to give you our death rolls." She was smiling at him, and he smiled back.

"You must have known that I'm a journalist," he said to Consuelo kindly.

"What's that?" She was interested in what he had to say.

"I write for newspapers. Or actually, I publish one. The *International Herald Tribune* in Paris. You won't have to read it till you're older." He smiled at them both again.

"My mother is a doctor." She was conducting the conversation with him entirely on her own, as Annabelle looked slightly embarrassed.

"Really?" he said with interest, and introduced himself, and said his name was Callam McAffrey, originally from Boston, and now Paris.

Annabelle introduced them as well, and Consuelo volunteered that they lived in Paris too, in the sixteenth arrondissement. He said that he lived on the rue de l'Université, on the Left Bank. It was near the college of Beaux Arts, and Annabelle knew the area well.

He invited them both to tea, but Annabelle said they had to get back to their stateroom to dress for dinner. He smiled as they walked away. He thought the little girl was adorable, and the mother very pretty. She didn't look like his vision of a doctor. He had interviewed Elsie Inglis several years before, and Annabelle didn't look anything like her, to say the least. He was amused at how liberal her daughter had been with their family information, somewhat to her mother's dismay.

He saw them in the dining room that night, but didn't approach. He didn't want to intrude. But he noticed Annabelle on deck alone the next day, walking quietly by herself. Consuelo had gone swimming with Brigitte. And this time Annabelle was wearing a hat that tied under her chin.

"I see you've anchored your hat on solidly," he said, smiling at her, as he stopped for a moment to stand by the rail next to her. She turned to him with a smile.

"It's breezier now than it was last month when we came over." It was the end of July.

"I love these crossings," he volunteered, "in spite of our respective losses at sea and family tragedies. It gives you a chance to catch your breath, between two lives and two worlds. It's nice to have some time out to do that sometimes. Have you been in New York all this time?" he asked with interest. He was pleasant to talk to.

"Some of it. We've been in Newport for the past few weeks."

He smiled. "I was in Cape Cod. I try to get back every summer. It takes me back to my childhood."

"This was my daughter's first visit."

"How did she like it?"

"She loved it. She wants to come back every summer." And then she volunteered a small piece of information about herself. "I hadn't been back in ten years."

"To Newport?" That didn't surprise him.

"To the States." That piece of information did.

"That's a long time." He was a tall, spare-looking man with salt and pepper hair, warm brown eyes, and a chiseled face, somewhere in his early forties. He appeared more intelligent than handsome, although his appearance was pleasant. "You must have been busy to stay away for so long. Or angry about something," he added, in the spirit of good journalism, and she laughed.

"Not angry. Just finished. I made my life in France. I went over to volunteer at the front, in a hospital, and I never went back. I didn't think I missed it. But I have to admit, it was nice to go home, and show old landmarks to my daughter."

"You're widowed?" he inquired. It was an easy assumption to make, since Consuelo had told him her father was dead, and had been for the whole seven years she'd been alive. Annabelle started to nod her head, and then stopped herself. She was tired of the lies, especially the ones she didn't have to tell, to protect someone else, or even herself from the unkind.

"Divorced." He didn't react to it, but looked puzzled. To some, it would have been a startling admission. But he didn't seem to care.

"I thought your daughter said that her father died." Annabelle looked at him for a long moment, and decided to throw caution to the winds. She had nothing to lose. If he was shocked and walked away, she didn't care if she never saw him again. She didn't know the man.

"I wasn't married to her father." She said it quietly, but firmly. It was the first time she had said that to anyone. In the circles she had grown up in, it would have been cause to end the conversation immediately, and ignore her from then on.

He didn't answer for a moment and then nodded, and looked at her with a smile. "If you're expecting me to fall over in a faint, or jump overboard rather than talk to you, I'm afraid you'll be disappointed. I'm a reporter. I've heard a lot in my day. And I live in France. It seems to be a pretty common occurrence there, although they don't admit it. They just have children with other people's wives." She laughed, and he wondered if that was the case and the cause of her divorce. She was an interesting woman. "I suspect it happens more often than we know or want to believe, even at home. People have children with people they love but don't marry. As long as no one gets hurt, who am I to say they're wrong? I've never been married myself." He was a very open-minded man.

"I didn't love him," she added. "It's a long story. But it turned out all right. Consuelo is the best thing in my life." He didn't comment, but seemed fine with what she'd said.

"What kind of doctor are you?"

"A good one," she said with a smile, and he laughed in response.

"I would assume that. I meant what specialty." She knew what he meant, but enjoyed playing with him. He was nice to talk to. He was open and warm and friendly.

"General medicine."

"Did you practice at the front?" He didn't think she was old enough to have done so.

"As a medic, after a year of medical school. I finished after the war." It was interesting to him that she didn't want to practice in the States, but he could see why. He loved Paris too. He had a much richer life there than he had had in New York or Boston.

"I went over to be a reporter for the British at the beginning of the war. And I've been in Europe ever since. I lived in London for two years after the war, and I've been in Paris now for five years. I don't think I could ever go back to live in the States. My life is too good here in Europe."

"I couldn't go back either," Annabelle agreed. And she had no reason to go back. Her life was in Paris now. Only her history was in the States, and the cottage.

They chatted for a little longer, and then she went to find Consuelo and Brigitte at the pool. They saw him again that night, as they left the dining room after an early dinner. He was just going in, and he asked Annabelle if she'd like to have a drink later on. She hesitated, as Consuelo watched them both, and then she agreed. They made a date at the Verandah Café for nine-thirty. Consuelo would be in bed by then, so she was free.

"He likes you," Consuelo said matter-of-factly, as they walked back to their cabins. "He's nice."

Annabelle didn't comment. She had thought that about Antoine too, and she'd been wrong. But Callam McAffrey was a different type, and they had more in common. She wondered why he'd never married, and he told her that night, as they sipped champagne at the Verandah Café, which was open to the sea air.

"I fell in love with a nurse in England during the war. She was killed a week before the armistice was signed. We were going to get married, but she didn't want to until the war was over. It took me a long time to get over it." It had been six and a half years. "She was a very special woman. From a very fancy family, but you'd never know it. She was very down to earth, and worked harder than anyone I've ever known. We had a good time together." He didn't sound maudlin about it, but as though he cherished the memory still. "I visit her family from time to time."

"Consuelo's father was British. But not a very nice man, I'm afraid. His mother is terrific though. We'll probably visit her in August."

"When the British are great, they're fantastic," he said generously. "I don't always get along as well with the French." Annabelle laughed ruefully, thinking of Antoine, but said nothing. "They're not always as straightforward, and tend to be more complicated."

"I think I'd agree with that, in some cases. They make wonderful friends and colleagues. Romantically, that's another thing." He could tell just from the little she said that she'd been burned, presumably by a Frenchman. But Consuelo's British father didn't sound like a peach either. It seemed to him as though Annabelle had had more than her fair share of lemons. And in his day, so had he, other than Fiona, the nurse he'd been in love with. And he had been alone now for a while. He was taking a break from romance. His life was simpler that way, which was the same conclusion Annabelle had come to.

They talked about the war for a while, politics in the States, some of his experiences in journalism, and hers in medicine. And if nothing else, she thought he'd make a nice friend. He walked her back to her stateroom eventually, and said a friendly but polite goodnight.

He invited her for a drink again the next day, and they had a very nice time. He played shuffleboard with Annabelle and Consuelo on the last day of the trip, and she invited him to dinner with them that night. He and Consuelo got along very well, and she told him all about her dog, and invited him to come and see her, while Annabelle made no comment.

They had a last drink that night, and out of the blue, as he walked her back to her cabin, he said that he'd like to come and see the dog. He had a Labrador himself. Annabelle laughed at what he said.

"You're welcome to come and see the dog anytime," she said. "You can even come and see us."

"Well, my main interest is actually the dog," he said, with a twinkle in his eye, "but I guess it would be all right to see both of you too, if the dog doesn't mind." He looked gently down at Annabelle then. He had learned a lot about her on the trip, more than she knew. That was his job. He could sense the pain and trials she'd been through. Women of her upbringing didn't leave their homes at twenty-two, and volunteer to go three thousand miles from home, to serve in a war that wasn't theirs. And they didn't stay there afterward, and take on the profession she had, unless some pretty bad things had happened to them at home. And he had a feeling a few more had happened since. She wasn't the kind of woman, he felt sure, to have a child out of wedlock, unless she had absolutely no other choice. And she had clearly made the best of it, and everything that had happened to her. She was a good woman. It was written all over her, and he was hoping to see her again.

"I'd like to call you when we get back," he said properly. She wasn't stiff, but she was always ladylike and correct, and he liked that about her too. She reminded him of Fiona in some ways, although Annabelle was younger and prettier. But what he had liked most about Fiona, and now Annabelle, was what was inside. You could tell she was a woman of determination and integrity, high morals, with an enormous heart, and a fine mind. A man couldn't ask for more than that, and if a woman like Annabelle crossed your path, you didn't miss the opportunity to get to know her better. Women like her didn't come around often in a lifetime. He'd already been lucky enough to have one in his life, and he knew that if he ever had the good fortune to meet another, he wasn't going to miss the chance.

"We'll be in Paris," Annabelle said to him. "We might go to Deauville for a few days. I promised Consuelo we would. And maybe to England to see her father's family for a bit. But we'll be around. I have to get back to work, before my patients forget that I exist." He couldn't imagine anyone doing that who had ever known her. And he didn't intend to lose track of her.

"Maybe the three of us could do something this weekend," he said pleasantly, "with the dog of course. I wouldn't want to hurt her feelings." Annabelle smiled in answer. The weekend was only a few days away, and she liked the idea. In fact, she liked everything she had learned about him on the trip. And she had a good feeling about him, of solidity, integrity, warmth, and kindness. Their respect for each other was mutual so far. It was a good start, better than most she'd had. Her brotherly friendship with Josiah should have told her something she didn't understand at the time. And Antoine's dazzling fancy footwork right from the beginning covered an empty heart. Callam was an entirely different kind of man.

They said goodnight outside her cabin. And the next morning she got up and dressed early, just as she had when she arrived in Europe ten years earlier, when she had left New York in despair. There was no despair this time, no sorrow, as she stood at the rail and watched the sun come up. She could see Le Havre in the distance, and they would dock there in two hours.

As she looked out over the ocean, she had an incredible sense of freedom, of finally having shed her shackles at last. She wasn't burdened by the yoke of other people's opinions, or their lies about her. She was a free woman, and a good one, and she knew it.

As the sun rose into the morning sky, she heard a voice next to her and turned to see Callam.

"I had a feeling I'd find you here," he said quietly, as their eyes met and they both smiled. "Nice morning, isn't it?" he said simply.

"Yes, it is," she said, her smile deepening. It was a nice morning. They were both good people. And it was a fine life.